down the unmarked roads

by

joan finnigan

Published by

GSPH GENERAL STORE PUBLISHING HOUSE

1 Main Street Burnstown, Ontario, Canada K0J 1G0
Telephone 1-800-465-6072 Fax (613) 432-7184

ISBN 1-896182-73-9
Printed and bound in Canada

Cover Design by Hugh Malcolm
Design and Layout by Derek McEwen
Cover photo: by Joan Finnigan, "The Lane to Constan Creek, McWilliams-Gibeau house (removed) at Dacre on the Opeongo Line."

The General Store Publishing House
Burnstown, Ontario, Canada

Canadian Cataloguing in Publication Data

Finnigan, Joan, 1925 –
Down the unmarked roads

ISBN 1-896182-73-9

I. Title.

PS8511.I55D68 1997 C813'.54 C97-901101-9
PR9199.3.3F532D68 1997

First Printing October 1997

Dedication

"Every life is a story, some told, some untold.
Every life, long or short, is a pilgrimage.
Every story you enter becomes a rediscovery that
you are not alone; for ultimately story-telling
binds together all the pilgrims on the road to
Compostela."

from Aphorisms & Absolutes
by Joan Finnigan
(unpublished)

Table of Contents

The Cherished Woman

The first political warmer-upper in Pontiac County was a woman, yes, a cherished woman named Jenny Brennan Killoran from Lost Nation, Quebec. And her story needs telling not only because it is so unusual and so true but because it needs to be told in this day and age when the libbers would have you believe that, back in those early pioneering days, the women were all downtrodden, tied to the cookstove, taken to early graves by childbearing and in general "worked their fingers to the bone," while the men all sat on their asses, told stories and chewed tobaccy. The truth is that men killed themselves with hard physical labour or, at least, broke their backs lifting, heaving and pulling while the women created works of art like children, signed quilts, and crabapple jelly.

I'll tell you how it all happened that the remarkable Jenny Brennan Killoran became the first political warmer-upper in Pontiac County.

Jenny Brennan was born at Lost Nation, Western Quebec, 1908, the third youngest daughter of Bridget and High Bernie Brennan, the village blacksmith. Now when High Bernie was just a young lad beginning to stretch up, it was his legs which grew and grew while his body stood still. And, of course, he *would* go into Conway's store one day when some of the lads were sitting around on the barrels and stools, chewing tobaccy, spitting into the far spittoons and talking about bad weather, good horses, the crop situation, the political scene and the latest choice bit of gossip.

Yes, that's another one of the misconceptions about the old-timers. Gossiping was always laid at the feet of the women but, in actual fact, the men were just as bad, or worse. Indeed, in Brennan's Blacksmith Shop which served, as it did in every village, as the Men

Only Private Club, the men talked about the terrible things the women always shushed—like the castration of poor Patrick O'Neil by six friends of Theresa Fitzpatrick, the girl he knocked up.

Well, anyway, one day in 1892 the old lads were sitting jawing away in Conway's when Bernie Brennan, at the awkward age, came into the store and up to the counter. Xavier Sweeney, Liam Poirier, the only Frenchman in Lost Nation, Hans Burgomaster, the only German in Lost Nation, and Paddy O'Meara, the village wit, were just waiting for the train to come in. They all looked Bernie Brennan up and down as he stood there giving his list to Conway.

"By the Lord Jesus! That boy of Willie Brennan's is getting to be tall," said Liam Poirier to Paddy O'Meara.

"Oh, not at all, not at all," said Paddy O'Meara. "That boy is getting to be HIGH!"

Now, Lost Nation had so many Brennans in tribe that people had pretty well given up trying to distinguish them all by name and, for the last couple of generations, had separated out the Brennans by initials: M.T., son of R.T. out on the Fifth Line; P.S., son of B.S., south of the village; R.O., T.M., L.D., and J.A., all up towards Lost Nation. So, in the fashion of the country, the nickname "High Bernie" was a welcome relief from all the initials. And it stuck.

In due course High Bernie filled out, married Bridget Doyle—no, that's not the Doyles from Lost Nation but the ones from below Chapeau on the Eighth Line—and in 1900 began his famous family of blacksmith's daughters.

High Bernie's father died young; they found him in the shop stiffened over the anvil—so stiff, indeed, the undertaker couldn't straighten him out and he had to be buried as he had been in life, bent over crooked. And the transition period between the father's death and the son's takeover was no longer than the usual Irish Catholic wake in the country in those days—perhaps five or six days, a week at the most. Old Brennan had wisely taught his son everything he knew about blacksmithing, and right after the wake was over and he had sobered up, High Bernie stepped into his father's (horse) shoes—that's straight from Paddy O'Meara, the village wit—and life went on in Lost Nation uninterrupted, babies being born, and lovers wedding, and old folks dying.

Regular as the mass bells at St. Isadore's, over the next sixteen years every twenty-four months Bridget produced another daughter for High Bernie Brennan, the village blacksmith. Conceived after the Chapeau Fair, they were all born in May or June. Almost without exception, gathered on the step of St. Isadore's after mass, or at a quilting bee, or on the benches at a wake or dance, the women of Lost Nation would voice their approval of such good planning on the part of Bridget Brennan.

"Spring babies get a good start before the next winter," they would all agree, and then begin again the mournful tallies of all the badly-planned winter babies dead of croup, pneumonia, tuberculosis and polio.

"Yes, almost all winter babies," one would intone. And the rest would nod.

Bridget started out with exotic girls' names she had been exposed to in the Women's Romance series in the *Ottawa Journal*—Colombe, Genevieve, Mathilda, Lilith, Veronica. But, worn out with the taxation on her ingenuity, by the time she got to the sixth, seventh and eighth girls, she conceded to fatigue and simply named them Jenny, Jane and Sara.

Now High Bernie Brennan was a good, hard-working man, a strong and able blacksmith in the days when every farm around Lost Nation was green, productive and run by horse-power, teams and teams of horses. Some farmers who contracted for the lumber camps had thirty, forty, even fifty horses in their stables.

More than that, in the fall hundreds of teams of horses with their teamsters, sleighs and supplies left Chapeau and Lost Nation on their passage to the lumber camps of the Ottawa Valley, to the far reaches of the rivers of the Upper Pontiac and to the rivers of the Ontario side above Pembroke. Then there was a line-up outside High Bernie's blacksmith's shop and on down the main street past the two hotels, Kirby's and Marcotte's. Sometimes, bored with waiting in line, the teamsters would take off to the hotels and tie one on, leaving their poor horses tethered to a post on the main street. Then High Bernie would water, feed, sometimes stable them overnight, for he loved horses himself, had a driver which won prizes at all the fairs and a trotter, Darkie Hal, which usually cleaned up at the trotting races, even the ones on the ice at Ottawa.

Yes, the village blacksmith was a happy well-off man with enough cash for his wife and growing collection of daughters to order materials and fine ready-made dresses from Eatons in Toronto. Nevertheless, once a year High Bernie joined all mankind and, during the Chapeau Fair, closed up his shop and went on a bender in Marcotte's Hotel. There in a huge men's bar crowded with celebrants in the same mood as himself, he would cry into his beer about Bridget's inability to bear him a son to carry on his business, to help him as he got too old to pound out the shoe on the anvil or lift the foot of a skittish horse.

"What have I done wrong, Lord!" he would cry out in the bar, surrounded by all the fair-timers, lifting his eyes heavenward and pretending to peer through the heavy settlement of smoke towards the outline of the Heavenly Father, somewhere beyond the ceiling.

His friends, neighbours, even strangers in town for the fair were quick to give him advice.

"Change position."

"Try it from the back."

"Eat more potatoes."

After the same advice given year after year without variation, talk would turn to the Morriaritys who had produced six sons and then six daughters.

"Better go talk to them," someone would advise. "They must have the right recipe."

"You could reverse it maybe," said Paddy O'Meara.

And High Bernie would take it all in and eventually reel down the street home, bed down with Bridget, try it from the back, or hanging from the rafters, and produce another daughter.

By the time Jenny was born the Brennan household was overflowing with daughters, more than enough to clean, cook, mend, patch, polish, wash, daughters enough so that the "spickery and spannery"—that was Paddy O'Meara's—of Bridget's house was the envy of the women of the village.

"Where am I to get such help? What about me, Lord?" High Bernie would wail as he allowed the younger daughters to overflow into the blacksmith's shop.

"I guess I'll have to make some of them into he-women or she-men, like that famous Philomene Bergeron of the Opeongo Line," he would say to whomever was listening in the Men's Club. And there was always somebody there. And there was always somebody there to laugh.

And so it happened that what had been forbidden to the older daughters—No Entry to the Men Only Club—was permitted the younger ones and they began to spend time there, particularly Jenny.

From the time she was six and going to school, Jenny hovered like a spirit in the blacksmith shop, watching her father at work, trying to help and being told it was "not women's work," learning about horses, and listening to the men, always, always listening to the men. Eventually she blended into the background and many of the village men, who might have otherwise been self-conscious enough in the presence of a female to curb their tongues, became used to and finally almost unaware of Jenny lurking in the background. For her part,

Jenny was like a wolf on the edge of a clearing, present, watching, listening, but rarely ever seen.

She heard the stories of all the unsolved murders since 1840 in Pontiac County. There was the badly decomposed body of the man in the big beaver coat and beaver hat found near Holden's Swamp.

"That was no tramp," Liam Poirier would insist. "The police came up from Hull for that one. My God, I saw the body! But what could you do? It was just a huge pile of fur with bones inside it."

"Who killed Big Jack McLeod, the only Scot in Lost Nation?" somebody would ask again, and they would go on for hours with their endless theories about that unsolved murder. It was an Indian. He'd been messing around with the Indian women at Trout Lake. No. It was one of the Merciers with an old grudge about fence lines. No, it was an Assyrian pedlar passing through—.

Jenny heard all about the catch-colts, a seemingly endless recitation, Bridie Murphy's second child—horror of horrors—belonged to Alfie Hodgins, a Campbell's Bay Orangeman; Ted Murray was the illegitimate child of a roll in the hay between his father and the hired girl. Billie Keily actually recognized his catch-colt by Nonny Burke; he always nodded to him.

The first time she had heard the story of how Amy Kelly was stood up at the church by her groom-to-be, Howie Quilty—or how Amy had stood up her groom, depending on your point of view—Jenny had run to her sisters with the delicious tale.

"Just before the priest opened his mouth at the front of the church while Amy Kelly stood in all her pure white Pembroke-bought gown beside the trembling groom, she asked Father Harrington if she could have a word with Howie. Father Harrington, thinking that something like a broken garter had occurred, gave approval with a nod. Amy whispered in Howie's ear. He paled. He turned and left the altar. Apparently, she had told him she had a two-year-old boy—a two-year-old catch-colt—at home for him.

"'I saved it for her,' Howie was said to have later declared as he got drunk in Kirby's Hotel. There was a great bawdy roar from the men in the bar because everyone knew it was a goddamn lie. 'But she didn't save it for me,' Howie wailed.

"The next morning he went north to the mines and never returned to the scene of his betrayal."

Jenny and her sisters speculated far into the night as to why Amy didn't tell Howie *before* the wedding.

Jenny heard about who rustled timber and who ran the stills and who loaned money. Father Renaud loaned it out at 50 percent. She heard ten versions of the Ridley murder at Demer's Centre and she carried in her memory the names of ten suspects who entered into the story of the murder of Sheriff Tom Sloan. There were dozens more reputed to have been laying for him.

Every once in a while in the blacksmith's shop when the talk slowed down to the point where you could hear the forge spit, someone would drawl out, "Now, who do you think killed Sheriff Tom Sloan?" And another two hours of heated speculation and opinion would follow.

The stories about the long succession of priests who had served the parishioners in a one hundred percent Catholic community were a continual reality test for Jenny and early in the game implanted a deep ambiguity in her towards her religion and the priests who were, in those days, such absolute enforcers of it.

Father Henry was such a womanizer that the diocese never left him longer than two years in one parish. Even at that, he left a trail of offspring behind him. Father Grenier openly lived with a woman and had children by her all the time he was parish priest in the county. Father Harrington had a manager who ran his huge farm where he bred prize cattle, and Father Blais at Deux Rivières ran a whorehouse. All enough to make a young girl reconsider the gods of her family.

Now, in time, it began to sift in to Bridget that her third youngest daughter was not only becoming a purveyor of gossip, story and legend for a country-wide feminine underground—including all her other daughters—but she was also becoming a recognized expert on bar-room language.

"That tongue of yours is going to get you into trouble," she more than once warned Jenny in private. Bridget also spoke firmly to High Bernie about banning Jenny from the blacksmith's shop when that whole painful exercise became unnecessary. Jenny, at the age of eleven, wrote her entrance exams in Fort Coulonge and sailed off to high school in Pembroke. There she boarded with Bridget's sister, Aunt Jessie, and came home on the weekends, when she still managed to sneak into her father's shop to garner more stories to take back to her new captive audience at Immaculata.

"That one's way ahead," Paddy O'Meara often used to say as he watched Jenny helping her father to quiet down a frightened horse.

"Yes, a young lad will have to watch that one," Paddy would warn as the other men laughed. "She may outrun him."

"Or put out her foot and trip him," another lad would add.

And the men would all laugh together in a kind of male conspiracy, remembering from their youth that different breed of girl, the wild kind, untamed, untameable.

While she was at high school in Pembroke, Jenny discovered sports, excelled in them all, but particularly hockey. She was indeed so good and so out-distanced the rest of the girls on her hockey team that there was a running joke between Chapeau and Pembroke.

"We're going to put Jenny Brennan on the boys' team and see if they can beat the Boyneville Bears."

A couple of the real progressives in town, the grade eight teacher at the protestant high school and a returned First World War veteran who painted pictures and sold them in Ottawa, combined to start a movement to *put* Jenny on the Pembroke boys' junior team.

But Father Darlington quickly crushed that revolutionary movement.

"That's not a young girl's place," he snapped. And because his word was law, that ended that.

Jenny also had a serious run-in with the sisters who taught her at the Convent of Mary Immaculata. Every month the convent had an assembly at which the marks were all read out loud to the audience and which always included a special dignitary as speaker. Sometimes it was the Bishop from the cathedral in Pembroke with his two aides.

"Oh, how the Mother Superior bows and scrapes and kowtows!" Jenny told her family on the weekends at home. "You'd think he was the King of England!"

Actually Jenny hated the bowing and curtsying she and the other girls had to do, too. There was always an address from the Mother Superior to the Bishop which began, "Monseigneur"—and, at that signal, all the convent girls in their black uniforms with white turn-over collars and cuffs, with one accord as though in a drill or chorus line, curtsied to the Bishop.

One day in the Bishop's absence—he was on an extended holiday in Rome—the guest of honour was Judge Monahan. From her days in the blacksmith's shop in Lost Nation, Jenny knew all about Judge Monahan. He was known as "The Drinking Judge" because he had never sat sober on any case. Moreover, he was involved in all kinds of back-room politics, mostly crooked, and worst of all, he had black-marketed sugar during the First World War, smuggling it out of the Petawawa army camp—it was never rationed in the Canadian training camps in Canada and shipping it to England where it was black-marketed to the shops of London.

Jenny didn't refuse to bow to the judge; she simply stood while all around her the rest of the convent girls flopped over in accordance with convent custom. This act of defiance did not escape the Mother Superior whose one eye, Jenny always said, "saw more than anybody else's two." Jenny was severely reprimanded for insubordination, threatened with expulsion, and called to a further meeting with her parents in the presence of the Mother Superior. After a lengthy session on the values of recognizing authority, honouring the institutions, and knowing one's place as a young girl, the Mother Superior, on the basis of Jenny's excellent scholastic standing, allowed her to remain at Immaculata to complete high school.

"I always said she was going to be a hard one to harness," pronounced Paddy O'Meara in Brennan's shop as the whole matter was being aired.

When Jenny graduated from high school with honours—she also won the debating prize along with Delia Shannon—that's of course the daughter of the lumbering Shannons—there was talk of her going to the States to train as a nurse. A couple of Pembroke and Chapeau girls had already left to enter nurses' training in hospitals south of the border.

But, as it turned out, High Bernie wasn't too keen at all on that idea. He had his own secret reasons.

"After I spend all that money," he proffered, "she'll just go off and get married. It's not that I don't have the money but—"

"It won't be easy to marry that one off," Paddy O'Meara countered. "A hard horse to break in, a hard one to break in."

High Bernie kept on hiding the fact that his back was beginning to bother him, always a blacksmith's occupational hazard from all that lifting and anvil-smashing, holding, tugging and pulling. Besides, he wanted to keep one daughter at home as a surrogate son. And who better than Jenny who was beginning to know something about the business?

Out of school with nothing much to do in Lost Nation or Chapeau, most of her friends married or left town, Jenny, bored, restless, inwardly waiting and hoping for something new and strange to happen, took to riding her father's thoroughbred through the countryside. Hair flying, skirts flying, tearing over the countryside at a gallop, she became a familiar, and somewhat scandalous, figure from the mountains to the river, from north to south.

One day she rode home to her father's shop yard, brow sweating and her horse in a lather. There she met Paddy O'Meara coming out of the Men Only Club.

Paddy O'Meara took one look at her.

"Lord bejesus, Jenny!" he exclaimed. "That horse is white in the face."

"And you'd be white in the face, too, Paddy O'Meara," Jenny snapped back, "if you'd been so long between my legs."

For the first time in his life Paddy O'Meara, the village wit, had no retort. But the one-liner spread through the countryside like hoof-and-mouth disease and, at the end of its circle, came to the ears of Bridget and High Bernie.

"That girl has got to marry soon," Bridget said to her husband, "or we have trouble on our hands."

"Easier said than done, my girl," said High Bernie. "How many young men do you find at our gate seeing her home from the dances?"

Then, one morning as he was about to get up and start his day's work, High Bernie's back locked and he couldn't move out of his bed.

The caravans had started to move into the Booth, Gillies, Bryson lumber camps in the Upper Pontiac taking supplies in for the horses and the men.

High Bernie was very upset. "In this world of sin and sorrow a man who can't work can't earn," he cried out. "What will we all do?"

"Never mind, Father," Jenny said. "I will hold the fort." And she walked into the blacksmith's shop, lifted the foot of the first waiting Clydesdale, and took his measure.

By the time High Bernie's back had unlocked with the help of a visit from Dr. Keon, word had spread throughout the countryside, by phone, by word of mouth, even by mail, that Chapeau had a young woman who could blacksmith.

"Yes," said Paddy O'Meara, "her father's son. A boy at last."

"High Bernie can now stop eating a peck of potatoes a day and trying to do it upside down," Paddy O'Meara remarked one morning after mass in Lost Nation when all the lads had retired to the shed back of the hotel to wash out the taste of the bad communion wine with a quart or two of Black Horse.

After High Bernie's recovery and return to work, Jenny found herself once again with nothing to do and took to riding the mare farther and farther each afternoon, up to the foot of the mountains, around the lakes and even up the lumbering roads into the wilderness.

"Too big for her britches now," Paddy O'Meara pronounced.

Bridget and High Bernie were beginning to talk in whispers late at night about the need to marry Jenny off when word spread through the village that Black Dan Killoran was on his way home from the North. His cousins had had a letter and he had phoned his family long distance to meet him in Pembroke at the station. Black Dan was not called Black Dan because he was black Irish—although the Killorans may have been a little of that, too, as well as a little of the Algonquin Giddygaw—but he was the only black-haired son amongst the six red-haired sons of Big Ben Killoran and his wife Fiona Donnelly. Black Dan had gone North after his affair with Sarena Sweeney from back in the Brulé. The Brulé was a backwoods foot-of-the mountain settlement of French who had become Irish and Irish who had become Indian, and it generally had a reputation as a place "where you could get it anytime and then go back nine months later and pick out the ones that looked like you."

Sarena Sweeney was a beauty—no man alive questioned that—but from the wrong side of the fields, and Black Dan was generally conceded to be the best-looking man that ever walked the streets of Chapeau. Indeed, it was said that men stepped off the sidewalk and into the curb to watch him going by, and give him room. When Black Dan and Sarena, headlong with the kind of passion that you can't believe when you get older and can't even remember when you get really old, bedded down in some historical hayfield they got themselves with child and "no ring on the finger." Of course there was no thought of marriage between a Sweeney from the Brulé and a Killoran from The Front. Black Dan's older brother Alec, a prospector in the North, paid for the back-room abortion in Montreal.

"I heard it was $600," Paddy O'Meara said to the lads in Brennan's Shop. "I could have bought the Lynch place for that."

As soon as Sarena Sweeney was recovered from the trauma and the shame of a back-room abortion in Montreal, despite all the threats of the Killoran family to banish Black Dan from the farm and all the threats of the Sweeney family to clean up the Killorans, she and Black Dan, as young people will do, got into the horizontal position again. There Black Dan and Sarena, attempting to make up for lost time, went at it so hard again that the bed fell in Marcotte's hotel, the echoes of its collapse reverberating throughout the countryside. And not too long after that word came down that Sarena was pregnant again. The Killorans refused Black Dan permission to marry. The Sweeneys ganged and met the Killorans in Kirby's hotel yard where the battle went on for days and one of the Sweeneys had an eye gouged out. After that Donnybrook, black and blue all over, Black Dan went North to the mines and Sarena had her catch-colt, a boy who looked so much like Black Dan that nobody ever thought of a blood test.

"My God bejesus," Paddy O'Meara said to High Bernie in the shop one day, "A boy! Imagine that! You and Bridget should try one of the beds in Marcotte's hotel—one of the collapsing ones!"

Now, weary of the dark mines and longing for God's country of Lost Nation, Black Dan was rumoured to be returning to take over one of the Killoran farms, Big Ben and Fiona having reached an age where they could no longer do the physical labour required to keep a large farm running properly.

Jenny Brennan hadn't forgotten Black Dan. He had seen some of the world and she knew he wouldn't be threatened by a forthright feisty woman like herself who was very much like his own mother, an Ottawa girl who had come to Chapeau to teach and had met Big Ben Killoran, then in his fortieth year, having seen the world as far as Seattle and the Yukon and ready to settle down.

"Timing is everything," Paddy O'Meara would repeat in the blacksmith shop. "Timing is everything..."

Jenny Brennan made up her mind to have Black Dan Killoran. She was not the first girl he took to a dance on his return to God's Country, but she was the last. When he made the move on her she laughed and said,

"Not till you put the ring on my finger. Get it in the Brulé, or better still—the Gatineau."

Black Dan roared with laughter at her sass, and asked her out again to the Fall Fair dance at Chapeau, one of the biggest events of the year. Jenny bought a new dress in Pembroke that accentuated her waist and bosom, and a fine comb for her hair. She also sharpened her tongue.

Bridget looked her third youngest daughter over as she waited for Black Dan Killoran to pick her up.

"You're setting your cap for this one."

Jenny held her tongue.

"If a Sweeney wasn't good enough for a Killoran, maybe the blacksmith's daughter won't be either."

Jenny's neck snapped as she whirled to reply,

"The Killorans always choose women who can stand up to them." She flared around and left the room to wait outside on the verandah.

"Well, then, keep your legs crossed," her mother threw after her.

"I'll cross them until I'm ready," Jenny retorted, full of anger at still being treated like a child.

Fair-time in Chapeau was always fight time. Old scores were settled, revenge exacted, anger expiated, old challenges revived, new champions crowned. It was one of the busiest times of the year for the parish priest, Father Harrington: not only did he have to act as peacemaker, village bouncer, justice of the peace, censor of morals, he often also had to intervene before a Sweeney killed a Killoran or a Berrigan killed a McCooey in old feuds, some of whose beginnings had been forgotten but whose spirit had not only been carried on but often aggrandized. It was believed that a record was set at fair-time in 1919 when 26 fights were counted going on at the same time in Marcotte's hotel yard.

Paddy O'Meara partially accounted for that record when he said later in Brennan's shop, "There were a lot of lads back from the war who had it in for the lads who didn't go."

At fair-time the Orangemen came up the line from Boyneville "looking for it." They picked up a heavy contingent of legendary strongmen, the Horners, the Hodginses, the Hannas, the Prendergasts, the McCords, and a few muscled strays who were spoiling for it. And they arrived in a blended corps to visit the Chapeau Fair, attend the dance and settle old religious scores deliberately imported from Ireland by their forefathers so there would be some form of manly entertainment in the New Country.

The Orangemen from Boyneville were always perfect gentlemen at the dance, so perfect you would never dream what they carried in their fists. Generally they never laid a hand on the "Mick" boys' women, just stood on the sidelines, drinking Orange Crush, watching the stuff and making the odd lascivious remark amongst themselves.

But unbeknownst to the gentle folk of Chapeau, fair-time, 1931, they had made a bargain amongst themselves that one of them would ask a Chapeau girl to dance. To go forth on this dangerous mission they had chosen by vote Larry Hanna, big, black-haired, with curls that twirled down on his forehead giving him the appearance of a little steer, so muscled and strong he could lift a horse by the belly. To compensate for the dangerousness of this mission—an Orangeman being sent forth to ask a Roman Catholic girl to dance with him—the Boyneville boys voted that Larry could choose any girl he wanted.

Now Larry loved to dance. And he was a great dancer. When he entered the dance hall anyone would think, "Well, here comes the bull into the china shop." But once he stepped onto the dance floor, the music raised him onto the balls of his feet and he floated through the round dances so that his partners said it felt like "being wafted away." In the squares he could stomp the loudest and swing the highest. So, that historic night in Chapeau, September 1931, what Larry Hanna was looking for amongst the Chapeau girls was not the prettiest, nor the whoriest, nor the one with the biggest teats, or "legs like a thoroughbred," but the best dancer. Of course, that was Jenny.

At a signal from the Boyneville boys, Larry Hanna moved. He walked over to the benches lining the wall of the dance hall, bowed a gentlemanly bow to Jenny Brennan, put out his hand with a great show of gallantry and said, "May I please have the next dance?"

He had asked the right girl. Jenny hesitated a moment and then put her hand in his. There was a silent falling back of the rest of the dancers as Jenny and Larry floated out on to the dance floor alone.

Then, there rose a murmuring in the crowd, like a gathering of wasps.

"A sacrilege," some were saying.

"Great dancers," others were saying as, mesmerized, they watched the scene unfold. In horror and fear some dancers fled the floor. Some of Black Dan Killoran's friends moved in close to him. People lined up along the edge of the dance floor. The faint-hearted left the hall.

Then the murmuring crowd opened to let Father Williams through. Very wisely the band kept playing. They had played through Donnybrooks before. Father Williams marched up to the lone dancers, tapped Jenny on the shoulder and motioned her off the dance floor. The dancers slowed politely. Outraged, Father Williams put his hand under Jenny's elbow preparatory to lifting her off the dance floor and out of the arms of the heathen from Boyneville. Jenny, carefully, slowly, deliberately removed the priest's hand, said something to him—there were various reports later about what her phrasing was—and the dancers moved off together again. That was how Jenny Brennan became the first Roman Catholic girl in Chapeau history to dance with an Orangeman in public.

On the way home in the buggy, Black Dan brimmed with mirth, groaned, broke down, tried to talk, broke into laughter again.

"What did you say to him, Jenny Brennan, Jenny Brennan?"

"That's between him and me."

"You'll be excommunicated, Jenny Brennan."

"Let him try. The old fool. Times have changed."

"Not in his parish, not in *his* parish. Come on. Tell me what you said to him—I'll tickle you until you do."

Black Dan tried to tickle Jenny in the places where he knew she was ticklish but she held his hand immobilized. He had to drive with the other and nearly went off the road.

"I told him to go to hell."

Dan broke down in the sheer joy of it, the pure vicarious ecstasy of it.

"Father Williams is sixty six and finally somebody told him to go to hell!"

He stopped the car. "Oh, Jenny. I think you're my match. Shall I put the ring on your finger?"

Jenny held out her left hand, chuckling as she did it.

After Jenny and Black Dan Killoran were married they moved to the village of Chapeau where Black Dan invested all his savings from his work in the northern mines in a general store on the main street across from Marcotte's Hotel.

"Sure, I never intended to farm the old family farm really at all,"

Black Dan said later. "Jim can have it all. And I've had my fill of the mines. No, the money is to be made in service to the farmers."

Jenny became co-manager of Killoran's General Store.

"Just like home," she sighed often, looking around at the old general store with its benches and stools along the counter where, once again as in Brennan's blacksmith's shop, young men and old-timers alike dawdled the time away, aimed at the spittoons, told and retold the stories. The big old pot-bellied wood stove in the centre of the store was kept warm from September to April and remained, as it had been since the turn of the century, the gathering place of community hockey fans for the NHL games on Saturday nights.

It wasn't too long before Killoran's General Store was one of the most popular places in town—and that had a great deal to do with the personality of Jenny herself, a great listener, a good storyteller, and a quick sharp tongue to boot, one that could invent a sassy retort on a moment's notice.

Jenny and Black Dan had three daughters very quickly, within three or four years, and then Jenny gave up and got herself a pessary. She had to go to Ottawa to get it.

"I'm not going to wear myself out like my mother did, trying to have a Killoran son," Jenny said to Black Dan, "and I've got other things I'd like to do. Three's enough. Right?" And Black Dan agreed.

"There are enough Killorans spread across the country already," he said with a laugh and gave Jenny a supportive sendoff for whatever else she wanted to do with her life.

Jenny took off like a whirlwind. She began to take her B.A. by correspondence from McGill University; history, law, political science. She joined the Women's Catholic League and the following year was elected president. From this platform she began talking about birth control, women's rights, getting out to vote and lobbying for the women's right to vote. Ontario had given women the right to vote in 1911 but Quebec, still under the sway of the Roman Catholic church, had not yet recognized this inalienable right, this recognition of their equality with men.

It was about the time, and certainly in the same year, that Jenny finished off her Honours B.A. that Jake Rutherford was running federally. He was a terrible speaker but unlike most of them, he knew it. Like the majority of candidates in Western Quebec in those days he was an Englishman without a word of French; yet in this election which was going to be close—the incumbent was Hiram Harper, a hotel-keeper with money to spend on his campaign and places to get more if he needed it—Jake Rutherford felt he really needed to court the

French vote in towns like North Bay, Mattawa, Bryson, Fort Coulonge. Jenny had become active in back-room politics for the party and her reputation as a public speaker was growing. So Jake hit Jenny up to come with him to a big rally in North Bay and warm up the crowd before he killed them off with his wandering monotone. After much coaxing, finally, "for the sake of the party," Jenny agreed.

"But just this once," she warned.

That was how Jenny became the first political warmer-upper in Pontiac County. She was outrageous and they loved it. She told racist, religious, sexist jokes. If she was with the Catholics she told anti-Catholic jokes; if she was with the Protestants she told anti-Protestant jokes.

She'd yell out at the Frenchmen, "If Frenchmen are such great lovers, how come the Quebec government always has to pay you to have babies?"

And then she'd tell a story on the Liberals:

"You know, of course, all about the Liberal who got very animated about his Liberalism and his party policy. And he was up on the platform telling everybody why he voted Liberal.

"'Yes, yes,' he shouted. 'My father voted Liberal. My grandfather voted Liberal. My great-grandfather voted Liberal. We've always been Liberal. And I vote Liberal.' (Boos and cries from the audience).

"'Furthermore,' he shouted. 'My father was a Catholic. My grandfather was a Catholic. My great-grandfather was a Catholic. And I am a Catholic. And I am going to be Catholic to the end of my days.' (Use Protestant here in a Catholic area. Boos and cries from the audience).

"'Yes, yes,' he went on. 'I do what my proud forefathers did—right down to the last letter. I'm a bachelor. My father was a bachelor. My grandfather was a bachelor. My great-grandfather...'"

And then Jenny would be drowned out by the hoots and boos and delighted cries of her all-male audience.

Jenny had other talents, too, which enhanced her popularity as a political warmer-upper. In talking to and rousing up what was in those days an almost entirely male audience, she would use even her great figure to turn a laugh or make people sit up and take notice. If many in the meeting were French-Canadian she would say, "I guess de first ting on de program, I take off my dress." And of course, the men would yell gleefully, "Take it off. Take it off." And Jenny would yell back, "Don't say that-because I might!" And the meeting was off to a hilarious beginning.

Besides her great figure, Jenny also was endowed with a

formidable memory, which had been further expanded and exercised by going to school in the days when "memory work" was frequently prescribed by teachers on the theory that this part of the brain was enlarged by use and shrivelled by disuse. "If you don't use it, you lose it" was an underlying philosophy also applied in those earlier days to this part of the human anatomy. Jenny could quote appropriately and at length from Tennyson, Shakespeare and Robert Service. She knew almost all of William Henry Drummond's *Little Baptiste* poems and endeared herself to the French-Canadians in her political audiences throughout Pontiac County by reciting them holus-bolus on every opportune occasion.

Jenny became a consummate actress moving across the stage of Pontiac County politics with her sense of timing perfected and her intuition poised to pull from her repertoire the exact story or joke for each situation, every audience. She became adept at disguising what she considered real issues (like sex education in the schools, birth control in Quebec, legalized abortion, using Canadian books as textbooks in classrooms) and rolling them into her speeches under the umbrella of humour so that her audiences were almost unaware of what was happening to them.

She was such a dynamic speaker she was invited to speak on both sides of the Valley. When she was in Ontario, she harangued her audience to get out and vote.

"Don't sit there like a bunch of ninnies. Get out and vote. And don't vote the way the minister or the priest tells you. And don't vote the way your husband tells you to. Get out and vote your own way, according to your own conscience."

When she was in Quebec, she harangued her female audiences to lobby for the right to vote.

"Don't sit there like a bunch of ninnies," she'd yell at them. "Get out and picket your Members of Parliament. Write letters to your government. Picket the priests' houses—if you have to. Form lobby groups. Do something to join the human race and assert your rights!

"What did our foremothers fight the battle for? Pankhurst, Sangster, Stowe, Nellie McClung? So that you could stay at home on election day and mop the floors?"

Jenny was so dynamic and effective, and her renown as a speaker spread so far and wide that she began to be invited to address all kinds of women's groups, from the WCTU to political meetings, from Women's Institute meetings to Women's University Club meetings, on both sides of the river, in both Ontario and Quebec. She was the instigator for the first Literary Club in Chapeau knowing full well that across North America and even in England Literary Clubs had been "fronts" for the suffragette movement. And it certainly was that in the village of Chapeau.

"Let them think that we are doing readings from the Bible and studying Zane Grey," she would yell out gleefully at her audience while, in actuality, she was passing out suffragette tracts and books.

"Someday you'll do more than vote," she'd yell at the women in the halls. "Someday there will be women in parliament and a woman playing in the NHL."

Statements like this, wildly extravagant, were made more for laughs than conversions, and they worked to drop seeds of ideas, ridiculous as they might seem, and dealt with so derisively by most of the men in the community. She withstood all their chaffing in the store, downed them with rapier retorts, and continued to have the backing of her husband, even although some of the men, alone with him in the store, gave him a very hard time of it.

"If that was a woman of mine, I know what I'd do with her—" was the oft-repeated strain of their snide remarks to Black Dan.

But Black Dan would maintain a totally unruffled countenance and go about his business. Sometimes with a little mischievous grin he would say. "Yes, quite a girl, my Jenny, quite a girl—now how much binder twine would you be needing, Floyd?" Or, if pushed too hard about her unorthodox behaviour and her reformer image, he'd finally go so far as to repeat, "Well, you have to remember I married her because she was the first Roman Catholic in Chapeau to dance with a Protestant—"

From her years of listening in the blacksmith's shop and her years of carrying tales to her fellow students at Immaculata in Pembroke, Jenny had become a natural storyteller and collected her own repertoire of anecdotes for every occasion, jokes about the Orangemen for a Roman Catholic audience, jokes about alcohol for the Women's Christian Temperance Movement, jokes about the Liberals for the Conservative audiences, jokes about intellectuals for the Women's University Clubs, jokes about greenhorns and ingenues for the Farmer's cooperatives and 4H Clubs, jokes about the Englishmen for the Frenchmen, jokes about the Frenchmen for the Englishmen, jokes about those two immortal Irishmen, Pat and Mike, for everybody.

The Chapeau Literary Club had cell mitosis and comparable "reading clubs" sprang up throughout the Valley, in Quebec to lobby FOR the vote in Boyneville, Campbell's Bay and Aylmer; in Ontario to lobby the scaredy-cats to GET OUT AND VOTE, in Pembroke, North Bay, Arnprior, Cobden, even in Renfrew. From the village of

Chapeau, Jenny provided lists of underground reading material for all these groups, and volunteered her services as a speaker. Eventually she evolved two very popular pieces entitled, "I Vote the Way John Votes," and "Sex Is Not a Sin."

Since Ontario had had the vote since 1911, Jenny's most popular piece on the Ontario side of the Ottawa River was, "I Vote the Way John Votes."

"Remember, girls," she'd yell at the women, "I don't care how old you are—I was young one time myself—I don't care what age you are. It doesn't matter. You are still girls, aren't you? You are not boys. Are you? (and this always got a laugh out of the men in the audience). There are 51 percent voters in Canada who are women. Most of these women—but not *you* of course—are under subjection to their husbands" (and this would always pull a great groan and denial from the men), "yes, under subjection to their men and a great many of them—but not *you* of course—say, 'Well, I always vote the way John votes.'

"A lot of women when they get in that polling booth (tomorrow or next Friday) will do whatever their husbands tell them to do—well, not *you* of course—but all kinds of foolish, unwise women. They are the kind of women who do just what their husbands tell them to do—always. If he says, 'go to this church' they go. If he says, 'You can go to Boyneville to shop on such and such a day,' why that's the day they go. If he says, 'This is all the money you can have,' that's what they take.

"Yes, by jeepers, these women do what their husbands tell them when they go behind the curtain on election day. They are the ones who take the pencil up and say to themselves, 'This is how John would want me to vote.' And they vote that way. But not *you*, of course. Remember when you go behind the curtain on voting day you have 51 percent of the voting power in this country. And when you get in behind that curtain, forget that you were ever married. And put your X in the right place. Because he'll never know! He'll never know!"

And then after Jenny had outrageously harangued the women in her audiences, she would proceed to bring down the entire house by saying, "Well, let me tell you right here, I vote the way my husband Black Dan Killoran votes."

And she would fold her hands piously and look heavenward.

"Of course, I don't have any trouble at all voting the way Black Dan votes. Because he always votes the right way. He always knows how to vote the right way. He votes Liberal!"

"Who told you sex is a sin?" she'd yell out for an opener when she was delivering her piece on "Sex Is Not a Sin."

"Your mother? The minister? The priest? Sex is not a sin, not even in the Holy Bible. Just as you have suspected all along, sex is good for you. Sex can be fun. Enjoy. And who told you it was only for procreation? The minister? The priest? Nonsense. Get yourself some birth control and enjoy it. Mr. Goodyear invented the rubber condom in 1839 and the rich have been keeping it a secret for a hundred years. And the priests have been keeping it a secret from the poor for a hundred years. Get with it, girls and boys! Mensinger invented the pessary in 1881. Get with it, girls! If the Holy Father says birth control is against the Roman Catholic religion and the sale is outlawed in Quebec, take the train to Ottawa. That's what I did."

Jenny began preaching the need for birth control clinics for ordinary everyday people, for women to take control of their lives, for sex education in the schools.

Inevitably, the village priest of Chapeau went to see Black Dan and they had a brief very private conversation.

"Well, for God's sake," Jenny cried out to him after the meeting as they got ready for bed. "What did he say to you?"

"He said you were undermining the teaching of the Church of Rome and that he wanted me to tell you to stop."

"And what did you say to him then?" Jenny cried out.

Black Dan laughed.

"I told him he had to start moving with the times, that the Roman Catholic church was losing ground every day—"

"And what did he say then?"

"He said that I should have more control over you, that good Catholic wives obey their husbands—"

Both Jenny and Black Dan were laughing together by this time.

"And what did you say then, Dan?" Jenny asked.

"I told him to go to hell."

The echo of the conversation they had had 20 years before when Black Dan had proposed to Jenny had them both rolling with laughter. They laughed so hard they fell on the bed together.

"Let me tickle Adam's rib," Jenny cried out, tearing at Black Dan's shirt and grabbing for his groin.

"No, No!" Black Dan cried out. "Sex is a sin."

Eventually, perhaps even inevitably, the party association asked Jenny to run for a provincial seat but she replied that she didn't want to give her teaching up or put that kind of expense on her husband. "And besides, it will be years before Quebec is ready for a woman MPP. My God! Women haven't even got the vote yet in Quebec!"

And things began to change. At her school Jenny was threatened with firing for her outspoken stance on sex education. She was accused of being a "a racist" and "a bigot." She was castigated for her "sexist" jokes. To a certain extent, she fought back.

"We used to have freedom of speech here and we all used to be able to laugh at ourselves—even, yes, even the English whom the French-Canadians always called 'Les Glacées'—could sometimes laugh at themselves.

"I used to tell that story when I was warming up an audience which had a goodly number of French in it. Yes, I would often say to them, 'I have a relative who lives up in Resolute Bay and he says Resolute Bay is the ideal place to live; there are no mosquitoes, no humidity and no Frenchmen!'

"Well, everybody would hoot. Including all the Frenchmen.

"But not any more. I'm accused of racism. And can you imagine what would happen nowadays if I changed that story around and said 'no mosquitoes, no humidity and no Englishmen?' Big Brother is not only watching you now but he has your sense of humour about yourselves strictly censored.

"Brian Mulroney has perfected the political art of saying nothing." she proclaimed. "And soon the rest of us will only be able to speak freely in sign language, Esperanto or pig Latin."

Although Jenny continued back-room work for the political party, and lived to see women in Quebec get the vote in 1948, she gave up political warming-up and became a lay preacher.

"One of the extraordinary paradoxes of this country today," she said in a speech at Aylmer to the English Alliance in Quebec, "is that one is still able to speak freely from the pulpit."

She took all her issues on the road from church to church, sex education in the schools, legalized abortion, equal pay for equal work.

When she was 74, Jenny wrote her memoirs, *The Truth About the Cherished Woman*, published by McClelland and Stewart, in which she stated, "I'd rather be cherished than liberated." The book was blackballed by the entire formidable underground network of the Women's Movement in Canada. Female reviewers tore her to shreds, proclaiming that she had "betrayed women in Canada" and by that one simple statement "set the whole movement back twenty-five years."

Despite the hostility that surrounded her later years, and the forces that made her obsolete as a woman, a teacher, a back-room politician, Jenny was nominated for the Senate in the year of our Lord 1984. Newly-elected Prime Minister Brian Mulroney on the advice of his closest cronies was trying to dilute his patronage image by giving appointments to people in political parties other than his own and it was thought that, since there was so much pressure from the Women's

Movement to boost women into politics (although most of the saner ones didn't want to go) that Jenny might have a chance to become one of the first woman Senators in the history of the nation.

But the answer from Mulroney came back "No." He said they were on a new quota system in the Senate, "French this time; English the next time. West this time; East next time. Man this time: woman next time. Visible minority this time; invisible minority next time." His advisers had informed him that this time he had to appoint a visible minority black woman and, of course, Jenny didn't fit into that category.

"The truth is, my dear Jenny." Black Dan said, feeling that she might need some consolation, "You really don't fit into any category."

"You're right, my dear," Jenny said. "I shall probably only go down in local history as the first—and the last—political warmer-upper in Pontiac County. And so be it. I've lived my whole life with the only man I ever loved. And I've had it both ways, always."

Bad Blood

I had first met Amaryllis MacInnis with her companion, Betty Barker, at a heritage conference two years before in Ottawa. Although Mrs. MacInnis was then 89, I was struck by her beauty and dynamism. She looked 65 and I remember thinking to myself at the time, "For a number of reasons, other women must hate her." Moreover, I had expected this woman to be a pale shadow of her famous late husband, Willie MacInnis the Third, the last of one of the greatest of the Ottawa Valley timber dynasties. But, as I observed her from the sidelines I realized that this was a woman in her own right, resonating the strength of true core femininity and the beauty of courage, as well as exuding the pride and self-confidence of a woman long cherished and well-loved.

Prior to that first glimpse of Amaryllis MacInnis I had talked with Betty Barker, explaining to her that I was doing a book on North American Timber Barons and that I really must interview Mrs. MacInnis as one of the last links with the MacInnis family. Betty had agreed to introduce me. So, after one of the morning coffee breaks at the conference I moved towards a group of people of all ages with whom Mrs. MacInnis was animatedly holding forth. I waited until the Grand Dame was nearly finished expressing her views and the listeners beginning to move off. I moved forward into her circle; Betty introduced me and Mrs. MacInnis graciously acknowledged the introduction.

"I'm doing some research into the great lumbering families of North America," I explained. "And I've already taped some of the descendants of the Davies, Frasers, McCools, Houghtons, Barnetts—some of the people like Tommy Bailey and Jackson Cornett—I'd very much like to—"

Mrs. MacInnis turned her great grey eyes full upon me in righteous indignation.

"You taped Jackson Cornett! Then you'll not tape me! Anything you want about the MacInnises you can get from the book. *White Pine Saga*."

My heart sank. The book was a well-known commissioned whitewash full of statistics, cloying righteousness, academic dullness, without a shred of the human interest that makes history live.

"But Mrs. MacInnis," I stammered, "I can't do a book without—"

But she had already turned to someone else who had come up to talk with her.

I looked towards Betty Barker pleadingly.

"Bad blood there," she said. "Some kind of a crooked deal, I think—"

"What will I do?"

"You'll just have to wait," Betty replied, "Until she either changes her mind or can be convinced."

As it turned out, I had to wait for two years. In the meantime Amaryllis MacInnis had gone on an extended trip to Europe, had had a bad fall, broken a hip, been hospitalized for months. She was, indeed, still convalescing at home when, through Betty's intercession, she was convinced finally that I did not want the tired old commercial story of the MacInnis Lumbering Company but rather her woman's story and her story alone.

And so it was that I finally found myself on my way to Lochwinnoch.

For 60 years the MacInnises had been living on the Ottawa River at the centre of the capital city in a primeval woods so deep and so protected that few people except close friends, relatives and business associates ever knew that the Lochwinnoch estate existed. Although Willie MacInnis the First, a hundred or more years ago, had stripped the timber off thousands of acres in the Upper Ottawa Valley in order to make his incalculable fortune, intending to build a summer place that would be the envy of Ottawa society he had kept for himself this choice riverside stand of white pine and maple, hemlock and beech. But he had died before he fulfilled that dream.

His eldest son, Willie MacInnis the Second, had married Princess Maria Theresa Bastudo of Spain. Not surprisingly, her tastes had not run to retreats in the Canadian woods but rather to the ballrooms and government galas of Ottawa, Washington, London, Paris and Madrid. It had remained to Willie MacInnis the Third and his wife Amaryllis to build their "dream home" in the midst of this astounding paradoxical urban forest.

On a perfect day in June, as I had been instructed to do, I gave my name to the gate-keeper at the south entrance. He nodded me forward and as I passed between the Grecian urns on the gateposts I realized how excited I was to be one of the few members of the Third Estate ever allowed into the hallowed grounds. After two years of planning and frustration, I was finally on my way to talk with Amaryllis MacInnis!

The forest of Lochwinnoch estate is frighteningly dark even on a summer's midmorning. The giant trees tower over a hundred feet into the air and in the full fresh foliage of early July cut off almost all light at ground level. I found myself shrunk to the knee-high size of childhood expecting to meet in these magical woods the wicked witch of Grimm's Fairy Tales, to hear far-off a chorus from the Seven Dwarfs, to catch a glimpse of a white knight on his way to rescue the beautiful princess from the heart of darkness. Driving slowly along the winding lane with my neck craning out the window I partially understood the emotional phenomena which the people of the North describe as "bushed"—the sudden rising of fear in one's breast that the forest will never end.

But at Lochwinnoch the forest does end after all (there are only 27 acres of it, the waterfront and forest probably combining in real estate valued in the millions). The road curves upwards suddenly, the lawns open out and the Timber Baron's stone mansion comes as a surprise, an intrusion of civilization in God's primeval world. Three-winged, many gabled, the MacInnis house sits on a high cliff overlooking the Ottawa River amongst its manicured lawns, formal gardens and carefully designed glens of rare trees which Willie MacInnis during his lifetime imported from all over the world. He had died in 1968 leaving his widow alone in the big house with their servants.

I took my time getting my papers and my tape recorder out of the car. While I mentally reframed some of my questions, I wanted to savour the house of Willie and Amaryllis. Obviously architecturally designed. A warm stone with browns in it rather than the cold Glasgow grey of Kingston and Perth. Large. But not pretentious. Snug. In this process I guess I must have been standing so long on the pillared porch that the gardener in his rose beds stopped his work to look at me, perplexed by my dawdling. Lest he think me an unannounced intruder, I quickly rang the bell. Several dogs barked inside. Betty Barker answered the door.

"How is she?" I asked when we greeted each other.

But I did not know what Betty's shrug meant.

"She is waiting for you," she said as she lead me up the wide white curved staircase to a sunlit suite on the south-east side of the house. In the huge bedroom the twin mahogany sleigh beds had been pushed to one side to make room for a hospital cot with sides on it. Propped up on pillows and wearing a pink bed jacket Amaryllis MacInnis lay looking out the far windows. Her skin was a pale yellow. She had lost a great deal of weight.

"Oh, no!" I groaned to myself. "I am already too late!"

There was a fire going in the marble fireplace. The room was a gallery of personal photographs. I glanced at the bedside books; the Bible and something called *The Art of Prayer*.

Betty spoke to Mrs. MacInnis and she slowly turned in my direction. There it was! That rare and beautiful smile. But I knew by her eyes, her speech and the way she extended her hand to me so slowly and uncertainly that she was heavily sedated.

"Please," I prayed, "Don't let it be too late."

"You can leave us, Betty," Mrs. MacInnis said with a wave of her hand. "We'll be fine. We met before."

Tripping over my own anxiety and haste I fumbled about trying to get the tape recorder plugged into the nearest socket, to site it on her bed close enough to catch her voice but not so close as to make her uneasy. It wasn't going to be easy; her voice had faded to a fragile whisper.

"That dreadful Jackson Cornett!" she said.

I looked at her sharply to see if I had heard alright. Could she really remember that?

"I hear there was bad blood between the Cornetts and the MacInnises. A crooked deal?" I said, taking the bull by the horns.

"Oh, there was probably that, all that," she said with a little laugh. "But that's not part of MY story. No. Jackson Cornett was a heavy drinker and he used to come calling on people all over town when he was blind drunk. One time he came to our house and the poor maid let him in. I guess she couldn't hold him back and he barged in and insulted me in front of Will. Called me 'Miss Proper-bum.' And Will just took him by the coat collar and the seat of the pants and threw him over the front verandah railing out there and Jackson landed right in the middle of one of those huge low spreading hemlock bushes. He wasn't hurt at all but he just lay there cushioned in the hemlock looking up at the sky. And he was the funniest thing we had ever seen. And we just closed the door on him, and leaned on each other, and laughed for fifteen minutes."

"Tell me more about this house."

"Oh, you wouldn't believe the things and people this house has seen! Including a Prince of Wales! It was just as well they got Edward off the throne, you know, because he wouldn't have made much of a king. When he made his tour here in 1909 the Ottawa Timber Barons all got together and had a real lumberman's feast for him in the old Russell Hotel in Ottawa—it's gone now—but that was a real hotel. Dinner was preceded by a ride through the timber slides at the Chaudiere Rapids on a square-timber raft. The prince was afraid to make the trip so they got a man just his size and put him on the raft in a princely uniform with instruction to keep his head down. The real prince was waiting in the bushes at the bottom of the slide and the two exchanged places and Edward went on to the ceremonies. You often see old photos of that ride with the prince sitting in the middle of the raft and Gentleman Paddy Dillon and Fighting Jim Bailey on the oars—they got the best rivermen in the business for that royal ride—and I often laugh over it. The caption says, 'HRH, the Prince of Wales and his party riding the Chaudiere Rapids.' You know, he took a great fancy to our upstairs maid, chased her down the front stairs one night. We fired her on the spot, of course. But when he left we rehired her right away. Poor Nellie! I don't think to the day she died she ever understood.

"It hurts to laugh," she said, holding her side. "But you want MY story, not some bumbling prince's. Isn't that right?" She had a twinkle in her eye she intended me not to miss.

"Shall we begin then at the beginning?" she asked, anxiously leaning towards me. "There is so much to tell—and I haven't got very long to tell it."

Mrs. MacInnis was repeating a phenomenon I had encountered a number of times in my tapings. People who had previously been reluctant or disinterested in telling their stories became eager and anxious as they sensed their death approaching. They manifested an urgent need, it seemed, to set the record straight, to leave behind a summation of their lives.

"My maiden name was Jennifer Amaryllis Gillespie—and as if that wasn't long enough—Courtwright Gillespie. My Courtwrights, on my mother's side, were distinguished United Empire Loyalists."

"The Courtwrights of Kingston?" I queried.

"Indeed, yes, distinguished UEL settlers at Kingston. There are various distinguished Courtwright houses preserved there still. My father's side, the Gillespies, came from Scotland and settled at Falkirk, north of Kingston. But when they were growing up the Courtwrights did not know the Gillespies. In those early days, even if you had money you travelled very little, and you did not even get to know the people who lived more than ten miles away from you.

"My mother was Penelope Courtwright of Kingston and her mother before her, my grandmother, was Eliza Fairfield, another very early distinguished UEL family that settled at Bath near Kingston."

"Ah, the Fairfields. They brought their negro slaves with them when the came, didn't they?"

"Yes, indeed, and their linen and china, their silver and glass, and their haughty high-class noses—which I inherited. Will always used to say I had 'the snoot of a snoot.'"

"Tell me more about your early people!" I said, quietly steering her back to her unexpectedly fascinating forebears.

"In the 1880s my father, Joshua Gillespie of Falkirk went West by rail. That was the only way to go West for a gentleman—or otherwise—in those days. He was a railroad builder and he built the first track out there between Winnipeg and Brandon. When he was in the West, somehow or other, perhaps through a relative or a colleague, he saw a photograph of my mother, Jenny Courtwright of Kingston. He fell in love with her instantly. She was very beautiful. Ever afterwards when we were growing up he could be heard saying, 'She was very beautiful. But the best part of her was that she didn't know it!' Then he would take her in his arms and twirl her around the room as though they were ballroom partners. It is nice to remember your parents always dancing—I think they were always in love.

"Anyway, at their beginning, when my father saw that photograph of my mother, he took the next train to Kingston, booked a room at the British-American hotel, searched Kingston until he found her, was introduced to her—properly, of course. She was just recovering from a love affair with another young man named Burwell—another distinguished UEL Kingston family—who had died of some dread disease of the times—TB, I suppose. She was in a heart-broken state. But when you are young, the heart mends quickly. It is when you are old and left alone that the heart stays broken—"

"Where were they married?" I asked, gently leading her back.

"Falkirk. In 1886. It was a very fashionable wedding. In Falkirk would you believe! Drive through it today. Who would believe it! My grandmother—she of the Courtwright-Fairfield connection—she knew how to do things up royally, even if she was annoyed at her daughter marrying a Scot in kilts, even if she was annoyed that the wedding had to be held in Falkirk because grandmother Gillespie was bedridden and didn't want to have the wedding anywhere else. My

Courtwright grandparents hired every livery carriage and horse in Kingston and the wedding guests were driven by uniformed liverymen to the house in Falkirk.

"My mother's dress was Honiton lace; it came from a couturier's in London. The champagne was imported in cases direct from France. There were twelve bridesmaids all in cream peau de soie, all of the Courtwright-Fairfield connection. The only thing that came from Falkirk was the groom! And the gifts! The Richardsons of Winnipeg sent Crown Derby in barrels. And the Molsons of Montreal Irish Waterford settings for thirty-six. My mother wore a going-away suit trimmed with sable. I think both that suit and her wedding gown are in some costume collection in a Kingston museum today. Their honeymoon was a six-month tour of the continent. She told me she took thirty-four trunks of clothes and fifteen hat boxes. Those were the days! Dressing for the occasion was an art and an event."

"And after the honeymoon?"

"When they came back to Canada, they went out West to live so that my father could be near his work building railroads. He also contracted to build American railroads and for a time they lived in Chicago. But then my father decided that Chicago was no place to bring up three red-blooded Canadian boys. My parents moved back to the Gillespie estate at Falkirk, to the great old country stone, up on a hill just west of the village. There I grew up. Being an only child my mother decided that she would carry on her family name through her children. So my brothers were called George Courtwright Gillespie, David Courtwright Gillespie and William Courtwright Gillespie. And I was the youngest, Jennifer Amaryllis Courtwright Gillespie MacInnis— How will they get it all on the tombstone? Big stone or small print?"

She laughed to herself and went on.

"Even before I met my husband, my family had a lot of history of their own, you know, were very important people—" Here her voice trailed off and I realized that someone was coming up the stairs. Betty was bringing us both juice on a tray.

"I need that!" said Mrs. MacInnis. "I haven't talked so much since Will died!"

She very carefully watched Betty leave the room, begin to go down the stairs, waited until she was sure her companion was out of earshot before she resumed.

"You always have to be careful about the servants overhearing things," she whispered to me with a wink. "Now where was I? I have lost my place."

"You were saying that your family had a lot of history of its own—apart from the famous Gillespies. But tell me, how did the Courtwrights make all their money?"

She looked at me aghast.

"My dear! In Kingston in those days you didn't make money. You simply had it!"

She laughed as she said it and sensing this was not the time to press the point of family finances, I urged her to continue.

"Davie was brother next to me—we were only a year apart and always very close when we were growing up—Davie was killed in the First World War. The story was told afterwards—I don't know how true it was but it sounds like Davie—that the officer-in-charge ordered Davie, a sharp-shooter, to go out and check on another soldier who had been holed up a long time in a gun-site. Davie did this and reported back, 'He's an older man and he looks very tired. I will take his place.'

"Davie did. And was killed shortly afterwards. In a little village in France. We have been back to the grave many times. Will was always so good about taking me whenever we were in Europe. The letters of sympathy to my parents absolutely covered the grand piano in the drawing-room. After we received word of Davie's death, I moped about for weeks until finally my parents in desperation—my depression and grief was probably heightening their already heavy load—they suggested that I get away somewhere, get my mind off it all with a change of scenery. The Dewar Robinsons, my cousins who owned a great big stone mansion on the Ottawa at Hawkesbury, were recommended and I decided to take everybody's advice and go. The Robinsons welcomed me warmly. And there I met Will.

"He was living at Cliffside at the time, the third generation running a vast lumber business established in the 1850s by his grandfather. As you can tell by the pictures in this room, Will was a huge man. He had just come out of the bush back of Fort Coulonge, the Swisha, Chapeau—some of those legendary places a Timber Baron's lady heard of but never saw. In his bush clothes he looked like a gigantic bear, fur coat, fur hat, great plaid wool shirt, pants with braces, mammoth gum rubbers.

"I don't believe in love at first sight and all that nonsense. But the attraction was so instant that the Robinsons sensed it immediately. They teasingly tried to get me to confess that I remembered meeting Will before. In actual fact we HAD met before at a family wedding but Will had paid no attention to me whatsoever. Well, I played the teasing game with them all for a while. At first I claimed I had never never laid eyes on Will MacInnis before. Then I said it was Peter his brother I had met before—Peter looked very much like Will only he wasn't nearly so big—but finally I gave in and said, 'Oh, if you must know then, I do, indeed, remember meeting Will before at the Fairfield-Dalton wedding. And I'll tell you why I remember him. He had the biggest hands I had ever seen. And he ate three lemon meringues—which I was brought up to know was very bad manners!'

"Several weeks later I went back to Falkirk mended considerably and Will went back to the bush. He wrote me every day until he came to propose. He used to send the letters out by his teamsters to the nearest post office which would be miles away from his lumber camp. I have them yet here right beside me."

She opened a drawer at her bedside. I looked in. There neatly tied with ribbon was a little packet of letters.

"Will knew what he wanted and he didn't hesitate about it a second. He was like that in everything he did. He could make big decisions with a snap of the fingers. I knew my family wouldn't be happy about my choice. But I had no idea how unhappy. I can remember the scene as though it were yesterday instead of sixty-some years ago. My mother was in the Flower Room making an arrangement for a sick friend in the hospital. She loved to make her arrangements and I felt she would be in a receptive mood.

'Mother,' I said, 'Will MacInnis has asked me to marry him'.

'I never heard of him,' she said absent mindedly. 'So I am sure you will not'.

'But I've already said yes.'

'What does he do?'

'He's a lumberman'.

"She dropped her roses. 'Amaryllis! You're not going to throw yourself away on a man who cuts wood!'

'No, no, mother. A lumberman. He owns a lumber business. He employs hundreds of men in the bush. He has a mill at Cliffside on the Ottawa and another at Chelsea on the Gatineau.'

'Where does he live?'

'Ottawa,' I replied.

'Slabtown!' she groaned. 'He lives in Slabtown! Just full of nouveau riche. Dreadful people. Totally without culture—'

'His family has an estate—'

'I will hear no more of it. Do you understand?'

'Mother, I am going to marry Willie MacInnis. I love him. You loved David Gillespie. And you married him—'

'That was different. You'll have no blessings from Kingston, my girl,' she said, her lips drawn in fury. 'We didn't bring you up in the best schools—with the best people—to throw yourself away on some woodcutter from Slabtown.'"

"Well, I was just as stubborn as my mother. We were married. Will wanted the wedding to take place in Ottawa, so that all his friends could come, including his favourite shantymen from the bush. But my mother nearly collapsed at the suggestion. In those days you know my dear, Kingston, Perth, Toronto, yes even Brockville were fashionable. But not Ottawa. Ottawa was considered to be full of people without any breeding, blue blood or background, people like the Booths and Eddys who put up monstrous showy houses—utterly declassé. Ottawa was famous for its 'recreational violence,' brawls on the Lebreton Flats, the stench of the E.B. Eddy plant in Hull, rows and rows of workers' houses, fires in the lumberyards. According to my mother's standards, nobody of class lived in Ottawa, much less married there. Well, Will would not be married in Kingston. So we compromised and were married in Toronto. That was sixty-five years ago. I was twenty-seven. Whisper it. That was getting on in my day. That was Old Maid!"

"Tell me about the wedding."

"Well, it was in Bloor Street Presbyterian. Where else? It was not a 'white wedding' but it was large. Being a very practical person, I wore my going-away suit—well, there we are in that photo (here she paused to point to a very large photograph over her bed of a tall young couple) and Will, being a very practical person as well, combined our honeymoon with many business activities. We crossed the continent, even down into the States, even up into Alaska. The MacInnises had speculated on vast tracts of land in the prairies, even had timber stands throughout British Columbia. Indeed, they were amongst the first Valley lumber people—if not the first—to develop timber stands in the West as well as the East—"

"This is to be YOUR story," I reminded her. "Not the MacInnises."

"When we came back from our honeymoon we lived in an Edwards mansion for a number of years until Will had this house built and ready. He hand picked every stick of lumber in it himself. And the stone came from Portage-du-Fort. He said he wouldn't have a Kingston stone in it—after the way my mother acted about our marriage. But you know it turned out I was really a small-town girl and I longed to live in Cliffside up the river. I felt that one of the large MacInnis Mills was there and Will would be close to his work. But he was away a lot in the bush and he thought I would be lonely in the little town, not very many stimulating people, or people of my class. But finally we compromised. He built me a summer place, a huge rambling gracious frame, a twenty-four room cottage. That was our hideaway, our retreat. We spent long summers there. Oh! lovely long summers! That was fifty years ago, fifty swiftly-moving marvellous years. Where did they all go?"

She became lost in her reminiscences. I waited a little in comfortable silence then said, "Tell me about the social life in Ottawa. It must have been a wondrously colourful era—all those timber barons and their ladies—all that money."

"Oh, my, yes!" she said. "And how Mrs. Dufferin Brighton resented me when I first came here! She had been the reigning Queen Bee in town and she didn't want another Queen Bee entering the hive, I tell you! Often as social leaders in town we would be asked to sit at the opposite end of the table to pour at Government House functions, church affairs, IODE teas. And do you know what they used to do?" She began to laugh to herself here.

"Tell me what they used to do."

"They used to put big banks of flowers in the middle of the tea tables so that Mrs. Brighton and I wouldn't have to pretend that the other one wasn't there! One day someone forgot that flower barrier—I think it was at the tea at St. Andrew's Presbyterian on King Edward Avenue—and I sat down at my end of the table and looked right into Mabel Brighton's face! I smiled at her ever so sweetly, so sweetly, indeed, that she poured hot tea all over her lap and had to be helped out to the ladies' room, dancing all the way as though she had ants in her pants—"

Mrs. MacInnis was lost here in giggling to herself.

"You and Mrs. Brighton didn't get along very well?"

"I think the other reason she detested me so much was because Will and I were so obviously happy together—it's funny, isn't it, how people, and women especially, can hate you for being happy? Everyone in Ottawa knew that Mabel Brighton's husband Henry had a mistress he spent most of his time with—a widow in Sandy Hill and would you believe it?—French as well. Everyone in Ottawa knew, too, that the Brightons had forced their only daughter Penny—to marry—they called it an 'arranged marriage'—Harper McCuldrick, the heir to the lumber mills at Trois Rivières. That was some marriage!"

"How come?"

"That marriage put together in the same bed the children of two of the biggest lumber companies in North America at that time. Outsiders considered it the match-making coup of the century. But it backfired. Penny left McCuldrick—some even said before the marriage was consummated. And she came back to Ottawa and lived openly with the man she had obviously always loved and chosen, Jasper Bradley, a young lawyer in town. The Brightons were beside themselves. Not only had she spurned all that money but she was living in sin. I know young people do it today with reckless abandon. But in those days! Well, it was the ULTIMATE immorality!

"Penny and Jasper lived next door to some friends who were friends of friends of ours, the Beatons. And the Beatons said that Penny's father and mother persistently pounded on Jasper Bradley's door, trying every ploy to get Penny back to her lawful husband in Trois Rivières. They even went so far as to appear on the doorstep with Harper McCuldrick himself and there was evidently a terrible scene, fisticuffs and all that, Jasper throwing them all out on the lawn and Penny screaming at them. They said she said things to her parents that no child would ever dream of saying in those days, accused them of living together without love, called them whore and whoremaster—"

"What do you think of all that?"

"Well, as a child of my times, I couldn't possibly condone living common-law. But then I suppose I am always on the side of True Love. Anyway, you couldn't convince a small town like Ottawa—and so provincial in those days—still is for that matter—that Penny and Jasper were not depraved sinners, setting a bad example in the community. Socially ostracized, they moved to Toronto. I suppose they thought the Big City would absorb them more readily. And finally a divorce came through for Jenny. Everyone has forgotten how hard it was—even for the rich—to get a divorce in those days. How rotten and degrading it was. Anyhow, they got married and legitimized their children. Oh, what a cruel harsh world it was for them! Can you imagine being married off to and living with a man you didn't love, didn't ever love? Can you imagine it!"

But I didn't need to answer that rhetorical question. She took off in another direction.

"Because of our social position, Will and I had to entertain a lot. But I don't think very many people in Ottawa realized it was only because it was expected of us. Given the opportunity, Will and I always preferred to curl up together with a good book in the evening. You can see what a library we have collected over the years—yes, we were really very simple people with very simple likes and dislikes.

"Of course, Will dealt with all the other lumbering people in his business operations but another reason we didn't have much to do with them socially was that so many of them were such heavy drinkers. We were tee-totalling Presbyterians. And they were all so extravagant! Thirty-nine dollars Mabel Brighton paid for a pair of shoes! In the days when they only cost ten! And that brother of Henry Brighton's, Darby, the one who never married but womanized the length and breadth of the Ottawa Valley! And Europe, too, they say. Whenever Darby used to go on a European tour—which was at least once and maybe twice a year—he always shipped over his Cadillac and his chauffeur. Can you imagine the expense of that!"

"Did you and Will travel a lot?"

"Oh, yes! Not having any children, Will and I travelled all over the world together. Well, I guess I should say all over the British Empire. We never went to and wouldn't ever go to places like China and Russia and that sort of Communist thing. But we usually spent about half our year abroad on Will's business. We made friends everywhere. We used to especially like to go to Will's cousins' country estate near Balmoral in the Highlands. And we had so many friends in England! I have an enormous collection of postcards collected over all those years from all those countries. And photographs. And letters. Scrapbooks full of clippings about the Gillespies, the lumber business papers, a houseful of mementos for sixty-five swiftly-moving marvellous years—.

"We always had such fun together. Good GOOD companions. A most remarkable happy marriage. Gone like that! Sixty-five years of a happy marriage is over before you catch your breath. The only thing Will ever did in his life to hurt me was to die before me. Gone like that. And I am left to mourn."

"This happy marriage. Tell me more about it."

"What is there to tell about it? It was happy. That is all. Happy. That is everything."

She fell silent.

"Somebody once said that a happy marriage has no story. Or was it that a happy woman has no history? Something like that. What do you think of that?" I asked her.

"Well, yes, that is right. All I can say is we had a happy marriage. I can't describe it for you."

"Well, can you tell me how this miracle occurred? What do you think makes a happy marriage?"

"We liked the same things, did them together, yes, often even read the same books together. We laughed at the same things. Even across a crowd in a room we would see something we both thought was amusing and we would lift an eyebrow at each other. And probably laugh over it at home later. Our tastes were alike—with a little cultivation on my part. We were very good at compromising with each other. And we both went to the same church. Originally Presbyterian. When Union was proposed, we studied the proposals together very carefully. And then we decided to throw all our weight with the United Church of Canada.

"We were equals. I think that is so important. I can't describe to you the tremendous feeling of equality we always had. He loved me dearly. He wanted always to make me happy. I loved him dearly. I always wanted to do the same for him. One ahead of the other. Yes! That's one of the great secrets. Anyway, without even knowing it, Will put Jenny ahead of himself, and Jenny put Will ahead of herself. There is a 'beyond oneself,' a going beyond oneself, that is a very special part of a happy marriage."

I interjected, "A famous Frenchman once said, 'Love, when it is total, becomes religious.'"

She caught her breath.

"How beautiful! What a lovely lovely thing you have given me! I never thought of it that way. But yes, a great marriage is a spiritual experience. When you're going through it, living it, you may not be aware of that. But looking back on it—yes, yes. It starts in the gut, moves into the heart and, in the end, enters the soul."

Her eyes went around the photos on the walls as though she were drinking them all in again, maybe for a last time.

"Do you think all your money made any difference in your marriage?" I asked.

"Not a dot. I had had money all my life. I was entirely unaware of money, of having it, of using it. As Scots Presbyterians both Will and I had been taught as children to be careful. We were both also taught that we must share our silver spoons, give back in return for all our gifts. Will gave the skating rink and a park to the town, left funds for a hospital wing—and nobody will ever tally up how many old shantymen he took care of, helped out, like children, like sons.

"When Will died I knew nothing about the business. He had protected me from anything and everything he thought would take my mind off him! So I knew nothing. But one thing he did do for me while he was still alive; he taught me whom I could trust. So when he died, I knew who to go to, what to do and say with each one. The cousins and the nephews took the business forward. Will had trained them and versed them in the lumber business so that there would be someone—however far removed—of the MacInnis bloodline to continue the MacInnis traditions in the lumbering business."

"How do you feel about not having any children?"

She paused so long I thought she was not going to answer this touchy question. Then she turned and looked me full in the face.

"THAT was our tragedy. Our tragedy was not having any children. That was the only way I ever hurt Will; not having any children for him. We were so fortunate. The Good Lord gave us so much. But that was our tragedy."

"Perhaps the Good Lord feels that two people can't have EVERYTHING on earth, not absolutely everything?" I tendered to her.

She seized upon it. "I never thought of it that way," she said. "But you may be right. Will has been out of my world for ten years. I still look for him, still miss him every day. I hear his voice. He is very close to me all the time, almost watching over me. I said to the cook just the other day, 'Will will be around for me soon.' None of that reincarnation stuff, you know, that second sight business and all that. But he is very close to me all the time. And he ought to be around soon—"

"What was the most beautiful thing that ever happened to you in your long life?"

She looked at me with a certain incredulity in her gaze, an intense disbelief.

"What was the most beautiful thing that ever happened to me in my long life?" she repeated, savouring each word slowly. "That's easy. That's just so easy. Meeting Will. In spite of the fact that he had the biggest hands I ever saw! And I am left to mourn. But I'll do the best I can."

At this point in our conversation, Betty came in with the lunch tray. Mrs. MacInnis protested; she wanted to talk, not eat. But Betty invoked doctor's orders. I turned off the tape recorder. I knew she was tiring and I did not want to be responsible for putting too much strain on her frail constitution. She played with some Jello and a little soup while I packed up. When I went to leave she held my hand tightly the way old people do when they sense they may not see you again. But also because we liked each other so much, had had some instant unplumbed accord.

"What was that you told me again?" she asked sharply.

I knew exactly what she was referring to.

"Love, when it is total, becomes religious," I repeated for her.

"I want to keep that with me. Betty, write that down for me."

"Right now?" Betty asked.

"Yes, right now," she snapped.

"You must promise me to come again," she said to me.

"I really would like to come again," I said.

She finally let go of my hand.

Ten days later while out of town on a research assignment I sat down with an Ottawa newspaper, and guided by some inexplicable intuition, turned to the obituary pages, a section I very seldom glance at. The top obit on the first column said, "Jennifer Amaryllis Courtwright MacInnis." And I couldn't believe it. I read it again. And again. Trying to make myself realize that Will had come around for Amaryllis so soon.

My work took me off in other directions and my busy schedule made it impossible even to contact Betty to find out the details of the Grand Dame's death, funeral, bequests. But one day several weeks later, back in Ottawa I had an unexpected phone call from Peter MacInnis, Will's younger brother. He and his wife Sarah, both of whom had been very fond of their sister-in-law Jenny, had heard via the grapevine that I had taped her only ten days before she died.

"Would it be possible to hear the tape?" Peter asked. "Maybe get a copy?"

"I would be prepared to try and do both," I had answered.

"Why don't we meet this afternoon at Lochwinnoch? Peter suggested. "Sarah and I have been willed a few MacInnis mementoes and we will be at the house this afternoon to pick them up."

We agreed that would be a good central place to meet. And at two o'clock I turned into the Lochwinnoch forest for the last time.

It was a shock to find that in a few weeks the house had been stripped. The McInnises watched my face as I looked around. Paintings, sculpture, china, furniture, rugs, all had been taken from the once warm and inviting rooms. All that had been left intact were a few pieces of pedestrian furniture, a number of books and a few copies of photographs. I was thinking to myself that such haste suggested greed, distant relatives who didn't care a dot for the long married life of two very special people.

"Yes, the Courtwrights made short work it, didn't they?" Peter MacInnises' voice came through to me. "They finally had their revenge on the MacInnises," he continued. "When Jenny left everything in the house to her Courtwright and Gillespie relatives in the Kingston area, around Falkirk and Bath."

"I knew there was bad blood there," I said, "but not THAT bad."

"The Courtwrights never forgave the MacInnises for being so rich and having so little blue blood," Peter said wryly.

"What happened to all of the MacInnis' lumbering papers, documents, records, photographs, lumbering memorabilia?" I asked, stricken.

"The Courtwrights and Gillespies shoved it all into plastic bags, hired a truck and had it carted off to the dump," Peter answered. "So much for Canadian history."

I gathered myself together enough to put on the tape. The three of us sat together in a strangely disparate communion listening to the voice of Amaryllis MacInnis up from the grave speaking for the last time in the rooms of her beloved house, telling us about her life with Will. At one point part way through the tape, the MacInnises reached out for each other's hands and held on until the end. When the tape was finished we three sat in silence. Finally Sarah cleared her throat.

"It is a beautiful tape," Sarah MacInnis said. "But Amaryllis left out a few things. When they had given up all hope of having any children, she begged and begged Will to adopt. He finally gave in but they had to adopt older children because of their age; they were both well into their forties by then. Like a lot of men, Will couldn't accept the children, let alone cope with them. His masculinity was threatened, I guess. And he wasn't much of a father anyhow—away so much—and all that. And they had to give the children back to the Children's Aid. I think it nearly killed Amaryllis."

Peter spoke for the first time. "After that she always swore that everything she had in the house would go to her side of the family because at least they had some children to hand her things down to—you see, the MacInnises have virtually died out in the Valley—we have no children—neither does my brother Alec."

"And she never travelled with Will after that," Sarah said. "He went on all his business trips alone."

"Oh, really!" I gasped in total confusion.

"Mrs. Courtwright, the old bitch, never forgave Amaryllis for marrying a Slabtown Scot with no breeding or proper credentials," Peter said with rising anger. "Even on her deathbed she turned away from Amaryllis—there is something so cold and unforgiving about those UELs—tough, indestructible, incorruptible, principled—but so cold and unforgiving and formidable—the money all went to a brother who didn't need it. Not that Amaryllis needed it but she did need a sign of forgiveness and she got none. It was so sad. Even at the end Will went in to the old woman dying to intercede for his beloved Amaryllis."

"Til the day she died," Sarah continued, "old lady Courtwright never put a foot in the house of Will and Amaryllis. Amaryllises' brothers visited betimes, grew to be really fond of the big bushwhacker their genteel sister had married."

"Did you know they buried Amaryllis in Kingston?" Peter asked.

"No. Impossible!" I gasped. "Apart from Will!"

"Yes, Amaryllis wasn't much on technical details, business stuff—and there were no specific instructions in her will. So they carted her back to the Courtwright crypt at Kingston."

"How dreadful!" I exclaimed. "Almost sacrilegious. But what about this house? Do the relatives on Amaryllises' side have it as well?"

"No," Sarah answered. "This house was left by Will to Amaryllis but, on her death, was to go to the United Church to run a home for adoptable children."

I gasped again. Death reveals all the secrets, intrigues, buried passions, unexpurgated hurts, hidden motives.

"And that's not all," Peter continued. "The United Church has refused the house, can't afford the upkeep. According to Will's will the Falkirk and Bath relatives on Amaryllises' side, out of Will's money, must maintain Lochwinnoch estate and all the servants until the United Church takes it over."

I sat dumbfounded and confused. "So often," I observed almost to myself, "it seems that revenge recoils upon itself—"

"Yes," Peter answered, picking up on my musings. "It's always difficult to say who wins—"

Outside, the three of us stood and looked back at the house of Will and Amaryllis MacInnis, a house now in complete limbo.

"Well," I said. "There's one good thing about it."

"What's that?" Peter asked.

"An empty house is so much easier to haunt. The ghosts of Will and Amaryllis will not have to fight off any newcomers. They will have the whole place to themselves."

"Yes," Peter laughed, "Amaryllis has probably already come up from Kingston."

The Language Inspectors

Prologue:

Once upon a time about four or five centuries ago there began on this ancient planet a strange anomaly of a country called Canada, so named after its Native Peoples who were honoured in this manner because it was intended that they be dispatched as quickly as possible. This queer little quixotic quirk of a perpetually quarrelling country was actually made up of what was left over from the creation of what was truly to be the richest, most over-consumptive, most exploitive, most polluting and therefore most powerful country in the world—the United States of America.

Now in the very beginning, you should be aware, Canada was mostly made up of immigrant French who had heard about Canada's gourmet delicacies, Jerusalem artichokes, edible pickerel-weed and wild blueberries, all new and exotic fodder to be exported to the great dining-rooms of Cordon Bleu cookery in the best parts of Paris. The early French were also slightly interested in furs.

After the French came the English who were primarily concerned with the extension of the British Empire and the implantation of the British flag on out-of-the-way places (which Canada certainly was then) on the face of the globe. The British also were slightly interested in furs.

Following fairly swiftly on the heels of the annihilation of the buffalo and the beaver came the Irish refugees from the potato famine, primarily interested in survival. In time they opened stopping places every twenty miles throughout the Ottawa Valley, both sides of the Ottawa River, cut down the trees to make fiddles, imported their songs, dances, stories, and pretty generally had a good time. When they developed a better potato the theory was widely held that progress in this area of agriculture was motivated through race memory of Death by Hunger. But in actual fact potato improvement was accelerated by the phenomenal growth of still and distillery. Furthermore, for decades the Irish in Canada kept it an underground secret that the potato functioned as an aphrodisiac, a secret not revealed until some idiotic Celt blabbed it on the Internet in the 1990s.

About the same time that the starving Irish climbed on board to sail for Canada the Scots were routed out of Scotland through the use of a tricky little device called The Clearances whereby absentee English landlords replaced real live Scots on the landscape with less demanding sheep. On arrival in Canada, the canny Scots quickly saw their way up in the New World, opened schools, began libraries, started universities, instituted Big Business. The Irish Canadian may have invented alcoholism, but the Scottish Canadian invented workaholism. Both were major contributions to the sound economic growth and future of what was to be Canada.

Then in the 1860s, despite the fact that the lines of communication, culture and humour had developed north and south on the East coast of Canada and north and south on the West coast of Canada, a group of politicians dubbed The Fathers of Confederation (a surreptitious Protestant method of counter-balancing an over-abundance of Holy Fathers in Roman Catholic Quebec) decided to make the silly impossible sprawling and nearly empty land mass into a political unity, yea, a presence of power in North America. Ironically there were actually French-Canadians—then called "Canadiens," who backed this movement for union. (But this fact has been shielded largely by the Francophone rewriting of Canadian history now being deposited in the new $86 million "National" Archives in Gatineau, Quebec).

Although the Canadian sprawl was to be held together during the early part of the twentieth century by such modern day inventions as the railway and the telephone, in 1867 at the time of Confederation, the links were largely dog-team, canoe, stagecoach and bits and pieces of the Grand Trunk Intercolonial Railway lines. In both Upper and Lower Canada there was some thought given by the people designated inviters to invite some Western delegates from the colony of British Columbia to attend Confederation, if only to "see what the blighters looked like" as Joseph Howe put it in a conversation with Etienne Taché.

For union purposes the Confederation planners held that historical meeting in the most out-of-the-way place imaginable—Charlottetown, P.E.I. This of course was slyly plotted so that unwanted delegates would not be able to make the P.E.I. ferry—in those days it only ran once a week. Ironically, Lower Canada (later Quebec) was largely in favour of the Confederation of the sundry parts of Canada as evidenced in the Quebec Conference of 1846. However, this unity fever began to die out as soon as the Lower Canadiates (or Quebecers) found out that the Upper Canadiates (Anglo-Celt Ontarians) were to predominate in the new federal arrangements. On the other hand, it was well-known throughout the land that the brilliant and energetic Joseph Howe of New Brunswick was against any form of union and had stated this in his famous Botheration Letters. As it turned out, Canada was to confederate no matter who said what. But the Botheration Letters were generically important for future generations as the forerunner of what was to be called Royal Commissions, by definition strategic political devices used to avoid the truth of an issue, divest the Canadian taxpayers of millions of dollars, and fill filing cabinets. This device was to be particularly useful in shelving Native issues throughout Canadian history.

As it turned out both the advocates and the antagonists of Confederation on bits and pieces of the Grand Trunk Railway and the Intercolonial Line found their way to Charlottetown, P.E.I. to pound out the British North America Act, create a new country to be called the Dominion of Canada. "Dominion is untranslatable in French," Joseph Howe, the self-educated wizard, said to Eugene Tilley, his legislative pal, "and well may be useful in the future."

The reaction in the United States to the formation of this new country on the American border was mixed and low key. After all, the Americans had much larger issues to deal with like cleaning up a civil war, recovering from the assassination of Lincoln, suffering an interim period of vice-presidential rule, and persuading a general to run for president, a process they were to foolishly ritualize.

Canada's birth was reported only in major newspapers like the *New York Times* and then on the back pages, lower half. A few American diplomats expressed concern about an unarmed border and, even worse, the possibility of being posted to a backwater capital where rye was a favourite drink and winter was nine months long. Presidents of the United States and other wealthy Americans who regarded the Canadas as their private hunting and fishing preserve saw the Canadian union as no danger to their vacationing lifestyle.

A few far-sighted American politicians suspected that Canada's natural resources would eventually have to be pillaged for the survival of Americans "in the manner to which they had become accustomed." These pundits expressed the hope that the new country, made up of the Canadas (Quebec and Ontario), Nova Scotia and New Brunswick, would not be so foolish as to try to aggrandize by annexing the British colony British Columbia ("what a future power source! And the size of those trees!"), the vast prairie wheat lands with such potential for feeding Americans, and Newfoundland with those inexhaustible cod fishing banks.

Very few Americans, however, if any at all, had read in the *Ottawa Journal* an account of a speech given by that tiny tippling Irishman Thomas D'Arcy McGee to the annual Temperance Union meeting in 1865 in which he said of the proposed union, "I see in the remote distance one great nationality, bound, like the shield of Achilles, by the blue rim of ocean." A few readers of obscure news in both Great Britain and the United States wondered what McGee could have meant. What ocean? Well, obviously the Atlantic. The Pacific was far-fetched, indeed. And the Arctic? Inconceivable—except by Celtic dreamers.

After the British North America Act had been hammered out the Fathers of Confederation went back to their various bailiwicks in Quebec, Ontario, Nova Scotia and New Brunswick there to practise on a much grander scale paternalism, patronage, nepotism, spoilage and all kinds of other secular perversions, now woven so firmly into the fabric of our society and culture, but then fresh strategic novelties for anyone entering politics.

Amongst other wondrous things the newborn country was declared "a classless society." Everybody outside Canada believed this because it had been told to them, but everybody inside Canada knew this description was false from "sea to shining sea." In the beginning French Canada had two classes, the clergy and the peasants, and the one ruled the other. At one point there was a modest influx of French nobility from France carting in plaster sculptures, seeds for French pear trees, lace-trimmed court costumes. But after a little close observation of the scene at Hochelaga and Quebec City the French Counts and Marquises recognized the perks of living with the Indians, and took to the woods. For one thing the French Roman Catholic clergy under Laval was trying to make them marry, settle down, plough the fields and produce many children for the future of New France. Towards the end of the 17th century, it has been estimated, one third of the male population had deserted the seigneuries of the St. Lawrence, escaped rule by priest and were learning new games in the longhouses. Mohawk, Iroquois, and Montagnais genes entered the bloodlines of the *purlaine* French-Canadians.

Now, there were a number of unfortunate outcomes, negative influences, subsequent to the signing of the Canadian Articles of Confederation in 1867 amongst them not least the geographic fact that a number of good Anglo-Celts woke up to find themselves in the

Province of Quebec, regarded as the hated Anglais or *Les Glacées*, suddenly a minority group. A few Frenchmen as a consequence of the same boundary lines became the first Franco-Ontarians. For some years they were to be a minority in an Anglo-Celt wilderness but what had been lost on the Plains of Abraham was all regained in time by political stealth.

As early as 1818 the immigrant Anglo-Celts had settled Western Quebec, some taking up land as squatters and later, as the surveys went through, as legitimate settlers with deeds to land in what was later to become Pontiac County, Quebec. The river towns like Aylmer and Portage-du-Fort became thriving centres of Irish, Scots, English—and Orangemen! Some service centres like Boyneville, the heart of a rich farm settlement, grew and prospered in Catholic French Quebec, 100 percent English speaking, and 100 percent Protestant.

This was largely due to the influence of one James Prendergast, Crown Land Agent in Clarendon Township, Pontiac County, Lower Canada. In 1825, for his services in the War of 1812 James was granted 500 acres and got the appointment as Crown Land Agent at the same time. James had been born and brought up in the religious antagonism and violence of Ireland and decided that he would have none of this repeated in his territory in the New World. He decided to keep out the Catholics, make a pure Protestant enclave where there would be little cause for fighting and strife. *Ipso facto* when a party of immigrants arrived he would find out their religion and, if they were Catholic, make excuses like "Only swampland left" "No more room" "No land left for settlement." The excuses became barriers. Roman Catholics began to avoid Western Quebec as hostile and so there blossomed in French Roman Catholic Quebec a whole area of Anglo-Celt Protestants, later to become a thorn in the flesh of swelling Quebecois nationalism and that province's eventual espousal of the fascist principal—"the ends always justify the means."

In actual fact, it proved later, that the government officials at Quebec City had no idea where Western Quebec was, least of all Pontiac County. For most "Canadiens" at that time, the world fell off into heathenism at Hawkesbury and beyond that point the Jesuits were attempting to convert the Indians to a consumer religion and thereby promote commerce in Lower Canada. They confessed later they would have taken drastic action had they been informed that scores of pioneering Protestants were trekking up the Ottawa River, establishing Orange bastions, Anglo-Celt settlements.

As one Roman Catholic French-Canadian Jesuit historian wrote later in the annals of Catholicism, "If we had ever known what was going on in the territory at the border of what was later to be called the Province of Quebec, we would have moved to close off the infiltration of the anti-papists and kept all of our lands clean and pure for the Pope and the *purlaine* French." (This, like everything else in Canada nowadays, suffers in translation.)

Now one Dinny Dougherty (the "u" makes it Protestant) along with the McCagues, Dales, Hobbs, Hodgins, Armstrongs, Brownlees, McDowells, Starks, had already squatted on the Ottawa River about 50 miles up from Wrightville at a site they decided amongst themselves to call Paradise Springs.

Although most Canadians and even a number of Canadian academic historians don't know it, Boyneville, Quebec, was first called "Paradise Springs." It is obvious, without too much research, that it was named by an Irishman. Collectively, the Irish have for so long been invaded, looted, plundered, conquered, subjugated and oppressed that they are constantly on the look out for "paradise" in some new place on earth.

In one of his first winters as a squatter at Paradise Springs Dinny Dougherty had left behind in the log shanty his five young ones and his dear wife Moira whom he generously described to anyone who cared to listen as "The foinest woman God ever put a tongue in—but you can't live with her." The previous winter Dinny had gone to work in a lumber camp for timber baron Alexander MacDonnell on the Indian River.

"My God! That's work!" he said to Moira when he returned. "That could kill a man."

Dinny Dougherty had immediately signed himself on as a helper, or as the papers said "rod carrier" to Col. James "The Hammer" Prendergast. Prendergast was a hard, tough, silent man. Whatever events, adventures and trauma had occurred in those wars he had fought for the British Empire hadn't made him talkative. He spat out phrases and words as though they were bullets he was turning back. Although it was lovely weather and they were following a meandering old Indian trail along the Ottawa River Prendergast set his pace as though he were part of Napoleon's army marching on Moscow. When Dinny faltered and complained, Prendergast snapped, "Keep up. Or quit."

Surveyor's helper was considerably preferable to cook's cookee in a lumber camp—cold, flea-infested, isolated, no talking at meals, bed at nine—not Dinny's idea of enjoying life at all. With Prendergast he got to stay over at Symmes Inn in Aylmer—a grand place to sleep on the floor—and then at a widow's cabin near Luskville (where Dinny knew that, if Prendergast hadn't been there he could have had a memorable roll in the hay), and then on to the stopping-place kept by two weird cross-eyed sisters, both of them, on Ghost Hill. In a place called Quyon they stayed at Granny Bean's elegant stopping-place, later to bed down British royalty.

That first fall of work with Prendergast the two men walked fifty miles in three days and began the survey at noon on the fourth day. The next spring Prendergast hired on as helpers "Daddy" Tom Hodgins, Francis Armstrong and James Goodwin.

With the fearsome Prendergast pushing the men hard, the survey was completed in 1826. All the Irish squatters immediately took up lots in Clarendon joined by newcomers Moore, Mulligan, Dagg, and a lone Scot named Cuthbertson. Prendergast also went down in Canadian history as one of the first perpetrators of nepotism in Western Quebec. Amongst the very early settlers were two Roman Catholics, Denis Lynn and James Goodwin. For years they lived amongst their neighbours as lukewarm Protestants and the truth was not learned until Goodwin was dying and a Roman Catholic priest was dispatched from Portage-du-Fort for the burial.

When Prendergast was taken to task by the infuriated Protestant community he simply said, "Lynn and Goodwin were members of my old battalion in the War of 1812, and real good friends. In fact, Lynn saved my life and I could not refuse to locate them."

In revenge for this betrayal by one of their own the Protestant population joined forces to ensure that a Roman Catholic church would never be built in Boyneville. Protestant churches and Orange Lodges proliferated, but the great overwhelming silver spire of Papism never sprang at Paradise Springs or Boyneville as it became later. Racial and religious tension lay waiting for the moment.

Four-fifteen at the Beacon Hotel, Main Bar opening out onto the hotel-yard on Back Street in Boyneville. A steady beat of pick-up trucks and cars grinding to a halt on a mix of snow and dirt.

A Black Day in the Beacon. The *Ottawa Citizen* had just come up the line to Boyneville headlining the passage of Bill 178, an amendment to Bill 101, the charter of the French Language, passed by Trudeau in 1977.

As in the cycle of any ordinary day, the Beacon was beginning to fill up with men coming off work from the lumber mill, from the paper plant, from businesses and jobs in town, from farms and crossroad hamlets on the perimeters of town. Usually the town clowns and drinkers, characters and leaders greeted each other with boisterous openers and familiar one-liners like, "Getting any, Omar?" or "How the hell ya doing, Clarident?"

But on this particular day, December 21, 1988, both regulars and occasionals filed in almost silently, certainly glumly and slowly, as though they had just crossed the street from Argue's Funeral Parlour from whence they had buried their mothers, wives, brothers and best friends in a mass ceremony, the result of some Act of God rained upon the whole community.

Ken Findlay and Big Larry McCord, two regulars, sat down together. Faster than was his wont, Normie Hayes was by their side.

"You look as though you need some Christmas cheer—what'll it be, gentlemen?"

"The fuckin' bastards—" Findlay muttered to himself as though he hadn't heard Normie, wasn't aware of his presence. Then, suddenly, he pulled out of his trance and yelled out,

"By Jesus! I'll have a quart of whatever isn't made in Quebec!"

"Same for me," Big Larry added.

"'French outside, English inside'. What the hell do you think of that Mr. Hayes?" Findlay demanded.

Normie gave their table the usual required Department of Health swipe with his smelly grey cloth and set two Carlings on the table.

"I tell you this—they'll be one helluva long time getting me to change my sign—."

"My Findlays took up land here in 1828—from Prendergast himself."

"And the McCords were later—but not long after."

The two men sat pensive and glowering over their beers like a couple of old crony crows plotting an attack on an enemy hawk. Vinny Hodgins came in and joined them with a curt "G'day." Usually Vinny worked in class until five but word had sped up to the school of the passage of Bill 178, and he had left early. He ordered from Normie and fell into the unusual silence already wrapped around the table.

"It's as though we can't trust ourselves to speak—" he thought to himself as he unscrewed the cap on this beer.

Vinny saw Spittin' Sam Hodgins, Town Clerk Retired, at the barroom door and beckoned him over. Spittin' Sam usually read his newspapers in the bar in the relative quiet of the mornings there and seldom came in during the noisy four to six o'clock cycle.

"I can't believe it," he said as he sat down.

"Nobody can," Vinny snapped.

"You will when the Language Inspectors arrive," said McCord.

"It's Fascist!" Vinny yelled out suddenly, slapping the table with his open hand. "It won't stand. The Supreme Court will overrule it."

"We'll have to gather the big ones," Findlay pronounced in slow round syllables as though he were mouthing something rare and delectable like puff balls in June.

"Don't talk vigilantes," Vinny ordered, hitting the table again. "We have to abide by the Rule of Law—this is still a civilized country. We'll petition—we'll see our M.P.'s—we'll go to Quebec."

"I hope so, I hope so," Findlay muttered, remembering the burning of his barn with the Union Jack so proudly (and defiantly) painted on its roof.

Silence fell upon the table again as all three men watched their friends, neighbours, and relatives file into the Beacon, almost all of them descendants of first settlers, those intrepid Irish—some Scots and English—who had settled Western Quebec all the way up the Ottawa River from Bytown to Lost Nation.

"Say lads," Vinny suddenly hissed, "look around you—what do you see?"

McCord, Findlay and Spittin' Sam surveyed the bar now filling up to capacity as the bar clock moved towards the five-thirty peak.

"There isn't a fuckin' French Frog in sight," Findlay breathed out slowly in utter disbelief, word-and pause, word-and-pause.

"We've been polarized," Vinny said. "Absolutely polarized."

* * * *

And it was hard to believe because, although Boyneville had been 100 percent Anglophone since its settlement around 1800, during the 10 or 15 years succeeding the Trudeau regime, the town had begun to have a smattering, perhaps five percent, of French. Those filling Civil Service jobs like postmaster and the social services employees were now French. The Post Office was no longer one of the social centres of the town; people simply went in to get their mail, buy stamps, give a curt business-like nod to and maybe get one in return from the Beauchamp lady who had taken Reggie Hodgins place when he retired. The last two bank managers in town had been French-Canadians, one from Montréal and one from Trois Rivières. Consolidated began hiring what it called "bilingual workers" but in actual fact, if you weren't Québécois with a French name, you simply didn't get a job there, even a menial job, anymore.

Boyneville had a very active and effective AA, led by Burtrice Smith, which prided itself on the efficiency and speed with which it managed, through the Valley network of clans, to get jobs for its AA members when they were ready to try to make the long painful climb out of their addiction and into life again. But not anymore! AA couldn't give you a hand up unless you were bilingual; Québécois with a French name.

As the Francophone worker population increased in the area around Boyneville, more and more of them bought houses in Boyneville and commuted the few miles to work. It was often asked why they didn't buy in Portage-du-Fort or Bryson both of which always had had some French population, and Catholic churches besides. But Vinny Hodgins had the answers:

"If they can increase their numbers in Boyneville they can demand all services here in French—they will anyhow, eventually—and the other part of it is that the Québécois are in the throes of a revolution and one of the tactics in any revolution is infiltration."

Even although the community hospital in Boyneville had been built entirely from funds donated by the descendants of Boyneville's first settlers—the names were on a plaque in the entrance, McDowell, Eades, Hodgins, Horner, Shaw, Argue, Sharpe, Hobbs, Armstrong, Fulford, Kilgour—the hospital administrator was now a Sequin from Hull and the new superintendent a Charlebois from Montreal. She was supposed to hire bilingual nurses so that the Anglophone patients might make themselves understood from their disadvantaged position of weakness, pain and real emergency; but in actual fact most of the nurses Ms. Charlebois hired for her staff were Francophones with a little English, and some with none at all! This led to some dire circumstances and mix-ups such as when old Amy Hutchison from Quyon squawked out "Help! Help! I can't breathe! Get the doctor!" And was brought the bedpan. Unfortunately, when old Fanny Lester called for the bedpan one of the "illegally planted" Francophone nurses who didn't know a word of English brought her a wheelchair. Old Fanny was so outraged she sat down on it, and used it.

Bell operators spoke French first and managed to make the whole English community seethe with quiet rage as they waited out the superimposition of a foreign language upon their own. The Community hospital was listed in French only as *Hôpital Communitaire du Pontiac* so that, if you were in an emergency in English, you not only couldn't find the hospital listing in your own language but the operator would come on in French and give it to you first in French. People could—and did—die while "the bilingual thing" was being properly processed. The Health Department was hidden under *Commission de la Santé et de la Securité du Travail*, and social services disguised as *Un centre de Services Sociaux de l'Outaouais*.

It was even rumoured that a push was on amongst the Francophones of Boyneville to build the first Roman Catholic church. For as long as anyone could remember there hadn't been a Catholic within a 50-mile radius except for the Murphys at Maryland—and they always had gone to Quyon for mass—and the O'Learys at Clarendon who travelled to Fort Coulonge for service.

"I don't know who would sell them land for such a thing," someone like Ken Findlay would repeat in the bar whenever the topic came up. "Certainly not any of my neighbours or friends."

"They kept the Catholics from building in Arnprior for years," someone else would recall.

"Yes, but times have changed. Some people will do anything for money nowadays," Normie might say.

And somebody like Spittin' Sam or McCord might add: "Never could understand somebody going where they're not wanted—never could understand it at all."

Despite the deeply resented changes brought about by a "bilingualism" forced on a traditionally English community and despite Quebec's march towards French Only, Quebec nationalism and even separation, the French and English had managed—so far—to drink together in the Beacon and "the other hotel" without any real ugly interracial event occurring. There had been the fight in the Beacon yard the night Chug-a-lug had come up the line on his renowned Tour of the Valley, but that still had had the atmosphere more of "recreational violence" than racial antipathy.

But on this infamous night in the history of Canada, December 21, 1988, not a Francophone in town had put his head through the door of the Beacon Hotel.

"Even some of THEM must be ashamed," Vinny muttered into his beer.

"I doubt it," said Spittin' Sam. "They are now a race of people wholly devoted to the adage, 'The ends justify the means'."

"Yes, the straw that broke the camel's back," Vinny whispered half to himself and half to history.

"We'll have to gather the big ones," Findlay intoned again, looking down into his beer, preoccupied, far-off in a trance as though he were having a private déjà vu experience.

* * * *

The Ottawa Valley on both sides of the river had been settled predominantly by the Irish; in 1880 the Valley was 85 percent Irish. Not only had the Valley been settled by the Irish but it also was the home of a race of giants renowned in the history and legend of Canada, the Maloneys of Mount St. Patrick, the Jennings of Sheenboro, the Coltons of Pembroke—the list could go on and on.

Next to politics, giantism was the most popular subject for discussion and argument amongst the regulars in the Beacon. Spittin' Sam who read a lot and got three papers a week always held to the genetic theory.

"Why you take those Hayeses, for instance," he would say. "They settled first in the Gatineau and then they came over the mountains to Boyneville but no matter who you breed them with, east of the Gatineau Hills or west of the Gatineau Hills, you still get giants."

Big Larry McCord, shantyman cum farmer, held to a morphological theory.

"The land bred giants," he would declare. "Big timbers to fell, big rivers to run, big empty country to fill."

But Vinny had researched and read the historical source of giantism in the Valley and often passed the story on to his students in classrooms and his confreres in the Beacon.

"Before 1800 the English impressed all the giants in Ireland to work for them in the timber trade in Canada, to fell and bring out the giant trees for masts for the British ships. It was considered to be a terrible terrible fate to be dragged off to the cold cold shanties of the Ottawa Valley, but if the big Irishmen refused to go, they were simply taken off to Hanging Hill. Ireland was left with all its little men; the big ones like the Rafters, the Mulvihills, the Hogans, the Tierneys—they were brought to the Ottawa Valley."

And so it was quite logical that on the night of December 21, 1988, when the Sign Bill was passed in Quebec, that the lads would be sitting around in the Beacon in Boyneville and that somebody—was it Big Larry McCord or Normie Hayes, himself a giant of seven foot four?—would mutter to himself so that he could be well overheard by those around him, "We'll have to gather the big ones—"

* * * *

Following the fateful December 21 ruling, in the New Year the *Boyneville Informant*, three generations in the Corrigan family and the second oldest weekly in Canada, began a series of objective and passionate editorials on the Anglophones of Quebec, their settlement in Quebec, their history, contributions and rights. This was followed each week by numerous letters to the editor from angry, outraged—and articulate—Anglophones who loved their landscape, but hated what was happening to it. The Secession of Pontiac County was threatened on more than one occasion and the assassination of Brian Mulroney hinted at in various ways.

Petitions with hundreds of names protesting Bill 178 were gathered in Western Quebec and the Gatineau, presented to the English Alliance of Quebec which, in its turn, took them to the three English Members of Parliament in Quebec hoping that they, in their turn, would know what sympathetic Francophone ear might be found in the Quebec Legislature.

When the protesters arrived with their petitions two of the English MPs had their secretaries say "I'm sorry but he's just stepped out—No, I don't know when he will be back—"

But Maynard Miller, the Conservative member for Westmount met them in his office.

"Yes, I agree it's Fascist." he said, "and I'm going to do something, but I don't know what yet."

In actual fact, Miller had a meeting with Mulroney and then resigned on principle. He made a valedictory speech in the Quebec legislature that rivalled Lincoln's at Gettysburg. But it got so little coverage in the English media in Canada (and as usual none in the French media in Quebec) that Miller faded into history with no fanfare except in the Beacon bar and places like that.

"Jesus Christ!" Vinny yiped out in pain in the Beacon bar the night of Miller's resignation. "The only man in one hundred years of Quebec politics who has resigned on principle—and they put it at the bottom of page nine!"

All the presidents of the Conservative Party Associations from Aylmer to Lost Nation gathered their own private funds together and made some quiet little trips, first to Aylmer to visit their MP and MPP—both English, and then to Quebec City to see Bourassa. They returned home replete with platitudes, excuses and meaningful shrugs á là Trudeau.

They then instituted a broadly-based and consistent letter-writing campaign to the MPs, MPPs, and to Brian Mulroney. But except for Miller not a single politicians voice was heard in the land to protest the Sign Law and, worse still, not a word was heard from Mulroney.

"We now have the ultimate proof," declared Spittin' Sam in the Beacon Bar, "that he is totally a man of expediency. An English Quebecer, a member of the English minority in Quebec, and the only thing he cares about is being re-elected in Quebec."

"It is terrifying, indeed," said Vinny, "to think that the future of our country lies entirely in the hands of men of expediency."

All political mechanisms and devises were to no avail. One day, nine months after the passage of Bill 178, described by Vinny "like a gestation period in the womb of the Quebec Legislature" a new breed of Civil Servant never before seen in the land, the Language Inspector, sprang forth. Mr. Emile Bouchard (a cousin twice removed of the famous Bouchard Brothers of Mulroney's and Bourassa's cabinets) in his Quebec government car with its fleur de lis insignia flying on the side arrived in Boyneville and checked in at the Beacon.

He was not unexpected.

Watches had been set for him all the way along Highway 148, the ONLY highway in Western Quebec. It had been originally The Old Indian Trail along the Ottawa River but Quebec government officials in the Department of Highways, once they discovered far-off in Quebec City that Western Quebec was inhabited by "heathen Protestants" and "the hated Engleeesh," over the next 200 years had done very little to change the main highway from its original state as a trail. Furthermore, the Ottawa Valley remains to this very day a network of clans so it had been easy for the Boyneville Resistance Leaders to set up watches with cousins in Aylmer, uncles in Beechgrove and brothers in Quyon. Word of Bouchard's coming had come by phone to Boyneville long before his arrival.

"Just like smoke signals," someone said in the Beacon bar, and the place went up in roars of laughter.

Bouchard, after an uneventful night at the Beacon, the next morning began to make rounds of the businesses in Boyneville explaining to one and all that the English signs must be changed into French within six months; owners would be given one warning and then fined. He got various reactions.

Spittin' Sam, Town Clerk Retired, in his little watch and jewelery repair shop just looked up from his workbench, shrugged and spat on the floor.

Normie Hayes, contacted right in his own hotel, got out his great-grandfather's hearing aid, a big maroon-coloured horn shaped like an antler, put it to his ear and kept saying "Eh? Eh? Eh? What's that you say?" The entire body of men collected in the bar for the performance laughed so loud that they deafened Bouchard.

Ruben Kilgour, owner of the IGA grocery, and Moody Cowan, the IDA druggist were both "out of town on business" their wives told Bouchard, "Gone to Cuba and Sri Lanka" respectively, and wouldn't be back for an indefinite period.

"Definitely indefinite," they repeated with perfectly straight faces.

Hughie Armstrong who ran the lumber yard just stood outside right under his English sign, alternately nodded or shrugged but never said a single word.

Thallia Shaw was the third generation Shaw to run what was in 1989 the only blacksmith's shop left in Western Quebec. Even although he always joyously maintained that "horses are coming back," he supplemented his traditional trade with roofing and tinsmithing. However, the day Bouchard arrived Thallia made sure he was in. When the Language Inspector arrived at the door of his old log forge, Thallia just raised his shoeing-hammer over the anvil and glared. Bouchard got the message.

Indeed, the only person who ran amok was the person you would least expect—one of the foreigners in town, Alfie Schwartz, the only German in Boyneville. Alfie did a little moving and a little transporting, ran a taxi to the bootleggers in and out of town, did a little lawn-mowing and knife-sharpening on the side. Alfie barely managed to make a living for himself, his wife and family of eight children; and to be told, first in French and then in broken English, that he was to change his humble little sign to French was more than he could bear. He listened to Bouchard's ultimatums and threats of fines, and then blew his top. Picking up a knife off his counter, he brandished it threateningly at Bouchard, all the while swearing horrible curses upon him in Low German. The Language Inspector took off amid the cheers of all the shoppers, bystanders and shop-keepers along Main Street. Alfie chased Bouchard to the very door of the Beacon Hotel. Bouchard made it to his room on the second floor, slammed the door and locked it.

Alfie then calmly, knife still in hand, went into the Beacon bar and ordered a beer. As the events of the day were revealed and then repeated the whole bar collapsed in laughter and uproar. "My God, Alfie! Did you really chase him with a knife?" one lad asked.

"Yes," said Alfie, "but, mind you, it hadn't been sharpened."

At suppertime, a visibly shaken and considerably chastened Language Inspector supped quietly by himself in the hotel dining-room. Little did he know what lay in store for him or he would have jumped into his car and fled back to Quebec City the moment Alfie Schwartz chased him to the door of the Beacon.

Sometime in the middle of the night Bouchard was awakened by a tapping on his shoulder. When he opened his eyes he found himself surrounded by a group of men in black robes with stockings pulled over their heads, only the eyes cut out, all standing in a circle of light made by flaming torches held in their right hands.

The mouth of one of the stockings moved.

"Get out of town Bouchard," the mouth intoned in a deep rough disguised voice. "Get out of town and don't ever ever come back here."

The mouth of one of the other stockings moved.

"Fascism deserves fascism," it said.

"Stay out of town or else—" all the mouths intoned menacingly.

Some time in the middle of the night the Language Inspector disappeared from Boyneville. When Hayes sent his hotel bill to Quebec City it was promptly paid by the Department of Language Inspection, no questions asked.

Vinny Hodgins—belonging to one of the most prolific networks of clans in the whole Valley—had a brother teaching Political Science at McGill who knew the "token" Anglophone Civil Service Clerk in the Language Ministry at Quebec City and that's how the story came back that Bouchard had told his departmental boss that, even if it meant his job, he would never go back to Boyneville again.

"They were all giants. They were all giants, I tell you," he kept repeating, somewhat hysterically, as he retold the story of his midnight adventure in Boyneville.

The QPP did come up to Boyneville to ask questions about Alfie Schwartz and the knife-threatening episode reported to them by Bouchard. But nobody had seen anything, nobody had even been on Main Street at three o'clock.

"*Somebody* must have seen Mr. Bouchard being chased," the QPP insisted. "After all, it was broad daylight, three o'clock in the afternoon."

"Oh, you could roll a cannon through Boyneville and not hit a soul at three o'clock in the afternoon," Vinny supplied.

"Where is everybody at three?" the QPP investigator asked.

"Some working, some in the bar, some at home screwing—there's a lot of screwing goes on in Boyneville in the afternoons."

* * * *

To protect Bill 178 from court challenge, the Quebec government, hellbent in the losing game of language legislation, had invoked the Notwithstanding Clause of the Canadian and Quebec Charters of Rights and Freedoms. Nevertheless, the bill was tested in the Supreme Court of Canada and there, in the judges' ruling, language provisions were declared to be provincial jurisdictions.

"Get ready for another round!" Vinny warned in the Beacon.

"Yes, the crazy bastards will be riding up the line again trying to make us change our English signs," said Ken Findlay.

With the aid of four sons who had stayed on the ancestral land (the other two had gone West to the oil fields during boomtime and remained in Calgary) Ken guarded a large proud sign at his entrance gate, "Hilltop Farms, Ken Findlay and Sons, Ayrshires." He also displayed The Century Farm sign given out in 1967 to celebrate Canada's Centennial. Findlay had sworn that he would be burnt at the stake before he changed his signs to French.

"They can burn me at the stake," he would swear in the Beacon bar. "They burned my barn and they can burn me at the stake."

As a way out of the dilemma, the making and hanging of Reversible Signs was often and quite seriously discussed in the Beacon bar. Thallia Shaw was actually commissioned to begin working on designs.

"It would be easy," declared Big Larry McCord whose 25 years in the Gillies lumber camps had taught him infinite ingenuity and innovativeness. "I can fix anything and invent anything else," was one of his most-quoted bits of folk wisdom.

"Our watch dogs in Aylmer would just give us a bit of warning that the Language Inspector was 'riding, riding up to the old inn door' again, and everybody in Boyneville would just flip their signs over to French," he proposed.

"Not me," said Normie Hayes. "My sign's too heavy and it would cost too much money. If they want to change it, they can pay for it."

It was about this time that Normie turned off the French language TV channels in the bar.

"They can go across the street to 'the other hotel'," he said.

"As far as I'm concerned," said Vinny Hodgins, "they can go to hell. I say it's time for civil disobedience."

One of the French-Canadians in the town protested to Normie the censoring of his TV.

"This is a bilingual country," said the Québécois.

"Like hell it is," said Normie. "What about our hospital?"

"I'll go to the Human Rights Commission."

"Do that," said Normie, "it has a backlog of five years' complaints and it's run by a gang of feminists who'd as soon deball a man as have a cup of instant coffee."

Gradually through political intervention what had been a friendly tolerant stand-off between the English and the French minority in Boyneville became a polite but violence fraught truce. The French patrons in the Beacon bar gradually trickled off home to drink or to "the other hotel." With the bar virtually cleared of Francophones, table-top diatribes became—as Vinny loved to put it—de rigeur. In this situation Vinny flowered; as a teacher he was used to delivering monologues to captive audiences. Now, given enough to drink, he often climbed up on the table-top to rouse the troops with inspirational speeches, even diatribes.

"Brothers, let us unite in civil disobedience," he would cry out.

"Hear! Hear!"

"Bilingual today; French tomorrow. French outside; English inside. Do we want that to happen to us?"

"No! No!"

"The media keeps asking, 'What does Quebec really want?' Well, we know the answer to that. What does Quebec really want?"

"More! More! More!"

"And what do they want next?" Vinny would ask.

And the bar would explode with a variety of answers which made a cacophony of unintelligible noises.

"Well, I'll tell you what's next," Vinny would shout. "A referendum to separate. And I tell you if it is constitutionally legal for Quebec to separate from the rest of Canada then it's constitutionally legal for us to separate from Quebec. And we will! We want to remain Canadians and so does the Gatineau and so do the Eastern Townships and so does the Gaspé, and Ruperts Land was only deeded to Quebec. We will all secede. And where will Quebec be then?"

Boyneville had retreated into a period of freighted quiescence when one day the "French outside" sign went up on Reuben Kilgour's IGA on Main Street.

"Epicerie," it declared.

The Beacon bar that night was once again a seething mumbling and muttering as people tried to contain their anger and outrage.

"Epiceries be damned. I'll stop eating—or shop somewhere else."

"To think I'd live to see this day—"

"Piss on Epiceries."

Kilgour was charged with betrayal and right in the bar, too, where on one of his infrequent visits—he was a teetotaller, one of the handful in town—a group of Boyneville old-timers and cronies confronted him at his table where he was drinking a Diet Pepsi with his brother-in-law, Bertie Friend, from Aylmer.

"Kilgour, you've let us all down," said Hughie Armstrong.

"Come on lads, give me a break," Kilgour pleaded gently. "They came up from head office in Montreal. Said the sign law was about to be strictly enforced and it would be good PR to change my sign before things get ugly."

"I don't give a damn," said Ken Findlay. That's the end of my business at your place—after years and years."

"I'm my own boss," said Kilgour, "but I'm not, if you know what I mean. Policies are laid down—"

"I'm not marching in anywhere with my wallet under a sign that says 'Epicerie'."

The scene actually threatened to get nasty but Normie Hayes, in sympathy with any small businessman in Boyneville, intervened and said, "Come on, lads, Reuben has a problem—we've all been friends and neighbours for generations—."

And shortly after Kilgour's sign raised its ugly head on the Main Street in Boyneville, the *Boyneville Informant* reported on the arrival in earnest of the Language Inspectors in the Gatineau, in towns like Wakefield and Low where the English small businessman had always been in the majority.

Like Western Quebec, the Gatineau area had been largely settled by the Irish and the UELs who pushed up into the Gatineau Hills out of Philemon Wright's settlement in Hull. Its influx in the twentieth century had been largely Anglophone as well, Anglophone elite who worked in Ottawa as Senior Civil Servants, diplomats, businessmen, professionals who built superior homes amongst the hills, parklands, ski trails, Gatineau lakes, including infamous Meech.

As in Western Quebec some of the English business owners had been on site for generations. Some of them were interviewed on local TV-CJOH—Barbara Frum and The National, afraid of being accused of racism and prejudice, wouldn't touch anything to do with Bill 178 with a ten-foot pole—and some people angrily protested into the cameras, some wept openly and one man who owned a Wakefield General Store said,

"What can I do? Times are tough. I can't pay the fine."

"We're next," Vinny pronounced in the Beacon bar.

"We'll have to gather the big ones," Big Larry McCord said quietly.

For a week or two the Language Inspectors snorted and rooted around Wakefield delivering ultimatums and visiting small businesses. Everyone in Western Quebec cheered when one man who owned Chez Maxim's in Wakefield refused point blank to change his sign.

"Oh, no," he said, "that's already in French."

"Don't play games with us," said the Language Inspectors. "We know our own language."

"Well, I'll prove it to you," said the restauranteur.

"Have the sign changed within three months," said the Language Inspectors.

But the restaurateur challenged the Sign Bill in court. Four

French linguists were brought in from France to testify as to the validity of the Frenchness of the Englishman's restaurant sign.

The Francophone judge who sat on the case delivered a verdict in favour of the authentic Frenchness of the Englishman's restaurant sign, and the whole of English Quebec went up in one delicious roar of laughter. The *Boyneville Informant* ran the full story, even partial transcripts of the trial, but the event was pretty generally relegated to small paragraphs at the bottom of page nine in the *Toronto Star*, the *Montreal Gazette*, *Le Droit*, *The Globe and Mail* and the *Ottawa Citizen*. Although it was a precedent-setting case the story not only failed to make National TV but was ignored even by CJOH.

"The irony of the thing, of course," Vinny sang out in the Beacon bar, "the irony of the thing is that it could never have happened except that the Language Inspectors spoke Trois Rivières joual."

Nevertheless, the incident set up waves of anxiety again in Boyneville and volunteers organized to move the sign "The Old Village Cemetery" from its situation right on the sidewalk on Main Street across from the Presbyterian church. Begun in the nineteenth century on the edge of town, Boyneville had grown around and past its first pioneer cemetery, now full to capacity with 100 percent Anglophone bones.

In distant time, Thallia Shaw's grandfather had designed and built in his spare time at his forge the wrought-iron arch which designated "The Village Cemetery." The volunteers carefully and lovingly uprooted the arch with its beautiful decorative panels of birds and flowers intertwined, moved it back from the street into the middle of the cemetery and set it up again amongst all the ancestral tombstones.

"There now," said one of the volunteers, "English inside."

Two years after the passage of Bill 178 and one year after the visitation and spiriting away of Mr. Bouchard, two Language Inspectors, Mr. André and Mr. Masse, both distant cousins of André and Masse, leading Quebec politicians and separatists, left Quebec City for Western Quebec and Boyneville in particular. Prior to their departure they had been given special courses in Jujitsu, Parisian French and Mechanisms of Revolutionary Tactics. The two men left the capital of Quebec in a shroud of secrecy, in the dead of night, in an unmarked gray car and, by mid-morning, arrived at the Beacon to register for rooms there.

Normie Hayes had placed himself at the desk for the occasion.

"Oh, yes, Mr. André and Mr. Masse. We've been expecting you."

The faces of the two men paled visibly.

"Please sign here," said Normie with a greased smile. "That's rooms 101 and 102," he said in a loud voice, handing them the keys.

"I heard back in Quebec City, Mr. Hayes," said André, "that you were deaf."

"So far away and so misinformed—as usual," said Normie. "That's my brother, Eddie."

André and Masse left immediately to begin the rounds of the businesses in town.

Spittin' Sam, Town Clerk, Retired, in his little watch and jewelery repair shop calmly looked up from his work bench, listened to the Frenchmen's spiel, shrugged and spat on the floor.

Later in the bar he was reported to have said, "Well, I might as well use my disability to some good."

Hughie Armstrong, who ran the lumber yard, borrowed Normie Hayses' grandfather's hearing-aid, the big maroon-coloured horn curved like an antler, held it up to his ear and repeated, "Eh? Eh? Eh?" until the Frenchmen finished their spiel.

Thallia Shaw, third generation in blacksmithing, just raised his shoeing-hammer over the anvil and glared.

When they arrived at Ken Findlay's farm he was sickling the grass in front of his kitchen verandah. He never stopped, but just changed direction and sickled the two men around the feet, backing them up to their car. Slowly.

At Alfie Schwartz's little cubby-hole shop they never went beyond the doorstep but just did their spiel while, pop-eyed, they watched Alfie sharpen a knife. At 3:30—quitting time for all Civil Servants, at home or abroad—André and Masse returned to the Beacon Hotel where they presented Normie with a formal written warning about his English sign.

Normie looked it over and said, "Sorry, lads, no can read French. This is supposed to be a bilingual country. Get it to me sometime in English. At your convenience, of course."

In the middle of the night in their separate rooms, André and Masse were awakened by little tappings on their shoulders. When they opened their eyes they were each entirely surrounded by a group of men in black robes, stockings pulled over their heads, only the eyes cut out, standing in circles of light cast by the flaming torches in their right hands.

Not a word was spoken as André and Masse were quickly gagged and blindfolded, bound with their hands behind their backs, and carried down the back stairs of the hotel out into cars waiting in the darkness of the hotel yard.

From there they travelled but a short distance through town to the

Boyneville railway station where, without a single word being uttered by their captors, they were tied to the tracks.

The mouth of one stocking moved as its speaker looked down at the two figures lying prone on the tracks.

"The three-thirty should be in in a few minutes," the mouth of the stocking said. And even bound, gagged and blindfolded, André and Masse convulsed in their ropes on the tracks. Far off in the distance the sound of a train whistle was heard. It hooted as it came closer.

"Sure scared the shit out of them," one of the mouths in the stockings said to the others, his shoulders shaking with laughter.

A week later when the QPP arrived to question certain men known to be ring-leaders in Boyneville, nobody knew anything, nobody had seen anything and everybody had been in bed asleep. A handful of wives with very straight faces testified to this fact.

"We're very sound sleepers here in Boyneville, you know," reported May Armstrong when questioned about where Hughie had been that night. "That's because we have such clear consciences."

The QPP already knew from André's and Masse's report to them that, shortly after the train whistle had sounded far off in the distance (and scared them shitless) the two Language Inspectors, released from the tracks, still pyjama-clad, pounded down the empty village street to their hotel rooms where they had dressed, jumped into their car and fled like bandits after a hold-up.

The QPP took some of the big ones—Big Larry McCord, Ken Findlay, Hughie Armstrong, Big Harry Hodgins, Big Jack Horner, along with Normie Hayes, into the little side bar, once "the Ladies' Room" at the Beacon, for intensive questioning. They came down hard on Normie Hayes who, according to Quebec laws for Inn-Keepers, lived in a small suite in his hotel.

"Didn't you hear something?"

"Like what?"

"Like footsteps going up and down the stairs."

For the occasion Normie had borrowed back his grandfather's old hearing-horn from Hughie Armstrong. He put it to his ear, respectfully, each time the QPP spoke to him.

"Mon dieu!" he said, in token French, "everybody in town knows I am deaf. I can hardly hear a train whistle let alone somebody going up and down the stairs in the middle of the night."

"Masse and André reported to us they were abducted by gangs of giants, twelve-thirteen-fourteen-giants, and tied—"

"Oh, they must have been seeing things," said Big Larry McCord. "There are only maybe four or five men in Boyneville over six feet.

Most of the men here are Irish and sprung from a race of leprechauns—little wee men with hairy fairy ears—"

"They were abducted from their rooms and tied to the railway tracks—that's a felony and we intend to find out who did it if it takes us all year."

"Tied them to the railway tracks, you say? I don't think anyone in Boyneville would be that stupid. For God's sakes! Everybody in town knows that there hasn't been a train come down those tracks for the past twelve years!"

The QPP investigation dragged on and got nowhere. André and Masse resigned their $50,000-a-year Civil Service jobs. No one could be re-hired for the job of Language Inspector in the Western Quebec district, not a single man, not even a man-bashing fanatic Québécois feminist who would rather deball a man than have a cup of instant coffee. Indeed, the job became an infamous anomaly as the only Civil Service position, at that level, not filled by a *purlaine* Québécois. In time, the position was taken by one of the token Anglophones in the Quebec Civil Service at Quebec City. He was, as it turned out, a cousin of both Spittin' Sam and Vinny Hodgins and always phoned ahead before he made a visit to Boyneville.

A Tour[1] of the Valley

Daniel Connall O'Toole, Member of Parliament for Leeds-Grenville, had dictated his last letter to his complaining, outraged—and sometimes he well knew—betrayed constituents, and sorted through the weekly barrage of inter-departmental memos, press releases, info sheets. It was a survival ritual he tried to maintain on Fridays because so often he came in on Mondays hung over and really didn't get going until sometime Tuesday noon. The East Block was all hollow, echoing emptiness except for Gabrielle, one of the secretaries, who was still at her desk pretending to work but actually waiting for her weekend date to come down the tawdry, despoiled halls of government and pick her up.

When he had first come to Ottawa in 1984, a greenhorn Conservative, wet behind the ears, and still in a recoil of astonishment at his election, he had taken Gabrielle out to dinner at the Chateau Laurier and slipped her up to his room a couple of times before his wife insisted that they get a place in Ottawa so that she could stay with him while parliament was in session.

"I want you to have 'a home away from home' Danny Boy," she had said to him, pinching his ear, hard. But he knew that she wanted to keep an eye on him and, more importantly, to be in the Capital for all the glittering social functions that she believed belonged by divine right to the wives of MPs.

[1] Before drinking and driving became socially unacceptable, a "tour" of the Valley meant that you loaded beer and/or liquor into a car and went off, usually accompanied by drinking pals, to tour from town to town, house to house, hotel to hotel, all the while drinking in the car while driving, and drinking in each place you stopped.

Reluctantly, he suspended all operations with Gabrielle, knowing that it really didn't matter to her at all; as a married man he was simply another one-night stand. She had her sights on real game now—one of John Crosbie's bevy of "bachelor" parliamentary assistants named Edwin Pankhurst, one of the Pankhurst Pain-Killer Pill gang. O'Toole suspected he was gay and only dating Gabrielle as a "political" front.

"Anyhow," he thought to himself, "she will find out soon enough. Or maybe she already has—is doing her own 'political fronting' with a guy who has the money to take her to all the right places."

O'Toole went to his clothes cupboard, took out his overcoat and hat and slowly began to prepare for his descent into the Canadian winter, month of March. When Gabrielle looked up at him, he gave her the wink, the one they said had won him the women's vote in the last election.

"Where are you and Hanky-Panky off to this weekend?" he asked her with a grin that oozed conspiracy.

"We're off to Tremblant," Gabrielle countered, blithely ignoring his intended slur.

"Well, take a good look at the MP for Leeds-Grenville. It may be your last."

"How come?"

"My operation is Monday morning and it's a biggie. You'll either see me back alive or you'll read my obit."

"Geez, is it that bad?"

"Yup. That bad. CA of the colon—"

"Oh, you'll be back. Takes more than CA of the colon to kill a Valley Irishman."

O'Toole smiled and turned for the door.

"Have a good one," he said as he stepped out into the corridor.

Twelve-thirty. Except for a security guard, the long marble hall to the foyer was silent and lifeless. Everyone had fled what had been a hell of a week, a hell of a couple of weeks. Sault Ste. Marie had declared itself unilingual. Vander Zalm, like all the other first ministers, for his own partisan expedient reasons, had come out *against* the Meech Lake Accord, and Charest, Minister of Sports, had been so stupid as to phone a judge—not just any judge but the *presiding* judge—in a controversial sports case. The roars of the outraged Mulroney, Quebec's political hostage, still echoed in the halls from that one.

"Jesus Christ! Where do I go to get an honest one from Quebec?" he kept repeating in a voice that resounded through the hallowed halls. And the media had been quick upon it, Don Newman, Doug

Fetherling, Mike Duffy, Marjorie Nicolls all taking the tally; in six years of Mulroney's Rule and Mismanagement ten Quebec ministers had gone down on the count for crooked footwork, ten Quebec ministers incubated in "the politics of the shadows," as Geoffrey Simpson of the *Globe and Mail* had described it in *The Spoils of Power*.

The day of Charest's little faux pas a vast stunned silence had swept down all the corridors of power in Mulroney's block as he, a man betrayed once again, vented his rage on those around him. In his own hushed office, O'Toole had whistled through his teeth and said, "Sounds like an enraged bull at home in McTague's barn, tied up in the rutting season." It broke up the tension and got a laugh.

Now O'Toole, a son of the Ottawa Valley, fifth generation in Western Quebec, stepped out on to the steps of the Parliament Buildings of Canada. He never did it without a pause, a swelling of pride in being a Canadian, and an evocation of memories of growing up in the Valley. This afternoon with a Chinook blowing in from the far western mountains of his country, he stood longer than usual looking down over the northern city, the Capital of his country, so sadly in the throes of the National Capital Commission's relentless drive to emulate Washington.

He was here in power as an MP in 1990 because two young brothers, Fingall and Connall, had left Ireland, County Sligo, in 1840, sailed the Atlantic Ocean, got off at Quebec City, walked up the St. Lawrence River to the Ottawa River and, there at the junction, parted company. They had never seen each other again. Connall, it was always said in clan lore, walked on to the Crown Lands at Belleville, but Fingall having sighted the Ox Mountains of his homeland—the Gatineau Hills—turned north and walked up the east side of the Ottawa River.

"He sure as hell," O'Toole thought to himself, "didn't know he was walking into what would one day be separatist Quebec!"

Fingall O'Toole had walked up the Ottawa River for over a hundred miles, along the Old Indian Trail, following the mountains upriver, past the Protestant settlements, past Pendergast's holdings at "The Springs"—no Catholics allowed there—and on to The Lost Nation of the Irish, a tiny Irish Catholic enclave set down in the lake-filled "Inah Valley." There he took up his 100 acres of free lands and established himself in the community as the carriage-maker.

"Oh, lordy! The O'Tooles weren't famine Irish!" was a refrain that had come down the clan pipes, passed on in the oral tradition from generation to generation as if they were still in Ireland.

"Oh, the O'Tooles came with something! They came with skills!"

And succeeding generations of O'Tooles had maintained the tradition of skills—blacksmithing, harness making, carpentering.

"Yes, boys, those O'Tooles were all good with their hands."

Like everyone else in the Valley in the early years the O'Tooles had gone off to the lumber camps as shantymen in the winter when things were quiet and there was cash to be earned taking down the white pine.

"Oh, I'm off to White Pine College," O'Toole remembered his grandfather chanting.

According to clan legend, O'Toole's great-great-grandfather, Patrick, son of Fingall the First by Fiona Kilgoran, had walked down to Ottawa and brought the first cow back to Lost Nation. When she calved, Patrick had crossbred the mother and son. "And that," it was always said in clan lore, O'Toole reminded himself with a smile, "that was how incest began in the Valley."

Smiling to himself, he was suddenly reminded of another clan story he loved. One of the proliferating clan of O'Tooles, a cousin of some sort or other named Raleigh was so bright that the priests in the Upper Valley decided to send him down to study at St. Patrick's College in Ottawa. And it was an oft-told story in the clan that Raleigh's brother, an illiterate shantyman named Bernie, used to send Raleigh some of his meagre pay every year to keep him at his studies at St. Pat's and enable him to proceed into law.

Well, not only did Raleigh become a Bytown lawyer but he married into the McTavishes—the lumbering McTavishes, no less—built a mansion on Laurier Avenue near the Prime Minister's house, made very early in his career a national reputation as an orator, was elected to Parliament and managed to hold his seat there for some twenty-odd years. But at no time was Raleigh O'Toole's brother Bernie, a rough illiterate shantyman who had aided his brother's career so loyally in his early years, ever allowed to cross the threshold of his illustrious brother's mansion on Laurier Avenue!

"Well, that's certainly not in my cards," O'Toole said to himself, standing at the doorway of the House of Parliament in the footsteps of his clan relative, Raleigh O'Toole. "I *never* forget where I came from and I keep the common touch. Bernice may be a snob and a social climber, but I'm still 'one of the Boys'."

As O'Toole stood there looking over the capital city surveying his past, his heart cavity suddenly constricted and he knew he was afraid, yes, terrified of what lay ahead of him on Monday morning. As Dr. MacKeracher had said, the cancer was "still operable" and for that, he knew, he was supposed to be grateful. But, after an adult life of roughly 30 years at "Fort Whoop-Up"—drinking, touring, womanizing, divorcing, remarrying, five kids "scattered and screwy," a trail of premarital and extra-marital love affairs stretching across the continent from his Great Stud Period—he could now realistically face the fact that, even if he survived the operation and was granted respite with a shortened colon, his Rabelaisian days were over; he would most likely be condemned to a diet of oatmeal porridge and cottage cheese washed down with skim milk. He would be ordered not to drink. Worse still, he supposed he might become weakened, passive, and maybe even impotent.

Suddenly, he just didn't care. He was sick of sex often now and, he suspected, not very good at it anymore. He and Bernice had been "passionate pals" in the first few years of this marriage; but now, high living providing endless rich food and booze—and he was still smoking—weeks went by without an erection. And Bernice didn't seem to care any more than he did. Did she? Or was she busy having an affair with some younger man? Another parliamentary assistant? She was still, he thought, in her own unusual way, a good-looking woman with a great figure. But, thank God, not like Jill, his first wife. A Beautiful Woman with all the problems of A Beautiful Woman—one of them being narcissism and another being frigidity. Both lethal in any relationship, he had decided, when they were in the throes of separation and divorce, as well as a messy custody battle.

Now, back of everything else, lurking in his future was The Final Stroke that traditionally took out the O'Toole men as surely as alcoholism was in their genes. O'Toole's own father had died of a massive final stroke at 57.

"Exactly the age I am now," O'Toole noted with a twitch.

And suddenly, standing on the threshold of the Government Houses of his nation, a fifth-generation Canadian in the Valley, MP for Leeds-Grenville, new chairman of the Day Care Committee, he felt tears on his cheeks for his father who had worked his fingers to the bone, mortgaged his farm and his soul so that his two sons could go to university and move up—or so he thought—from the O'Toole's traditional Trades and Skills class. His mother—a Neville from Fort Coulonge—had gone back to teaching to put money into the coffers for law school and medical school for himself and his brother, Jim, now practising in Vancouver. He was an internationally renowned expert on drug addiction, had written books about it—one of them, *The Adult Children of Drug Addicts* was on the best-seller list not only in Canada but in the United States. There was even talk of translating it into French and German.

His father had lived to see them both graduate, the beginnings of their practices, Jim in Toronto and himself in a law office in Brockville. He didn't like the stuffiness, the underlay of UEL conservatism and "old money" in Brockville, but his marks hadn't been very high at law school—too many "extra-curricular" activities—and he hadn't had that many offers after his bar exams. Brockville was as close as he could come to staying in the Valley.

His father had died of his O'Toole Stroke several years before O'Toole had been catapulted into office. How proud he would have been! Yes, in the final analysis a man of honour and integrity. But how would his father have felt, what would he have said, if he had lived to know the truth about his son's ultimate backing of the Meech Lake Accord, or, even worse, his toeing the party line about the sign laws in Quebec?

In the beginning he had taken up the cause of his own people—the Anglophones in Western Quebec—and had led a little group of rebels whom the Ottawa press jumped on with glee and dubbed "The Dinosaurs." But then one day Mulroney had summoned him to his office, sat him down in front of his massive PM's desk, and said in that quiet restrained voice of his which masks so much anger:

"What is it you want, Dan? Off the back benches?"

They had made a deal—well, not exactly a deal at first. Mulroney had told him what would happen to him if he didn't toe the party line, and then he had promised that he would appoint him to a parliamentary committee.

Bernice had been elated, begun talking excitedly about a portfolio. But O'Toole knew his limitations. He was in the Big League now, but he knew he didn't have the ingredients to play on the First Team. For one thing, he didn't have the killer instinct. He was like the kid from the local high school in the Valley who leads in everything and then, with big head and inflated ego, goes to some major university like Toronto or McGill and finds out that although he might have been a star at home, he's just one of the "middle masses in the classes" at a first-rate cosmopolitan university. Besides, he knew he'd never really learn French; he was actually worse than Broadbent, and always would be. Secretly, he suspected his early childhood training in what was today called "racism" subconsciously prevented his tongue from bending itself to the elisions and nasals of the French language.

"Oh, well. Mulroney will ride VIA Rail out in the next election—with The Last Spike firmly driven into his spine—everybody knows that now. And me? Well, if I'm still alive, I'll be back to boring law practice in Brockville."

He crossed the parliamentary grounds towards the reserved

parking area and got into his car, fully intending to return to The Driveway condominium where Bernice was waiting for him to have a Jacuzzi—maybe if they were both in the mood, they'd do it together—a couple of drinks and then take her out to dinner at The Mill with the Priceyfields. Pete Priceyfields was Member for Algoma East, a man from the Mining North where, as he was wont to way, "The men are still men—and smell like miners." Pete kept his balls pretty well intact, knew how to kick up his heels and let down his hair. And like all Valley lads, he was a great storyteller.

But, instead of turning east towards The Driveway, O'Toole found himself going west, over the Interprovincial Bridge into Hull, for a ghost's age the traditional touring territory of every Anglophone drinking womanizer in the Valley. Recalling some of his own escapades there, he laughed to himself for the first time that day.

"Jesus! This is my first chance to see The Palace since Mulroney's government—MY government—the government "of the people, by the people, and for the people" put money into it. What a stink that was! A government business loan to what was essentially a Civil Service watering-hole and whorehouse!"

He parked his car on Le Promenade du Portage—it used to be Wolsey Street—and took a moment off to mourn the passage of all the unique heritage buildings in Hull that had been demolished by the NCC to put Federal Government buildings in Quebec, pump the economy of Quebec, and not just foster bilingualism but erect massive Federal Government buildings where French was *first*—the new Museum of Civilization being another case in point. These faceless monolithic towers of Hull were as everyone also knew, part of the NCC's plans to emulate glass and plastic Washington.

He entered The Palace's velvet-pawed garishness with its smells of nightlife—stale smoke, spilled liquor, perspiration—being cleaned up in the daytime, and its crazy strobe lights distorting reality, turning the gloomy inside world into a multicoloured night circus.

"There is nothing worse than a girlie joint in the daytime," he thought to himself. The place was almost empty, except for the bartender turning shades of yellow, purple, and green in the strobe lights and a cleaner in a white apron mopping the floors with what smelled like Lysol. O'Toole turned away, suddenly nauseated.

"This isn't what I want."

But back in his car he still didn't turn towards his assignation in Ottawa. The something driving him, the inner control, directed him again up the Valley. As he hit the old Aylmer Road out of Hull something clicked in him.

"My country! My country!" he said to himself in glee, hammering the steering wheel.

"Into my country! My clan country! The whole network of my clan country! Here I come!"

As he said it he remembered the wonderful story about how Chretien—then Justice Minister in Trudeau's Cabinet—lost his voice one time in the 1981 referendum campaign shouting, "My Rockies! My Rockies!" Yes, an incredible example of Francophone imperialism reaching out across the whole of Canada! O'Toole smiled maliciously to himself at the vision of Chretien going dumb from shouting, but he shuddered at the thought of Chretien as a possible Liberal leadership candidate in the not too distant future. Wasn't it Sweden's Count Oxenstiernia who is supposed to have asked his son, "Do you not know with how little wisdom the world is governed?"

He pulled into an old haunt on the Aylmer Road, the Gatineau Golf and Country Club, a real drinking and dancing dive in his youth. But the parking lot was empty, and ghosts of companions of his past benders there, some AA, some dried out, some even dead, drove him out again, away again, on again.

"I want a drink, but I don't want to drink alone," he observed to himself. In his mind he quickly went over a list of his old touring pals, but sadly realized some had quit drinking, some had quit drinking and driving, and some he had lost track of. The only one he could think of within possible reach was Buzzy Brennan, now mayor of Nepean. But he'd heard Buzzy had diabetes and was on the needle.

One of his old en route watering-holes in Aylmer, the Saint Charles on the corner of Main Street and Highway 148, despite its theological connections, had burned down a few years earlier, taking with it into hell all its barroom brawls, unsolved murders, clandestine sexual encounters. Looking at all the French signs on Aylmer's Main Street he found it hard to believe, even as an Anglophone, that Aylmer had once been 100 percent English, founded by the great English timber barons, Wright, Conroy, Egan, Foran, and that, as a young thrill-seeking adolescent, he used to come here with a Boyneville gang to the Twelfth of July celebrations, King Billy's Day and the Orangemen's Parade, looking for a fight.

It had been a matter easily arranged since the Aylmer July 12 celebration was one of the biggest in that part of the Valley. It drew King Billy's followers from all up and down the Valley, from all the English towns in Western Quebec, Beechgrove, Boyneville, Wakefield, Low, Bryson, Campbell's Bay; from Arnprior, Renfrew, Westmeath, Beachburg, even Pembroke on the Ontario side of the river, and from all the Orange towns around Ottawa, Carleton Place, Carp, Almonte, Pakenham, Merrickville, Smith's Falls. The glory of it all was that throughout the whole Valley for the remainder of the year whenever and wherever adversaries from the big brawl in Aylmer met, they would stage revenge fights.

O'Toole remembered a bruiser from Carp named Big Jim Sanderson who gave him quite a going-over in Aylmer. And then months later when he was on a "tour of the Valley" and chanced into the Almonte Hotel, who would be sitting at a table with a couple of friends? Yes, Big Jim Sanderson. O'Toole was with a couple of pals, too, so he went over to Sanderson's table and said quietly, "I owe you one. Would you like to step outside?" It had been a great brouhaha—one that still made him chuckle to himself as he remembered it.

Slowly he drove past the site of the old Saint Charles Hotel. On it now stood Aylmer's new City Hall, and he shuddered to think of the ghosts that must be haunting the ground there, men with knives in their backs, young girls gone to bed with beasts, truck gardeners and farmers robbed of their market and grain checks. There was even a castration story he had once heard.

He continued down Aylmer's Main Street—now renamed Rue Principale he reminded himself with a grimace—past a few stores and houses to the British Hotel, a historical Valley watering-hole now owned by what had to be called in the new "politicese," "a multicultural Canadian." That is, a Pole who regularly had nightmares about the Quebec Language Inspector riding in to town and demanding that, in accordance with Quebec's fascist laws, he change his huge rotating landmark $50,000 neon sign into some idiotic French translation like L'Hotel de Bretagne.

The British, a massive stone building, circa 1840, once the residence and business of timber baron Conroy, despite various bastard alterations, retained its grandeur and beauty and still exuded its importance as the social and political centre of Aylmer in its early days. He paused to read the heritage plaque on its cornerstone, still in English.

In this building was held the first meeting of
the Municipal Council of Aylmer, 1847.

Inside the hotel he found his way by rote into the Men's Beverage Room. It was typically dark, but once his eyes adjusted to the light he saw over in a corner a couple of UIC Frenchmen arguing in joual about the Wayne Gretsky trade—two years old but still a hot topic. The bartender was nowhere in sight. He sat down. The two Frenchmen stopped to gape at him, paused in their half-English half-French argument. He realized that he was too well dressed for the setting, an actor stumbled onto the wrong stage, into the wrong milieu or century. He considered flight but decided on a drink—even if it was alone. He was going to order a Miller Lite but found himself, when the bartender finally materialized, ordering a double rye and throwing the waiter a dollar tip.

"That looks like the beginning of a real old-fashioned Ottawa Valley tour!" he said to himself. "Yes, the good old way."

He raised his glass to the two Frenchmen.

"Here's to the Ottawa Valley!" he yelled over at them.

They both looked startled and then raised their beer glasses half-heartedly in a gesture of indulgence.

"They probably bloody well don't even know they are *in* the Ottawa Valley," he thought to himself.

The rye felt good. Bernice had been hound-dogging him off hard liquor ever since Dr. MacKeracher had issued his verdict.

A little half-assed glass of white wine here—a little light beer there—now rye, good rye is a man's drink—always was, always will be.

He raised his glass again towards the two Frenchmen, giving them a big phoney grin, all the while thinking, "The bastards probably think all of Quebec was always French, all French." He was tempted to yell out, "Here's to the English in Quebec, in Western Quebec, in the Mining North, in the Eastern Townships, in 'Moyyal.' All 100,000 of them!" But thought better of it. Instead, when he raised his glass again towards the Frenchmen he yelled out, "Here's to touring the Ottawa Valley!" One of them, fed up and mystified, gave him the finger.

Grinning to himself—because now he knew what he was doing—he drained his rye, slammed the glass down on the table top and walked out to his car parked behind the hotel, an inner compass now directing him up the Valley as surely as in his early days it had directed him to the Kazubazua for speckled trout. One on every cast in those days.

"Drunk or sober, in English or French," he thought to himself as he drifted along Highway 148 out of Aylmer, "this has got to be one of the most beautiful roads in Canada."

He wondered to himself how many hundreds, maybe thousands, of times he had travelled that route in all seasons of the year, in all stages of his life, yet never failed to be awed by its splendour and captivated in his imagination by its history as the road made its way north between the Ottawa River and the Gatineau Hills.

From Aylmer to Lost Nation where the road finally falls off into the Canadian wilderness that stretches north then to Hudson Bay, he could name many of the ancestral farms settled by the Irish, Scots and English in the dawn of his country; Pinks, Nesbitts, Davises,

McConnells, McKechnies, some of their descendants still owners of the first settlers' lands on the high plateau backed by the mountains and overlooking the Ottawa at a wide wide stretch of the river which he never passed except that he imagined the early explorers, missionary priests and fur traders paddling in wonderment, in astonishment at the land, the untouched, ethereal other-world beauty of the land.

"Or maybe," he thought to himself again this time, "would pagan adoration of beauty be a luxury they couldn't afford as they paddled under the gun day after day to reach the passage to the China Sea, the route to riches and power? Maybe it would sort of be like getting some of my constituents—men out of work because of the closing of the chemical plants at Cornwall—to think about the ecology."

"My country! My country!" he suddenly shouted to himself again laughing at the memory of Chretien going hoarse! And then the poignancy of his journey on this day contracted in his chest, and he wondered how many more times he would make this rejuvenating journey through Western Quebec to the source of his roots and the fountain of his being.

"True, one cannot live on beauty alone," he thought to himself, "but it sure helps palliate the smelly rat's underground of Canadian politics."

After a five-mile feast of river out of Aylmer, just above Ghost Hill the highway veers away from the water and moves very close to the mountains, running on a ridge high above the Eardley Flats—still some of the richest farmlands in the Valley—and here sit like designated guardians the great stone houses of first settlers Hurdman and McLean, surveying the original holdings on the Flats. He noted the old landmarks again—as he had a thousand times before on a thousand tours of the Valley—at Beechgrove Ira Merrifield's staunch General Store and his living quarters wrapped around it at the back and above it so that he could always be on duty, before, during and after hours, to help out and serve his community. Yes, a man as honest and open and tidy as the Eardley Flats below him, down the hill.

O'Toole used to drop in on the Merrifields sometimes when he passed—Ira was a great story-teller with a wry quick wit but they were both dead now—she had been a Halliday from Aylmer—both buried beneath a two-heart headstone in the little United Church cemetery at the head of Bradley's Hill, both Anglo first settlers' families going back to the Indians. So many of them were gone now—but the old General Store would stand like their memorial for years to come and echo those first NHL hockey games over the radio around the old pot-bellied stove in the middle of Merrifield's Store, the voice of Foster Hewitt still in high-pitched hysteria, "He shoots! He scores!"

Merrifield's sign now said Laflamme Marché Sûpreme and the store windows were all fogged in and filled with lop-sided cigarette ads and stacks of Pepsi cases.

Past the turn-off to the mountains at County Road 78 that led in to Wyman McKechnie's famous role-model farm where the generations had bred—and still bred—prize Ayrshire cattle that had established their reputations not only as "the best farmers in the Valley" but internationally as well. He contemplated how fortunate the McKechnies were that descendants, grandsons and great-grandsons, "took hold" and stayed on the land, continuing the farming traditions at a time when so many Valley farmers faced the heartbreak of selling their ancestral farms because no children cared to follow their way of life.

Past the McAra's place, now said to be the oldest log house in the area—Ira Merrifield had told him that once and Ira should have known because the first Merrifield children had played with the Indian children on the ice of the Ottawa river long ago. It was history, too, that the McAras when they came from Ireland had run the first river ferryboat and then—according to Ira—decided "there was more money in farming!"

Inside the old log house, still standing, slightly canted, lived "The Three McAra Boys," old Irish bachelors, still standing, slightly canted as well, but the last of their line. When they died the ancient Celtic name would die out as well, he observed to himself, and the "new" French will swarm over it and pretend that the Anglos hadn't settled Western Quebec—and the Eastern Townships—and the "northern townships" along the foothills of the Laurentians—and the Gaspé—and the north shore of the St. Lawrence River adjacent to Labrador—and Rupert's Land, that vast territory sold by the Hudson's Bay Company to Canada in 1870 and then assigned to Quebec—as an administrative convenience—and largely at the behest of the English-speaking provincial bureaucrats in Quebec City!

It was common knowledge in back rooms on The Hill that Quebec history was being re-written in the textbooks and re-taught in the classrooms and that data, like the extent of the Anglophone settlement in Quebec, was being eradicated.

"Ah, well," he mused to himself, "time mosses over more than tombstones—and all history is eventually fairy tale and legend."

Off 148, he took the first turn-off in to Quyon—there are three of them, all headed to the Quyon ferry—the last one left in the Valley above Ottawa—and went in the long way round to his next stop, Gavan's Hotel, a famous watering-hole. Over the years he had been there for numerous St. Patrick's Day celebrations, celebrations that drew people from all over Ontario and Quebec, and some from farther points east and west homewards again to a 24-hour non-stop fest of music, dancing, and drinking. In anticipation of Gavan's ceilidh, the great dancers of the Valley polished their clogs, and the great fiddlers of the Valley resined their bows and the great drinkers of the Valley prepared their bellies. He had been there when, as the gargantuan celebration reached crescendo, people danced through the chairs and table-tops, glass flew through the air, fiddlers collapsed and were revived with brandy, drinkers passed out whispering the name of St. Patrick. These celebrants were resuscitated with dippersful of ice-cold well water poured over their heads, or laid out in one of the empty rooms upstairs and, when those filled up, laid out in lines in the hotel yard like bodies in a morgue after a disaster.

Irishman Lennox Gavan, one of the twelve singing Gavan brothers of the Nickabeau Valley, owner of the hotel, had established the St. Patrick Day revelry and set the precedents for it 40 years ago or so. O'Toole remembered his first one there. He had only been 17. Before he had drunk himself senseless with his buddies, he had been led off into the bushes somewhere by one of the O'Leary girls of Maryland. "The Twelve Dancing Princesses" they had been called then, he remembered with a smile—where were they all now?

And Lennox was dead. The new owners were foreigners—whoops!—"multicultural"—and he had heard the place had changed. The town had changed. It had once been 90 percent English and was now about 60 percent French.

When O'Toole entered the Gavan's big bar he was greeted with a miasma of smoke and the noise of men together drinking, arguing, yelling, pounding the tables to emphasize a point they couldn't win. He knew by the stage they were at that many of them had been in the bar since its opening at eight, downing quarts of Bras D'Or and Labatt's. True it was Friday afternoon—TGIF everywhere—not just in the parliamentary bars and restaurants—but it occurred to him that the further up the line he went, the fuller the bars were in Western Quebec.

"Yup, makes sense," he said to himself. "More and more on UIC."

He found himself a little table for two and squeezed himself in. "Jesus! I've put on weight, but I'll be losing it fast now—as the CA eats me." Again, hearing Bernice's voice in his ear, he was going to order himself a light beer, but he decided perversely on a man's drink again, and ordered a double rye. He knew he should have something to eat, but decided that would only feed the Goddamn monster in his colon.

He expected someone to recognize him. After all, he was getting closer to home territory and his picture had been in the *Citizen* lately several times, even a cartoon.

"Christ! It's lonely at the top," he muttered to himself as he sipped his drink. He had left his hat in the car but he was still wearing—in this mob of blue jeans, green cotton plaids, and weather-beaten jackets—a Page & Price suit. He loosened his tie and tried to look ruffled, less "Federal payroll." But he was closed off by an invisible barrier. Some men even turned their backs on him as though to protect themselves from the evidence of too much money.

Finally he was approached. A fat man with a florid face, patchy red and white—stroke candidate—unsteady of foot, making his crooked way out past his table, stopped, gave him the drunkard's stare and slurred out:

"What in hell do we have here? A Member of Parliament?"

There were a few snickers as he passed on and out the bar door. But no other response.

He finished his drink. "Warmed to the asshole," he said to himself as he got up to leave. The further away he got from Bernice the more profane his language could become. His heart gladdened.

He had gone only a few miles past Quyon on the highway when he suddenly, again for no conscious reason he could describe later, pulled his car over to the shoulder.

"What the hell is the use of going on a Goddamn tour of the Valley—maybe my last—and going alone?"

He got out and stood beside his car. The Friday afternoon traffic was getting heavy as the commuters, out of government offices early, ran for home and the first drink, as the truckers, mostly empty-rigged, pounded down the highway trying to make deadlines, as the weekenders tried to beat the traffic up the line. He was thinking of his last meeting at Lost Nation with Tessie when an empty lumber rig, pup in tow, pulled in behind him. A grinning giant leaned out of his cab and yelled at him in an Ottawa Valley accent: "You in trouble, me lad? Need a lift?"

O'Toole hesitated a minute. What did he need? Where was he going?

He walked over to the cab. "Where are you going?" he asked emphasizing his Ottawa Valley accent which Bernice detested. "So backwoods," she always said. "So redneck."

"Oh, up the line, up the line for a good time," the giant sang out.

"Sure suits my pecker," O'Toole rapped back, and climbed into the cab.

The driver guffawed loudly, put her into gear and rolled out.

"I'm going up Chapeau way," he said.

"Fine by me, m'boy," O'Toole said.

They drove a little in silence, taking each other's measure. O'Toole could feel the truck driver trying to give him the once-over without turning sideways.

"You abandoning your rig me lad?" he said, finally.

"Yup," O'Toole said, realizing only as he said it that that was exactly what he was doing.

"I'm touring. Started in Hull. At The Palace," he proffered.

"You're not exactly dressed for it."

"I just left the office—"

"I hear The Palace is in big trouble."

"Oh, you mean, about all those government loans?"

"No, I mean about blackballing."

"Who's blackballing The Palace for chrissakes?"

"All the small businessmen like myself who can't get a loan from the Goddamn government—ever, ever, ever—when we need it."

He pounded the wheel.

O'Toole squirmed. Maybe this big guy would recognize him and throw him out on the road again, throw out the baby with the bath—.

"It must be tough," O'Toole conceded, and tried to change the subject. "Are you running lumber for Consolidated at Portage?" he asked.

"Well, I used to—but it's been bought by the Americans, you know. Free Trade and all that bullshit. They'll bring in their big machinery—like that stuff in British Columbia—and they'll tear our mountains apart, rifle every tree—"

"You don't believe in clear-cutting?"

"I sure as hell don't. This is my livelihood, and I like to work. When they strip every tree out of the Valley—which they will manage to do in a few years—I'll have to join all the sons-of-bitches on UIC—"

"But the deal was that they reforest—"

"That's horseshit! Who'll police that, for chrissakes? It's just like the fisheries down East—run into the ground by asshole politicians and the Feds not putting up enough money to police the fishing holes like the Grand Banks and keep the goddamn foreigners from cleaning it all out."

O'Toole began to feel uncomfortable again. This was very close to the bone.

Suddenly the jolly giant took his right hand off the wheel and held it out to O'Toole, turning sideways to look him straight in the eye.

"Say, my name's Kilgoran, Reggie Kilgoran."

He crushed O'Toole's right hand.

"I'm O'Toole. D.C. O'Toole."

O'Toole could sense that Kilgoran was mystified by the initials, as O'Toole intended him to be.

"You're one of those O'Tooles from the head of the Island near the Kennedys?"

"I live in Brockville, but I've been doing a little work in Ottawa lately."

"Moonlighting?" Kilgoran asked.

"You might say that."

There was another strained silence. O'Toole knew the Valley mind well enough, and especially the male Valley mind well enough, to know that this big bastard was sitting beside him thinking now, "What's up with this creepy asshole? What's he hiding? He looked okay."

O'Toole knew he had to try to rescue himself or he'd be out at the next truck stop—hitch-hiking up 148 again—only this time it might not be so easy.

"Say, Kilgoran," he said. "I read in the *Citizen* the other day that they blew up the weigh scales at Fort Coulonge—used a shot of dynamite—were you in on that? There must have been a damn good reason."

"There sure as hell was a Goddamn good reason," Kilgoran said. "I'll never admit to a stranger that I was in on it—but I sure as hell approved of it. My father was a dynamite expert—jigger in the mines at Kirkland Lake one time—and there's lots still around that knows about dynamite—."

O'Toole here held his silence. He knew that Kilgoran really wanted to tell this story.

"—Old Charlie Davis was on the weigh scales for years and years at Fort Coulonge, and he was the truckers' friend. You could count on old Charlie any time, anyhow. And then Charlie up and died. And they got this hotshot Frog from Quebec City who didn't know his ass from a hole in the ground—knew nothing about trucking and truckers—they said he had some degree from some community college in Quebec in Weigh Scale Operation—can you believe that crap? And he was taking everything down to milligrams, and really giving us all a hard time, and trying to do it all in French—all in French—so we blew up the son-of-a-bitch's weigh scales—we even considered putting him on them beforehand!"

Kilgoran laughed out loud at the thought of it.

"To be honest—and fair—I don't think they know that the Irish were here first. In 1880 Western Quebec and even the Gatineau was about 85 percent Irish," O'Toole said as a diversionary tactic.

"Sure, lad, my ancestors were here before that gang of French peasants armed with a few flintlocks lined up on the Plains of Abraham."

Here Kilgoran turned sideways to deliver his line.

"Sure, MY ancestors were here to greet Champlain!"

O'Toole had no difficulty with the innuendo and turned it back.

"Sure, there's 'a little of the Giddygaw' in all of us—here in the Valley," he said, and I don't know a Goddamn Frog here in the Valley that doesn't have a 'little of the breed' in him!"

"All those Scottish fur traders, all those Nor'westers—they all took native women to bed—"

"And sometimes even married them!"

They laughed together, remembering things from their own pasts.

"Yah, I've been reading all of Newman's books on those fur traders."

"Really?"

"Oh, don't sound so artsy-fartsy surprised, me lad. I read about five books a week—mostly politics and history."

O'Toole was digesting this surprise when Kilgoran said, "Okay, now, I'll ask you one. What do the city slickers think about Bourassa's 'French outside, English inside' crap?"

"Well—some of the big city folk, the English ones, think it's fascist, unconstitutional and regressive. In plain English, they think it's an asshole laughingstock! But the *French* big city folk—well, they think it's great. Another way of getting rid of reminders of the cursed English."

Kilgoran digested that a little and wheeled his rig.

"Say, did you ever hear down there in the big city what they did to the French Language Inspector the first time he ever went to Boyneville to do his dirty work?"

O'Toole knew all right. The news had reached Parliament Buildings the next morning—and the Press Club. But, of course, it had been all hushed up in the papers there wasn't a crusading journalist left breathing in the Fifth Estate in Ottawa and none of them would touch "The French Thing" with a ten-foot pole—they were all terrified of being called "racist" and "bigot."

"No," he said to Kilgoran. "What did they do?"

Kilgoran pounded the wheel in glee as he related the incident.

"They tarred and feathered him and tied him to the railway tracks. Of course the train doesn't run there anymore—or anywhere else for that matter now—but they scared the shit out of him anyhow. He never came back!"

They laughed together, both men now more relaxed, sharing an emerging sense of equality.

"Say, lad," Kilgoran sounded out, "Did you ever read that book *Bilingual Today, French Tomorrow*?"

"Well, I'd never admit it to a stranger—"

Kilgoran caught the inference, snorted and continued.

"Yup, Jock Andrews. That guy was a gypsy fortune-teller. If we Canadians don't get off our asses and do something, that is exactly what will happen. Right, O'Toole?"

He turned and looked directly at O'Toole, watching his response.

"Right. Right."

"They say that Trudeau closed down the press that printed that book and burned all the remaining copies—and I think that a guy who pulled the wool over our eyes and got us into this bilingual mess and the 'two founding nations' crap, and all that assholery sure as hell would be capable of book burning. Right, O'Toole?"

"Well, Reggie," O'Toole began lamely, "I don't think it's true that Trudeau closed down the press and burned all the books, but *Bilingual Today, French Tomorrow* must have struck a chord. It never got a review in all the Canadian media, and yet it sold something like—I think it was—around 150,000."

"That's a bestseller in Canada!"

"How do you know that?" O'Toole asked, grateful for what might be a subject changer.

"Shit! I've already told you! I'm a bookworm. I only have Grade Six, maybe a bit of Seven, but I read everything I can get my hands on—and I've read them all, Gwyn, Simpson. McCall, Woodcock, Brimelow, Berton. This country is going down the tube—and I want to know why—and I want my kids to know why—"

"Ever read Somerville's *Trudeau Revealed*?" O'Toole asked, hoping to defuse the conversation.

"Yes. Did you?"

"Well, it's almost required reading for every good Tory—"

Kilgoran turned and looked at O'Toole with a great spreading grin and almost jumped his truck off the road in his excitement.

"Jesus! I know who you are now! You're Chug-a-lug O'Toole, champion of Pontiac County—and you're a goddamn Member of Parliament!"

"Buy you a drink at Boyneville." O'Toole said sheepishly.

"It better be out of your own Goddamn pocket—and not the taxpayers'," Kilgoran gurgled, unable to contain himself. "Jesus! Jesus!" Kilgoran yelled out, pounding the wheel. "You're the leader of The Dinosaurs—against Bill 101 and the Notwithstanding Clause, and Meech Lake—and all that crap they're trying to shove down our throats."

O'Toole gulped.

"And we were so proud of you! We ARE so proud of you."

O'Toole gulped again. "I feel like a piece of shit!" he thought to himself.

Kilgoran pounded the wheel again.

"Wait until I tell the guys," he crowed. "Picked up this guy on the road and he turns out to be none other than Chug-a-lug O'Toole, the Honourable Member for Leeds-Grenville."

"And of course we're related," O'Toole jumped in.

"Of course, of course," Kilgoran yelled excitedly. "On the maternal side—"

"My great-great-grandmother was a Kilgoran—somehow or other—"

"Christ Almighty!" Kilgoran exclaimed. "I've got you trapped in my cab—and you know what is going on down there—you must know what is going on down there—besides graft and wholesale lobbying and patronage—you must know what IS going on down there!"

"Well, some of it—"

"And bilingualism is a boondoggle, isn't it? Isn't it?"

"Well, a lot of it is—"

"And it's costing the country millions, maybe billions—"

"Well, nobody's ever really been able to—"

"And you can't legislate language, can you?"

"Well, the Irish tried it and the Flemish tried it—"

"And they failed. Why do the stupid asshole Canadians think they can legislate language?"

"Maybe because they believe they can legislate everything."

"Oh, I can't believe this! Chug-a-lug—no, D.C. O'Toole—trapped in the cab of my rig!"

"I was just thinking of a relative of yours," O'Toole said, "Lornie Kilgoran—"

"He was a second cousin—"

"And I was just thinking about that lovely story they tell about him—"

"Which one?"

"Well, he was coming down from the mines in Sudbury one time—he worked there all his life—but he used to come home once a year to Chapeau. He'd 'tour' the whole Valley all the way from Sudbury to Chapeau—"

"Oh, God! Don't I know that! The whole clan would wait up all night and all day for him—he was such a storyteller—"

"But this time when he was coming down he knew he was dying. He knew it. And he said to the friends who were with him, 'Last year when I came home on tour, I stopped at every bar between Sudbury and Chapeau. But this year, when I know I'm dying, I've stopped at every church on the way.'"

The two men chuckled together.

"You and I don't need to make the church stops on this tour, do we?"

"I hope not," O'Toole responded.

"And now you don't need to tell me where you're headed. You're headed up to see Tessie Perrault. I know her. She was a Sweeney from Lost Nation—"

Kilgoran looked at O'Toole, saw that he had paled visibly.

"It's okay, lad," Kilgoran said. "We all love our wives but—"

"Jesus!" O'Toole finally gasped out. "I didn't know it was all over the Goddamn Valley."

"Well, believe me it's not likely to reach anybody on Parliament Hill."

They fell into silence, O'Toole wondering to himself if his goal really was Lost Nation and Tessie Perrault, his first love, his high school sweetheart in Pembroke, the girl he probably should have married. He'd promised her when he was accepted at law school in Windsor—he couldn't get in anywhere else because of his marks and Windsor was just beginning its law school there and they couldn't afford to be choosy—he'd promised her he'd be back for her. But Time, Distance and "All the Girls He'd Loved Before" had separated them. And he had heard that she had married one of the Perraults from Chapeau. He knew them; red-headed Irishmen with French names, long ago totally absorbed into the Irish enclave.

A year or so after he and Bernice had taken up residence on The Driveway in Ottawa, she had decided that she wanted a cottage up the Ottawa—or perhaps in the Gatineau—and finally he had acquiesced if only so that they would end up in some place of his choice—which was, without a question, Fort William, Quebec. On one of his subsequent sorties up there to look at real estate, in a bar at Fort Coulonge he had heard of Tessie's tragedy, and her widowhood. Rory Perrault had been killed in the bush back of Trout Lake while bringing a load of lumber down a mountain track. The brakes had failed, as they often did, and there's no way to stop a 100-ton hurtling missile. The men are taught to abandon their vehicles and jump clear. Perrault jumped, but not fast enough. And the truck door hit him. Fortunately, there was mortgage insurance on the new bungalow they had built at Lost Nation so Tessie lived there rather comfortably.

It was close to six years now since he first had begun dropping in on Tessie. It was his other world, his real, his honest world.

"Hell!" he thought to himself. "All the gossip-mongers, Mrs. Grundys, and probably Kilgoran himself, think it's a love nest—but Jesus! I'm not the man I used to be."

Aloud he said to Kilgoran, "Lookit. Tessie and I are just good friends—." But even as he said it, he knew that "good friends" doesn't have any meaning any more, or doesn't have the old right meaning, or has another meaning.

"How old are you, O'Toole?"

"I'm fifty-seven last September."

"I'm only forty-five. But I sure as hell know I'm not the man I used to be. Say, did you ever hear that old one about Father Harrington and the widow from Chapeau?"

O'Toole thought he probably had, but he said no anyway. Some of the old stories were so good you didn't ever mind hearing them again and again.

"There was once a famous lady of Chapeau who had been a widow for a very long time. But she had remained very active. She had six boyfriends. So, finally she died. And Father Harrington knew all about her so he decided that he would commandeer all her boyfriends to be her pallbearers. They all agreed. But it was a cold, icy January day and some of the pallbearers slipped on the steps when they were carrying her down the steps of the Chapeau Church. And Father Harrington, just behind the coffin, hissed at them, "Hold on to her, boys! You did it before and you can do it now!"

O'Toole had heard it before, but Kilgoran told it so well and it was such a great story that he found himself laughing from his belly.

"Oh, God!" he groaned. "The stories we grew up on! And the storytellers we grew up with!"

"I guess we all know who the famous widow of Chapeau was," Kilgoran said.

"Never let the name pass my lips."

"It's a real shame, isn't it? Women can go on forever—but men peter out—"

"You know that old story about Willie and Fanny Doyle on their fiftieth wedding anniversary?" O'Toole asked.

"I think it goes—'and after a long while Fanny said, Oh, Willie, my old back's going to peter out.' And Willie said, 'Never mind, Fanny, my old peter's going to back out'."

"That's the one! That's the one!"

"Here we are! 'Bienvenue à Boyneville'" Kilgoran roared out, pointing to a new French sign on the edge of town, erected at the entrance to the still 90 percent English town—except for some Consolidated workers, the few government services employees, and the odd bank clerk.

"Think of all our good clansmen and illustrious ancestors who settled this stretch of Western Quebec—turning over in their graves here as they read that bilge," Kilgoran raged, real anger in his voice for the first time.

"I think of it often," O'Toole groaned, recalling how recently he had betrayed those clansmen and ancestors.

"The graves-keepers say that at the rate of the turnover they can't keep grass growing anywhere—in the graveyards."

"Oh lordy!" O'Toole exclaimed.

Kilgoran pulled his rig up into the yard at the back of the old Beacon in Boyneville—the other hotel had burned down—or been burned down 'twas said—a couple of years before. So on this Friday afternoon the Beacon yard was jammed with cars and pickups. Kilgoran had to edge his huge machine onto the roadside just behind one of the hotel store houses right on the back street.

As they walked through the yard towards the hotel's back entrance, O'Toole thought to himself what a strange pair they must be—Kilgoran in his trucker's uniform and O'Toole in his what-the-best-dressed-Ottawa-MP-is-wearing-these-days outfit.

There was a little pause—or so it seemed to him—in the clamour of the Friday afternoon bar as they entered and peered about looking for empty seats. They spied a round table over in a corner near the men's urinal, and headed for it. Two or three men threw "Hi Reggie!" and "How's it going, Reggie?" at them as they passed. O'Toole hoped he was going to be able to maintain an anonymity that custom in the Valley always accorded to a famous native son returning to his home territory.

As he settled down into one of his favourite watering-holes—the town was filled with characters and wits—he quickly cased the tables around him. How things had changed in ten years! For almost 150 years Boyneville had maintained its 100 percent English *and* 100 percent Protestant structure. But now Consolidated Paper at Portage, the area's only plant, was hiring FRENCH ONLY. They had infiltrated and were buying houses in Boyneville, entering the Boyneville schools, and the complexion of the town, and the bar, had changed drastically. French rose on all sides of him; the table beside him was totally French. There was, of course, not yet any French or Catholic school or French-Catholic schools. But the push was on. And eventually, although they might only have handfuls of students, they would demand, according to the "Declaration of Bilingualism" French-Catholic schools.

"That's so they can be saved from ever becoming Canadian," O'Toole thought to himself. "Look at poor devastated Ottawa! Seven school boards! Oh, well, there will come a time when there will be a tax revolt—and then they'll have to do something about it. In the meantime, the quality of excellence deteriorates—and deteriorates."

He heard a voice above him, around him saying in English,

"Welcome, dear cousin."

It was Normie Hayes, owner of the Beacon and a cousin on his mother's Protestant Prendergast side. Normie generally worked the bar with his employees on weekends when the place was busy.

"And what will the House of Commons have today?" Normie asked, skimming his grey-black cloth over their table, giving it the required Department of Health swipe.

"G'Day, g'day, Normie," O'Toole said, putting on his Ottawa Valley accent. "My friend here will have—"

"A Bras D'Or," Kilgoran said.

"And I'll have—"

"Your usual double rye?" Normie filled in.

"Right. I'm not driving. My friend here is."

"And what would the Honourable Member for Leeds-Grenville be doing in this part of the country?" Normie asked. "Running away from the Meech Lake Discord?"

O'Toole laughed. "No, I'm just touring the Valley."

"Well, just make sure it comes out of your own Goddamn pocket and not out of the taxpayers' and small businessman's."

Normie turned and ploughed back through the crowd. Before the drinks ever arrived, men began moving towards their table, first Charlie Gervais, a veteran trucker from Fort Coulonge. Kilgoran immediately asked him to join them. No sooner had Gervais seated himself than Vinny Hodgins edged through to greet O'Toole like a long-lost brother.

A far-out cousin on his father's side, Hodgins was a high school teacher in Boyneville, taught history and was active in politics—Conservative, of course! Boyneville had been Conservative since the day Daddy Tom Hodgins had first squatted at "The Springs" or, as the new French sign says at the edge of town, "La Source." O'Toole had met Hodgins at various meetings numerous times and although he tended to always be a Devil's Advocate, O'Toole held him in high regard. He knew that Vinny, like most thoughtful Conservatives of the times, was torn in half, torn apart by Mulroney as leader of his party and Mulroney as the protector of Francophone rights, by his loyalties as a Canadian and his loyalties as an English-Quebecker. One half of Vinny was tempted to join a growing ROC chorus of "Let them go!" while his other, belonging to his ancestral roots in Quebec, was, the next day desperate to find a way to keep the country united.

Vinny slapped his half-finished beer down on the table.

"Well, what do you think of slime-ball Bourassa's latest fascist move, me boy?"

"Please, Vinny—"

"I hear the English Alliance in Quebec is taking the Quebec sign law to the Human Rights Commission—oh, not in Canada—here, it's in the hands of the feminists—but right to NATO."

"I'm just touring."

"Jesus! Isn't it just one amazing goddamn paradox—the 'breath of freedom' is blowing through all the Russian satellite countries—what a few months we have seen in Europe! And here we just keep regressing into fascism. 'Free people do not learn new languages at the order of their governments.'"

O'Toole thought of fleeing. But instead took a belt of his double rye. He thought it might help him tune out Vinny who continued to vent his frustrations and anger.

"It's a funny thing about that son-of-a-bitch Trudeau—he had brains enough on his left side, of course, to know you can't legislate sex, but not enough brains on his right side, of course, to know you can't legislate language—"

O'Toole felt nailed. No exit.

"Please, Vinny, I'm just a little old back-bencher trying to have a holiday—"

"You're here, for chrissakes, Danny Boy. I want some answers."

"Answers to what?"

"Did Bourassa really say that or not?"

"Say what?"

"Did he say, 'Let's get this Meech Lake Accord signed and then we can do anything we want'."

"Have mercy on me!"

"And all this crap about separating if they don't get Meech Lake passed—that's blackmail!"

O'Toole's liquor was taking effect and Vinny was fading out.

"The have-nots might separate—Newfoundland, the Maritimes, Manitoba, where the farmers are perishing—but not Quebec. Quebec is a have, have, have province!

In a sort of fuzz Kilgoran and Gervais came in on O'Toole's other side—they were talking about the Dye Report on government spending—the Science Museum north of Montreal was already $78,000,000 over budget—last year!

O'Toole looked down into his double rye and saw a surgeon in his mask. When he lifted his head again he was looking into the face of Ken Findlay, a five-silo farmer from up the line about three miles.

Findlay, descendant of first settlers in Western Quebec, had painted the Union Jack on the roof of one of his barns right on Highway 148 so that every Frenchman who passed by could see it. It had mysteriously burned down. Undeterred, every year now on Canada Day Findlay got up in the night and, with the help of some of his six sons, nailed the Canadian flag on every hydro post for three miles into Boyneville and three miles out of Boyneville. O'Toole had seen them.

"G'day, Dan," Findlay said, and gave him the nod.

"G'day, Ken. How's it going?"

"Can't complain."

Findlay didn't talk much. But he didn't need to. He was a living symbol of English protest in the whole of Western Quebec. "And we sure don't need him at our table, the way things are going right now," O'Toole thought to himself as Vinny nailed him again in a loud voice with:

"Just tell me, you ill-conceived bastard, is it true that Bourassa has gone on record as saying, 'Let's get the Meech Lake Accord approved and then we can do anything we want to'? Is it true?"

"No comment," O'Toole slurred.

Kilgoran phased in here and roared out, "Sure it was even quoted by a Quebec senator—what's his name?"

"Clouthier," Vinny filled in.

"On *Cross-Country Check-up*."

"No comment," O'Toole slurred.

O'Toole's feeling of being in the hot seat, nailed and coerced, forced into facing the issues and taking a stand was further enhanced by the arrival at their table of Spittin' Sam Hanna, Town Clerk, Retired. Sam got the monthly reports from the Dominion Bureau of Statistics and subscribed to three newspapers, the Boyneville *Bulletin*, the Ottawa *Citizen*, the Montreal *Gazette*.

O'Toole knew from earlier tours of the Valley and stop overs at the Beacon that Spittin' Sam—and he really did spit when he talked, poor lad, due to some strange undiagnosed physiological disorder—was plagued by the town's rednecks and that every morning when he came into the Beacon to read his newspapers one of the rednecks would crouch down low on the floor, sneak up and set fire to his paper at the bottom of the page. Such were Spittin' Sam's powers of concentration that the blaze would almost be up to his hands before he'd leap up, cursing, and throw the burning paper onto the concrete floor of the bar.

"Spit on it, Sam!" the lads would yell at him, and laugh as he stomped on it or poured some of his beer over it.

O'Toole had actually seen this daily soap opera enacted and he had had enough conversations with Spittin' Sam to know that he probably could write a thesis on Trudeau, from whom he believed all evils stemmed. He knew Spittin' Sam had crowded into this table because the conversation sounded enticing. Politics in the Valley had always been the main subject of bar talk but, in these times, politics was paramount, maybe singular.

"Trudeau was responsible for the ultimate division of Canada," Spittin' Sam immediately intoned. "Don't ever blame Mulroney; he's just a follower, putty in the hands of Quebec."

The effect was immediate. All eyes turned on Sam, and Vinny took up his challenge.

O'Toole was fogged in, feeling good. "I've probably reached the I-don't-care or the I-know-everything stage," he thought to himself.

"Welcome Farmer Findlay," he said, relieved that the conversational hot seat had switched away from him. "Are you going to blame the crazy weather this year on the Conservatives? Or the Liberals?"

"On God," Findlay said solemnly.

"Jesus! I thought it was the hole in the ozone layer."

"That's God's, too."

Befuddled somewhat, O'Toole looked down into his fifth—no fourth—well, maybe sixth—double rye—and saw Bernice's face, and then a shadow standing beside him.

He looked up into the face of Big Larry McCord, a burly weathered shantyman just turned 90, descendant of generations of shantymen "going up for Gillies."

He reached out his great paw to O'Toole as he settled into a chair.

"You know in the lumber camps there was silence at the trough."

O'Toole laughed. He knew what McCord meant.

"Nobody could talk at meals—cook's orders."

"How are you keeping yourself, Larry?" O'Toole managed to enunciate, thinking to himself, "Jesus! I'm down to short sentences or even phrases." The passionate buzzing around him was rising in pitch and intensity as alcohol converted conversation to monologue and one-word sentences.

"I'm going deaf," Big Larry said, "but it has its advantages, you know. I can't hear all the things I don't want to hear—like Vinny right now on the Ultimate Secession of Pontiac County."

They were into rounds now, each man at the table buying a round in turn. O'Toole had to go to pee. And even although the men's urinal was beside them—and he'd had enough to drink that the smell had faded out—he kept putting if off, unsure of where his feet were now, or how they would carry him.

"I don't know what's happened to this country." Big Larry was saying far off. "I think the politicians have ruined it. We all got on together in the lumber camps, the Indians, the Wops, the Frogs, the Polacks, the Irish, the Scots—even the Dogans and the Micks—"

"Yes," O'Toole tuned in passionately. "It must have been great then." And he meant it. "A great melting pot. Like in the States. They did it all right, those Americans—"

"But everybody spoke English," Big Larry said. "Everybody spoke a kind of English. Things have changed here. Things sure have changed," Big Larry repeated mournfully.

O'Toole looked down into this drink and saw Bourassa's face.

"I have a cousin here can't get a job at our hospital because he can't speak French—can't get a job as a *janitor* because he can't speak French."

O'Toole was suddenly angry for Big Larry's cousin—whoever the hell he was. His blood boiled, the blood of his ancestors who took up and cleared the land on which the hospital stood, the blood of his ancestors who had donated the money for the hospital itself. And he had another drink. "Drink doesn't destroy anger," he thought to himself as he downed another mouthful of his rye. "It only makes for a delayed reaction."

Big Larry leaned over towards him and O'Toole could see his false teeth move as he talked.

"And I'd like you to do something about it for me, pull some strings down there in Ottawa—he really needs the job—he's AA now."

O'Toole groaned. "Oh, my God!" he thought. "If this big honest Irishman only knew what really went on in Ottawa! How powerless I am to stop its course—or pull a little string against the French tide. I should really tell McCord 'I'm just a pawn in the game—and the game is out of control!'"

Aloud, he was about to say something as an excuse to Big Larry, something limp about being "just a little old powerless back-bencher," when suddenly the conversation erupted at the rest of the table. Vinny pounded the table top with his fist so that all their drinks jumped and silence flowed outwards around them to other tables—to the French tables.

"I tell you, they'll never separate! They've got their feet too far into the Federal trough—"

Normie and one of his bouncers, Dirty Jack Jennings, came up to the table.

"Quiet down, lads, or I'll have to ask you to leave," Normie said. Dirty Jack rubbed one big closed fist into the other for emphasis.

There was a momentary silence as they all fell aback into their seats.

In the momentary enforced silence, you could suddenly hear the uproar at the other tables. O'Toole noted that at two of them near them, the conversation—if it could now be called that—was entirely in French. Ten years ago on a tour of the Valley, Boyneville would have been 100 percent unilingual. He shuddered at his internalized use of the word. That was the next thing on the horizon, he had heard in Ottawa: Ontario towns declaring themselves, in self-defence, unilingual—and he could only imagine the backlash from that one!

Findlay managed to fill in the pause at the table. He talked little but he loved to tell a joke.

"Say, did you hear about the poll they took in Quebec last week?"

"Which one?" Vinny snarled. "There's one a week—and all fixed."

"They asked the Quebeckers if they approved of the Meech Accord and forty-one percent said they did. The other fifty-nine percent said they preferred the Honda Civic."

"That's racist," Vinny pronounced.

"No, that's funny," Reggie chimed in, laughing with the rest of the group around the table.

"I heard another good one at the Cobden Livestock yards last week. This Scotsman had his two fingers taken off in an accident in Almonte. The Almonte doctor told him to take them home and bury them in consecrated ground. If he didn't do that, the missing fingers would pain him all the rest of his life. So the Scotsman went home, but he didn't want to be bothered with burying his fingers in consecrated ground, so he just went into the barnyard and threw them into the manure pile. Well, it wasn't too long before the fingers started to ache something terrible and, unable to bear the pain, the Scotsman went back to the manure pile to try and find his two missing fingers. But he couldn't find them. Then he heard about this great Jewish doctor in Carleton Place and he went to him and told him the story and the Jewish doctor said to him:

"What nationality are you?"

"I'm Scots," the farmer replied.

"Well then, my good man," the Jewish doctor told him, "you just go home and put fifty cents into that manure pile and if those fingers are in there you'll soon see them start to work."

"That's racist," Vinny postscripted. "You'll be taken up before the Human Rights Commission for both of those. It's reaching the stage where censorship on all sides will make it only possible for you to talk only in the toilet or under the sheets at night. I tell you, this country is turning fascist and regressive—"

"—while the rest of the world is freeing its bonds, declaring for the Rights of Man," added Spittin' Sam.

"We don't have a democracy anymore," Vinny declared. "We have two totalitarian states, Quebec and The Rest, and Mulroney makes unilateral decisions for both, like the Meech Lake thing."

O'Toole joined in, "Yes, shir, if he brings in another crooked minister from Quebec he should be shot—"

"And the new abortion law," Vinny went on, "that was done for Quebec, to appease the Quebec Catholics, it has nothing to do with what the rest of the country wants."

"Or what women think they want," O'Toole added.

The pitch was rising again. O'Toole looked down into his drink and saw a mug shot of Mulroney's face.

"Say, I hear you're the Chug-a-Lug King of Pontiac County," he heard someone saying above him. He looked up to see a young Frenchman, probably thirty or so, standing over him. "How'd you like to chug-a-lug with me?"

There was a great pounding of fists on the tables surrounding O'Toole's.

"Yes, yes. We want Chug-a-Lug—We want Chug-a-Lug."

O'Toole's knees went limp under the table. He didn't know how many drinks he had had, what time it was, or where he was going. But, even drunk, he knew as an Anglo in Quebec, in the country of his birth, in the country of his ancestors, he couldn't lose face by backing down.

"Set them up," he said. "I have to piss."

On unsteady feet he arose. Reggie got up. "I'll go with you," he said. O'Toole pissed a long, long piss at the urinal, then threw some cold water on his face, slowly wiped it dry. While he was pissing beside him, Reggie said, "Give it to the bastard, O'Toole. He's young, but he can't chug-a-lug. I've seen him before. Remember, we won on the Plains of Abraham!"

Steadied, O'Toole walked back to the jousting table. They agreed on their seconds. The chug-a-lug mugs were ordered and brought on. The seconds—his was Findlay—carefully filled them with pints of beer. O'Toole asked for Miller Lite—he knew from experience it went down fast. The men in the bar, most of them, lined up in rows around the table. The seconds backed the spectators off a little, gave the signal to begin drinking. O'Toole had a moment of nausea before he put the mug to his lips. He was the pro. He knew all the tricks—how to open the throat so the swallowing device was under control; then drink like a baby—all straight down, non-stop.

In his ears, back of his mouth gurgling the beer down without stopping, he heard his crowd egging him on.

"Come on O'Toole. You can do it. Keep going! You're almost there!" Some English voice boomed out, "French outside, English inside. Horseshit!" It was meant as a goad.

Far off he heard Findlay intoning. "The Winner!" He felt his hand being held up. He didn't know what possessed him, but he remembered standing up, putting down the jug, hoisting an imaginary sword and yelling out, "And now to the Plains of Abraham, me lads!"

He heard the French voices yelling, "*Je me souviens!*" He recalled thinking to himself, "Jesus! Maybe I *can* be the first Prime Minister of Canada from the Ottawa Valley!" as someone caught him on the right side of the face with a fist. He swung out and contacted facial bone, heard the crunch. "Haven't lost the old power in the arms yet," he smiled to himself as he waded into a mass of male bodies swinging at each other, shouting obscenities in two languages, stumbling, falling, tearing each other's clothes. And then they were all being funnelled out of the bar by the bouncers—some by the very seat of the pants—and then the adrenalin flowed out into the hotel-yard as the mêlée continued and became a blood bath.

Some big lad hit O'Toole hard and he lay on the ground momentarily, catching his wind and looking up at a nightful of emerging stars. "My God! It's getting dark," he thought to himself, "and I'm supposed to be somewhere else." And he got up and pitched into the battle again yelling "Tally-ho!"

Big Larry McCord said it was the second best fight he had ever seen in all his 90 years in the Valley. "And I've seen a lot," he was quoted as saying later. "The best one, of course, was the big election fight in Campbell's Bay, 1911, when the crowd tore every stick of clothing off the great Larry Frost and left him with only his caulk boots. He headed for the river then and swam north to North Bay and never came back again for years and years."

But the Battle of Boyneville, 1990, ended when word came up the line via the signal stations in Quyon, Luskville and Wyman Station, that the QPP were on their way.

O'Toole staggered over to where Kilgoran was down on his knees on the ground pounding the hell out of a great big Frenchman.

"Jesus! Kilgoran!" O'Toole gasped out. "The cops! You've got to get me out of here. Can't you see the headlines!"

O'Toole could see them very clearly: "MP for Leeds-Grenville Found in Racist Brawl in Boyneville." At least he could spare poor Bernice that one.

They certainly couldn't hide out in the empty truck cab until the commotion died down. Suddenly O'Toole had a brilliant idea.

"In the back wing of the hotel there's a couple of rooms they always leave unlocked so the town drunks can sleep it off," he said.

"Let's go! I don't want to be caught for drinking and driving," Kilgoran said. He looked at O'Toole. One sleeve was completely torn off, his tie was gone, and his navy suit was grey with mud—all telltale evidence.

"Quick!" Reggie said. "We'll get some clean clothes from the cab—I always keep some extras—just in case."

They laughed together like old buddies.

As O'Toole had promised, when they slipped in through the front door of the hotel, up the front stairs, and down the long long, long hallway to the old back wing, a couple of the rooms were unlocked. There was even a sink in one of the rooms.

O'Toole put on Kilgoran's green denims and rolled up the cuffs, a clean plaid shirt, and a green denim jacket. He had to roll up the sleeves. Kilgoran was cut above the eye and they tried to wash that out. O'Toole knew when he looked in the mirror that he had the beginnings of a black eye. His right thumb hurt; he hoped it wasn't broken.

The cops arrived from Hull with sirens on full—they always give lots of warning so that everyone has time to escape and the cleanup job is simple—just a report from the hotel owner so he can claim damages. O'Toole and Kilgoran quickly stepped into the clothes closets in the two rooms. There were heavy hurried steps up and down the halls as the cops threw open doors making a pretence of looking for brawlers.

O'Toole had a queasy moment when he saw the headlines again: "MP for Leeds-Grenville Found Hiding in Beacon Hotel Closet during Raid!" But the QPP search was quick and cursory and the steps receded again.

Like a couple of town drunks, O'Toole and Kilgoran dropped onto the beds and slept. O'Toole didn't know what time it was when Kilgoran poked him awake.

"Come on," he said. "All clear. I have to get home now."

"What time is it?" O'Toole moaned.

"Oh, about ten-thirty." Kilgoran answered. "Dating time in the Valley."

They slipped out the front door, through the dark of the now-quiet hotel-yard to the truck.

As they drove towards Chapeau in a hung-over silence, both locked in their own reruns of the Battle of Boyneville, the moonlight of the March night contoured the beauty of the Valley, flooding the farmer's fields still slumbering in the snow, illuminating the guardian presence of the Gatineau Hills. For most of my lifetime—so far—O'Toole thought to himself, I've been coming and going on these roads well enough to know that spring is already working underground, that the mountain streams are stirring, that if I walked here on the land I could catch the blessed smells of beginning again.

"Yes, my country!" O'Toole cried out aloud, passionately. "My Quebec! I will be buried here, you know, with my Anglo-Celt ancestors—if they don't turn over all our cemeteries."

"I could have gone to B.C. Had an offer from a big lumbering firm there—far more money—but I couldn't leave the Valley."

In Chapeau Kilgoran turned his rig towards the hotel yard.

"A chaser to end the tour," he ordered.

When they entered the bar, cheers arose. Word of the Battle of Boyneville had already gone up the line ahead of them. There was a rush to start rounds of drinks.

"Thank you—but no thanks," Kilgoran said, holding up a hand. "We are suffering battle wounds."

The disappointed men shuffled off to their tables again. They really very badly wanted details of the Battle of Boyneville, firsthand.

"Who won?" a drinker yelled out with a French accent from across the room.

O'Toole and Kilgoran looked at each other, smiled, downed their chaser beers, and left.

Back in his cab, Kilgoran turned the truck towards the houses strung along the Ottawa River east of Chapeau, houses which had the luxury of water frontage, whose inhabitants had the privilege, too often taken for granted, of living with soul-restoring beauty.

"You know where I'm headed?" O'Toole asked.

"I know where you're going. It's where you've been going all day long—a roundabout route though," Kilgoran said, chuckling a little.

"I need to see her before I go under the knife Monday morning. I'm not the man I used to be but after Monday's clincher I may be only a shadow, a fading voice—"

There was a light on at Tessie's. But it didn't matter. He knew he would have knocked until she let him in anyhow.

"I'll get these clothes back to you," he said, climbing out of the cab, reaching up to grasp Reggie's hand.

"Until we tour the Valley again." Reggie reached down, and held on.

"If there's ever anything I can do—" O'Toole began. But even as he said it he was suddenly flooded with a sense of powerlessness. What could an Anglo-Celt MP do in Quebec for an Anglo-Celt logger in Quebec? Why he couldn't even finagle a job on the janitorial staff of their own hospital in Boyneville for Larry McCord's AA cousin.

"Just keep those government assholes from letting the Goddamn Americans cut all our trees," Kilgoran boomed out.

"I think I should just promise we will always be friends," O'Toole tendered. "Some wise man once said, 'Your life must be counted a success if you leave behind good friends.'"

O'Toole knocked at Tessie's door. He heard movements in the house. As he stood there, waiting, he had a flash of intuition, a realization that he wouldn't run again in the next election. And Bernice will probably leave me, he thought to himself.

Tessie opened the door, one hand holding her dressing gown together, looking sleepy. But her eyes opened wide. She gasped and then smiled a little when she saw his borrowed ill-fitting trucker's outfit and his blossoming black eye.

"Hi, girl!" he slurred. "I'm a little stinko but—"

"Bienvenue, Danny Boy!" Tessie laughed, taking him in with her smile, and then opening her arms to hug him.

"O'Toole turned and gave Kilgoran the wave.

"I'm in, Reggie!" he yelled. "I'm back in the Valley."

And despite the lateness of the hour Kilgoran gave the horn a celebratory blast heard throughout Western Quebec.

The Road Between the River and the Mountain

N*o blessed wonder all the children are a-day-dreaming today! I am myself!*

It was a smile of warm and sturdy acceptance that flashed across Sara Costello's face as she looked down on her 32 pupils, each one trying to hide the knot of excitement growing within at the approach of the noon-hour on a spring Friday. Momentarily, Sara's eyes strayed to the wide southern windows of the little one-room schoolhouse where siren blue skies beckoned everyone to dance with spring.

As an English-History major on "sabbatical" from her university Sara tried to think of some fitting Canadian poetry about the season. None came.

We can only write about fall and winter. After all, spring in most of Canada is only a weekend long—this coming weekend—the May 24 holiday weekend!

Someone rolled a marble down Aisle Five. Sara knew, without even turning her head, that it would be the class cup-up Tady O'Shaunessy sending a challenge to Lorne Eardley. Disturbed-dynamo, attention-getting Tady. Sara's eyes moved over her pupils as though she were seeing them that day last September 7, 1944, when she was the New Teacher.

Oh, how much children in school tell their teachers about their parents! Tell who is well-loved, who is emotionally starved, who is mother-tied, who is cowed and afraid.

Sara looked at the clock. Early in the school year she had learned to keep it on the desk turned in her direction. It now said three minutes to twelve. So she didn't orally reprimand Tady for the marble rolling, only slightly frowned at him to let him know that he hadn't put anything over on her.

Tady grinned devilishly, drew his head into his shoulders,

scribbled erratically in his notebook. He was the only child in the classroom who could actually dance in his seat while still sitting. For the two hundredth time that year Sara marvelled at this feat!

Remarkable how in a few months I have grown so fond of even this difficult one!

Across from Tady in the Front Row, Aisle Six, Entrance Grade, Beth MacLaren smiled empathetically at Sara as though to say, "Together we must be patient with this intolerable child!" Beth was a brown-noser. But she was a good student. She was going to be a nurse. Sara had decided she would make a fine nurse. Not only was she obsessive-compulsive but she was also good in emergencies.

Sara picked up her large brass bell and moved towards the door at the back of the room. On her first day when she had been a hopeless greenhorn she had rung the noon-hour signal from her desk, then watched helplessly as all 32 of her pupils stampeded out, the big hulks like Denny Wiley and Irwin Sally virtually running over the little Grade One toddlers, the Kilbride twins, Dolly Moynahan, Willie Eardley.

This lesson at least well learned over the school term, Sara moved quietly, at exactly twelve noon to the back, rang her bell, told her pupils to stand, lined them up in rows and filed them out onto their grassy school-yard, to their "pick-up" baseball games, to Alley-in-the-Hole, to the swings, to the skipping ropes, to their pea-shooters and sling-shots, to their bicycles.

In the empty classroom the silence and space-of-her-own spilled over a grateful Sara. She lifted the heavy wooden frames of her school-house windows to let "the room air out," stretched her arms high over her head, inhaled the fragrant Maytime perfumes of the Ottawa Valley, marvelled at the greening fields of fat farmlands rolling right before her very eyes down to the mightiest and most beautiful river in North America.

What a year to have lived through at nineteen! And in such a place!

In her entire eight months teaching Sara had never once grown weary of feasting her eyes. Elmgrove No.5 sat beside Highway 148 on a narrow plateau which rolled down to the Eardley Flats and the wide mighty Ottawa River. Not only was the little schoolhouse hallowed by a panoramic view of the Quebec and Ontario river borders to the south-west; it also backed right against the Gatineau Hills to the north-east. There, just over the school-yard fence, across the creek filled with trout and watercress, over a couple of fields and you were at the wild mountain's foot.

Sara knew that few, if any, of her 32 pupils realized the quality of their daily surroundings, that it would be many years before some of them came to conscious realization, that some would never arrive at appreciation. But Sara held that the human need for beauty is a basic hunger; it pleased her to think that at least this basic hunger was being satisfied in all of the young human beings she had grown to love and respect in her brief time amongst them.

While pondering these heavy aesthetic values at her window, Sara became aware of a little vignette in the school-yard. The day before, Beth MacLaren had been to Ottawa with her mother to shop. The rest of the girls were now grouped around her admiring and envying her beautiful city shoes. (Theirs came from Mr. McNevin's General Store at Elmgrove Corners). Although Ottawa was only 30 miles down a good gravel road, most of Sara's pupils had never been to the capital of Canada. Beth was one of the few who had. This made her Queen of the Schoolyard. She had even been to the National Museum, could speak with authority on Native Indians and Animals of the Canadian North, would do so if coaxed in a fittingly ingratiating manner.

I hadn't been here very long before I realized that the highway divides the community into its social classes.

Up from the Eardley Flats to Elmgrove No.5 came the children of the well-off farmers, the Eardleys, the Shannons, the Hodginses, the MacLarens, almost all descendants of those first Irish and Scottish who came up river and settled on the Quebec side where they would in time make the nucleus of an Anglo-Saxon bastion, an English minority within the Quebec minority of the Canadian mosaic. On the Eardley Flats the houses were large utilitarian brick, the barns of stalwart and steady frame with modern tin roofs. These farmers had telephones, inside toilets; many of them electricity. The Eardleys even had electricity in their barns. On rainy or stormy days, the fathers of the children from the Flats hitched their buggies or their flat-sleighs, came to the school and picked up a load of neighbours' children as well as their own. Most important, from early spring until late fall, these children rode their bicycles to school.

By comparison, scattered haphazardly to the back of the schoolhouse along the foot of the mountains were the poor rocky farms of the Irish and anglicized French, the Donahues, the Gagans, the Nugents, the Laidlaws, the Gervaises. The Laidlaws had originally been the Lamelins and, although Gervais still maintained its francophone spelling, it had long ago acquiesced to the pressures of English bastardization and was now always pronounced "Jervis." From these marginal farms and bush-lots came the children who were ill-clad for the weather, frequently cold, poorly nourished and, as Sara was to discover in time, often hungry. Some of these children like Joey Gervais had to walk five miles to school, three miles down a track from the foot of the Gatineau Hills and then two miles along the main road.

Sara looked about the school-yard for ten-year-old Joey. Marbles were something he could afford and he had become a champion marble player. He was usually off in a corner under the lilac bushes maintaining his reputation against older boys like Tady O'Shaunessey and Lornie Eardley. But he was not there. Then she saw him coming towards the schoolhouse.

"Probably headed for the washroom," she noted mentally as she watched him approach.

Joey Gervais was the kind of Norman Rockwell "regular boy" that any teacher—or parent for that matter—had to guard herself against lest she fall into the trap of playing favourites. Freckles all over his wide, open, round face, big brown eyes with heavy reddish lashes that matched his hair, slow wide grin, quietly mischievous, tough without being obnoxious and rowdy. But there the Rockwell qualities ended. Joey was often snotty-nosed, unclean behind the ears and on the head, smelly on damp days as his dirty socks and old running shoes exuded their accumulated smells. He suffered school with a quiet hatred, day-dreamed his way through all the "silent" assignments, only responded to arithmetic, at which he excelled. In wintertime he was almost always late, sometimes by as much as three-quarters of an hour.

Out of a winter storm or in from below-zero weather, he would arrive out of breath, half-frozen, his neck bare, often without mitts and, until near Christmastime, still wearing his old running shoes. His arrival was always disruptive, almost an event. Sometimes it seemed to Sara as though he were playing centre-stage and playing it for all it was worth. She knew she should say something, even punish him for being late. But her heart came up into her mouth at the sight of him, at the thought of the child's long trek. And she couldn't. In the end, all winter long, she and the whole class had a tacit agreement that Joey Gervais had it "rough" and shouldn't be dealt with in quite the same manner as the rest.

Standing at her window, listening to the sounds of spring, reviewing the past winter, Sara was suddenly aware of someone beside her. When she turned, Joey Gervais was looking up at her.

He cleared his throat, as though he were going to "speak his piece."

"Miss Costello," he stammered out, "you haven't forgotten?"

She sighed, looked at him tenderly.

"You haven't forgotten—" he cleared his throat again of its anxiety, "if I pass this year I get a bicycle!"

"No, Joey, I haven't forgotten."

Sara watched Joey run to rejoin his friends. Then she returned to her retrospectives. As well as being endowed with the most beautifully situated schoolhouse in the Ottawa Valley, Sara had also been blessed by the fortunate circumstance of rooming and boarding with Seamus and Catherine McNevin who ran the General Store at Elmgrove Corners. Both wise and warm in their ways, the McNevins had taken her in as though she were a blood relation. Seamus was Chairman of the School Board, had a sly teasing wit, way, and wink that was typically Irish. He never gossiped about her pupils but he did relay to her information he felt was necessary for her further understanding of their performance and behaviour. From Seamus she learned that Joey's father, Johnny Gervais, cut wood on the mountainsides, fiddled at square-dances and, most of the time, drank at the Quyon Hotel. From Mrs. McNevin Sara had learned that Mary Gervais "worked her fingers to the bone" and clothed most of her 11 children out of the cast-off box which Mrs. McNevin kept in her store and which was regularly contributed to by the well-off families from the Flats.

I should be putting work on the blackboard, geography for Grade Five, arithmetic for Three and Seven. You have to keep ahead of them, think ahead of them, plan ahead of them, always have something to fill in the gaps in order to prevent chaos.

Instead Sara went around her classroom putting her nose in all the flowers which her children had brought her. It was like a florist's shop and she revelled in every sweet spring scent of it, of lilac, of apple, cherry, chokecherry, crabapple blossom. Most of these came from the children who walked in from the foot of the mountain. Mary Donahue, the Bright One, had picked long-stemmed violets from the sides of a mountain stream and these Sara had on her desk along with lily-of-the-valley from Beth MacLaren's mother's garden. Carie Eardley had brought in early golden iris.

Restless with spring, Sara went to her windows again.

There, in his ancient buggy behind his old faithful horse, Peden Parsons was going by. They waved to each other. Peden was a venerable who came down from the mountains once a week to shop at McNevin's General Store. Sara smiled to herself as she remembered how he had been the first person last fall to make her fully realize (apart from being the New Teacher) what an enormous source of curiosity and mystery she was to the community.

It had been last September as she was walking her three miles home to McNevin's when Peden Parsons had pulled his horse up beside her.

"You the New Teacher?" he had asked, sticking his buggy-whip into its holder.

"Yes, I am Miss Costello."

"I hear you don't have a boyfriend," Peden Parsons said, looking her up and down.

"Well, no not here—"

"Never had a teacher here in 70 hears that didn't have a boyfriend." Mr. Parsons spat on the roadside.

"I have a friend in Kingston I write to—"

"Now what good is anybody to anybody that far away! Way up on the Front." He pierced her through with his sharp old black eyes. She began to feel that there was something awry with her. Then a kind of anger rose. The implication was that no woman—and she now considered herself to be a woman—could get along without a man.

"It isn't that you're not good-looking—" he began again.

She blushed, started to move off.

"Now, whoa there a minute!" the old man said. "I can fix you up with a couple of real good men, real good men—"

Sara had been about to open her mouth to protest when old Parsons pushed on with his match-making programme.

"There's Phil Poirier up there on the Mountain. Smart young lad. Big. Good looking. Only thirteen or fourteen when he finished his Entrance. Did well. But his father was killed up there in a bush accident a few years ago and he lives alone with his mother. Not much of a farm for farming but plenty of good bush. Bush-lot all the way up the Mountain and down the other side—"

"Really, Mr. Parsons," she said, trying to contain her anger. "I have all my preparations to do for tomorrow's classes."

And it was true. She had to spend at least three hours each evening without fail preparing all her board-work for her classes, boning up on her French textbook, organizing her schedule to run like clockwork so that when she was teaching intransitive verbs to Grade Eight, seven other grades would be occupied with written or silent work. Every evening she also struggled with the old Gestettner copier, setting up reading, writing and arithmetic exercises for her younger classes.

Mr. Parsons took up his buggy whip, flicked it over his old horse's back.

"Well, I meant no harm," he said. "I meant no harm to ye."

In a confusion of feelings Sara had watched him plod on down the road ahead of her. And she still well remembered how that night her class preparations had been intruded upon by recurring flashes of her conversation with Peden Parsons, by her reactions to it and by the dawning realization that the teacher did live in a goldfish bowl in any rural community but that she, more than any of the others before her, because of her unusual background, perplexed the community surrounding Elmgrove No.5.

Sara recognized that she was alien on a number of counts. She had grown up in Ottawa and was a City Girl. Her previous year in Arts at Queen's University set her further apart. Worst of all, she was not a "real teacher" but was working on a Special Wartime Permit created to fill the personnel shortage caused by the Second World War.

Prior to her arrival at Elmgrove to teach, Sara had been studying English and History at Queen's. Known as the "Poor Man's University," Queen's had the lowest expenses on the continent. But even there Sara had almost run out of money, money she had saved from the previous summer's work as a waitress at Bigwin Inn, a large Muskoka resort hotel.

The summer following her university year she had had difficulty finding a job in Ottawa that paid enough to save any money. Indeed, she had only managed to find a part-time government job as a typist and to supplement that, had taken on doing the books at night for the gas station owner at the corner of the street where she and her family lived.

Towards August Sara had seen the handwriting on the wall. Although the Second World War had brought some relief to her parent's family of seven—her father had joined up and attained the status of Staff Sergeant in Stores—still there were five younger ones at home—. Sara knew in her heart she would have to obey the unwritten, unverbalized rule of her times that the older children get out of the nest as quickly as possible and begin to earn their own living. In Sara's milieu, university was considered a frill for girls; if she chose to go that way, she would have to earn her own passage.

Sara accepted all that. She had to take a year out, leave behind her peer group, part with her university boyfriend, Robbie MacAllister, get herself a job that would pay enough to enable her to save enough for her second year at Queen's. She discovered that Ottawa Valley school boards, because of the teacher shortage, were paying $100 a month. Out of that she knew she would have to pay $20 a month for room and board. She had calculated that she would be able to save $800.

And that was exactly what Sara had been doing for the past eight months. It was all in the bank in Ottawa, deposited there by her mother. All $700 of it—with one month to go. All her monetary goals were being fulfilled. She knew that it would be years before she fully realized all the extra dividends of her years at Elmgrove No.5.

What a babe in the woods I was! How unprepared, naive, ignorant!

Standing at the window, Sara had to laugh out loud at some memories of herself. She had come to this road between the river and the mountains to make and save money, intending to do a passable minimal job of work without becoming involved to any but the most necessary extent with her pupils, their parents, the community. Moreover, her only credentials for teaching anybody anything had been that she was bright, that her mother before her had taught in a one-room Valley schoolhouse 25 years before. Sara had come to Elmgrove No.5 a "fool rushing in where wise men fear to tread," without the slightest conception of how much work is involved in running eight grades in one classroom, of the adaptability, innovation, improvisation, good instincts, fundamental psychology necessary as survival mechanisms. Nor had she had the foggiest inkling of the cultural gap between her urban-university background and the earthy simplistic one of the rural community.

I came as an idiot infant. In this one year I must be wiser by ten!

Despite her initial materialistic goals, Sara had not been able to fend off to the least degree involvement with the community and total dedication to her pupils. Despite Peden Parsons failure to match her with any of the local eligibles, nevertheless she had been invited to square dances at Luskville, Quyon, Shawville, even over the mountaintop to Lowe and Wakefield; to teas, wedding parties, anniversary celebrations up the Mountain and on the Flats. She had early gleaned that it was expected of her to set an example in the community as a church-goer and she had consistently gone quite happily with the McNevins to the little white frame United church beside her school.

Standing at her windows, Sara found herself recalling one of the major events of her year at Elmgrove No.5. She still winced at the memory.

Oh, my god, the Inspector's first visit!

He had come out of the snow unexpectedly in December when

she had all the desks pushed to the wall, indeed, was standing on her own desk directing a rehearsal for the Christmas concert play, "Snow White and the Seven Dwarfs." The whole scene was an unsalvageable chaos from which he exited quietly without any harsh criticism but over which she had agonized for months afterwards. By the time he had come again in March, she had acquired the good class discipline that comes of mutual respect, the self-confidence that comes of hard work coupled with many mistakes. He told her he had never in all his years seen such strides made by a young teacher in her first year and begged her to choose teaching as her career.

The Christmas concert cast an afterglow that lasted for months and will last in me for years and years to come.

The men cut a tree from the mountainside 15 feet high reaching to the peak of the Orange Hall, brought in chairs for the audience, carted wood for the great wood-stove, set up ladders so that the young people could decorate as high as the star that brushed the ceiling. The women baked, cooked, decorated, iced goodies for a feast to end all other feasts. The night of the concert the Lord sent a soft snow through which the flat-sleighs full of singers jingle-belled their way behind teams of great steaming Clydesdales to the soft lights of the concert hall.

There was a capacity crowd. Every pupil took part several times over, singing, reciting, playing parts, working behind the scenes. In order to incorporate everyone into the class play "Snow White and the Seven Dwarfs" was changed to "Snow White and the Fourteen Dwarfs" (no harm done to the quality of the script). It was on its way to being a legendary success when catastrophe struck. Someone had forgotten to bring the poisoned apple for the wicked witch. Quick as a wink Beth MacLaren put an orange in a red sock and passed it out to the distraught actress on stage who was saying in rising tones of hysteria, "Eat of my red apple. EAT OF MY RED APPLE!" That was when Sara had decided that Beth would make a good nurse.

Having the best Santa suit in the country, Seamus McNevin always played Santa Claus. To stuff his candy bag treats for one and all, he robbed every candy jar in his store, ordered in specials from Ottawa, bottomed each bag with a fat orange. In Sara's year, as a special event, Mr. McNevin made Joey Gervais into Santa's Helper, put him into a miniature red Santa suit with a red toque, tacked onto his upper lip a large white moustache which Joey learned to wiggle instantly, never failing to send the little ones into gales of laughter.

I learned this winter how easily one can die of snow.

Looking out at lilacs Sara found it hard to believe that she had nearly perished in the same country in a January storm. If she had read like the country folk the signs of the weather, been in tune with the natural universe, she would have known that day in mid-January that they were in for the storm of the year. In the classroom it grew dark by two o'clock. At three o'clock Hiram Eardley came up from the Flats with a big sleigh to pick up the children.

"Should close early, Miss Costello," he shouted through cupped hands, "looks like a bad one!" She did close early, but stayed herself to put work on the blackboard for the next day, then she had locked up the school, stepped down the steps and gone into snowdrifts up to her groin. To make matters worse, she had worn skirt and silk stockings that day, not pants, socks, snow boots. She began to plough her way out to the road. Every step was an agony as she sank to her hipbones. The fenceposts that demarcated the road were disappearing in drifts as the night winds came down from the mountains. She quickly realized that in the darkening, with all the wrong clothes on, she could easily lose her way, become bogged down, freeze to death. It can happen that easily! Fighting, floundering every step of the way, she made it to the first and only light she could see. Exhausted and frozen-legged she knocked on the kitchen door of the Nesbitts who lived next to the school about half a mile down the road. They shook their heads and took her in.

It was the Canadian winter which knit us into an entity, that made us into a cooperative fighting unit, that formed the igloo in which we survived.

Sara now recalled how during the winter she had discovered her pupils' starvation points and responded to their needs. Many of her youngest pupils, while they had been given farm chores to do since the time they could walk, had never been read to in all their lives. She made time in her schedule to do this—one of the most rewarding projects of her whole year. With money from the Christmas concert she bought the older boys some simple manual-training tools, let them go to it in the basement with wood supplied by Hiram Eardley and Seamus McNevin. When she was in Ottawa over the Christmas holidays, she bought for her older girls some Paint-by-Number Kits, the rage of the time. "It isn't a way to teach art," she rationalized, "but it's better than nothing!" With her own money as well she bought new books for each grade to put in the school "library." As a reward system she instituted Friday afternoon surprises, a nature study hike to the foot of the mountains, a sliding party, a skating party. The child in Sara took part in all these events with enthusiasm and joy; her pupils were delighted by her participation. As soon as the heavy snow had closed the road between the river and the mountains, she skied to and from school along the sleigh tracks. At noon-hours she allowed those pupils whose boots fitted her bindings to try to learn to ski a little.

Those who eat together are bonded together.

In the fall as the weather had grown colder and more and more of her pupils had crowded into the classroom at noon-hours, to eat their lunches, to play checkers or jacks, to gossip around the big wood-stove that heated the schoolhouse. Here it had been almost inevitable that everyone could see everyone else's lunch; and here Sara had seen again the social hierarchy. Those with the most fare spread it all out for everyone to see. Indeed, particularly the older girls, did it sometimes almost gloatingly. Those with sparse fare tried to eat unnoticed under their desks, taking out little bites, quiet as a mouse. That had been how Sara had discovered that Joey Gervais was physically hungry, that often he only carried bread-and-butter-with-brown-sugar sandwiches. And never any milk.

At noon-hours the hungriest of her pupils, those from the farms at the foot of the mountain—Mary Donahue, Erskine McCallum, Pete Laidlaw, Joey Gervais—found excuses to sidle up to her desk to talk, all the while eyeing with bright eyes the feast which Mrs. McNevin prepared and packed daily, thick roast beef and roast pork sandwiches with butter, mayonnaise, lettuce, celery, pickles, olives, great chunks of homemade cake, pies, squares, fresh fruit from McNevin's store, thermoses of tea and milk.

Initially, Sara was worried about her waistline. But then she began to feel guilty about having too much while those around her had too little. She was trying to think of diplomatic ways to get Mrs. McNevin to cut down without hurting her housewifely pride when suddenly one day the situation solved itself.

As a special treat Mrs. McNevin had put into Sara's lunch a Delicious apple, a real rarity in the forties, even in the big city, but almost unseen in the rural areas. Joey Gervais came up to her desk to peer at it.

"Half pear, half apple," he had said with his slow grin spreading from cheek to cheek.

"It comes all the way from British Columbia," she told him. "Would you like to sample it?"

She had cut him off a piece of the apple and he had rolled it around in his mouth with relish. She gave him the rest. After that, every noon-hour she kept a small part of the great McNevin lunch, wrapped the rest up in wax paper, set it on a far corner of her desk, turned her back on it to do blackboard work. Every day it anonymously disappeared. She knew that word would spread like wildfire throughout the community, get back to Mrs. McNevin. But if it did, Mrs. McNevin never mentioned it. Nor did she ever cut down on the lunch. Sara felt that they had been wordlessly joined together in a conspiracy to feed the hungry children.

If I pass I'll get a bicycle!

It was at one of the early winter noon-hours that Joey Gervais had first told her about this gentle bribe. When there was no one else around he had come quietly up to her desk, looked at her with great big brown soulful eyes and said, "Please, miss, if I pass this year I'll get a bicycle." Sara had almost choked on her celery. She knew how far he walked to school. She had seen the longing in his eyes as the other children wheeled away. She remembered her own nagging aching for a bicycle when all her other friends had one. She remembered the exact ecstasy of the moment of the day when she came home and found her first two-wheeler sitting under the elm tree in the backyard. And she knew that Joey, a borderline case in most subjects except his beloved arithmetic, was putting her over the barrel. Had he made it up? Had his parents made it up? No. She had to believe. She had to believe all of it.

Sara looked down her beloved road between the mountain and the river. She remembered March 20 when the snow plough came through. And opened the road. Everyone came out of their houses, lined up along the sides and cheered the man who had come with his big machine to let them all out of their cocoons.

She remembered the road a few weeks before on V-E Day, May 8, 1945, when the whole upper Ottawa Valley on the Quebec side flowed down to Ottawa to celebrate the end of the war. She had sat on her schoolhouse steps, the children all let out of school, and watched the honking, flag-waving procession, thinking of all her high school friends who had gone to war and wouldn't come back, of those who would come back, of one in particular.

Sara jolted out of her reverie. One-thirty! She had day-dreamed the Friday spring noon-hour away. No time for lunch, nothing more than a frantic few minutes to put some work on the board before she rang the bell for afternoon session.

* * * *

The last lap of the school term 1944-45 at Elmgrove No.5 flew past. Before Sara knew it, she was into exams and school was out. She had given herself a week to mark papers. The weather was so perfectly June that she had to lock herself in her room to keep on track. All her pupils with bicycles streeled up and down the road in front of her bedroom window over the McNevin's store, casting anxious eyes upwards, wondering what sort of fate was being decided for them in the upstairs room. The children without bicycles walked to the store on various pretexts, to buy one-cent candy for themselves, to shop for their mothers.

The McNevins kept her posted on who came in each day to put an ear to the ground. One day Mr. McNevin told her that Joey had walked in from the farm at the foot of the mountain to get some thread for his mother. Lornie Eardley had given him a ride back on his handlebars as far as the turn-off.

The next day Sara went to the schoolhouse, posted the results on the door. Joey Gervais hadn't been the only borderline pupil she had agonized over in her room on those hot June nights at the end. For his sake probably—although she was reluctant to admit it out loud—she had passed ALL the borderline cases. His name was at the bottom of the passing list for all to see.

Following the posting of the results, for two days she stalled leaving Elmgrove waiting for Joey to come down the road on his new bicycle. She was surprised at how much she cared; she was filled with longing to see the joy of new bicycle on his face. She went to the school and spent a day sorting papers, taking down drawings, cleaning out drawers, giving back paintings, compositions, notebooks.

She knew that the McNevin's knew, that everyone knew about Joey's bicycle. So finally she said to Mr. McNevin, "What can have happened to him? Where is he? Wouldn't he drive it down the road so everyone could see it?"

"Maybe he doesn't want to get it muddy," Mr. McNevin said, "or dusty."

The McNevin's relatives from New Brunswick were coming to visit and Mrs. McNevin wanted to house clean Sara's room, shine her whole house. Sara could stall no longer. She packed her belongings at night. Mr. McNevin had promised to take her to the station at Luskville the following morning to catch the train back to her home in Ottawa.

After an early breakfast she said her fond farewells to Mrs. McNevin, began to load her things into Mr. McNevin's market truck. He read her mind.

"If we leave a little early we can take a run into the Gervais place on the way to the station."

She hugged him, almost in tears with gratitude.

They whizzed down the highway and took the turn-off towards Joey's. The mountains loomed up almost beside them before Mr. McNevin said, "This is Gervaises'"

It was what Sara had imagined—a tumble-down insul-brick farmhouse, a yard full of discarded rusty machinery, old cars and parts of old cars, long straggly piles of split wood, wood chips and kindling, stacks of odd-sized, odd-length lumber reserved for some secret construction dream, all with flocks of chickens and children, cats and dogs scattered throughout.

At the gate entrance the familiar figure of Joey Gervais flew at them as though he did not want them to come any further or see any more. Somehow protective in his stance, he stood by the side of the McNevin truck casting anxious glances back towards his house.

Sara got out and went to him.

"Hello, Joey," she said.

He only smiled a little.

"Well, Joey, aren't you pleased you passed?"

"Yes, Miss Costello." He spoke hollowly, as though by rote.

"I was just wondering how you are—I came to say goodbye—I'm going back to the city—"

Another silence. Joey looked down at his bare feet, looked again towards the house. He squared his shoulders.

"I didn't get my bicycle," he said.

She bent down, was about to put an arm about him. But the thrust of his chin made the gesture unsuitable.

"I'm sorry—there must have been a good reason."

He gave none. No excuses. No accusations. His loyalty was unflinching.

She held out her hand. But he did not take it, instead backed away a little.

"I will see you again, Joey. I will be back—you know I have relatives of all kinds up the Valley—and a family cottage—and I'll come again—drop in—to see the McNevins, of course—." She found herself gushing to cover up her mix of feelings.

Joey said nothing, looked anxiously towards his house again.

No one appeared. Sara opened the truck door.

"We have to go now, Joey. I'll miss my train."

Mr. McNevin started up the engine, made a turn around the farmyard, slowly headed towards the Gervaises' gateway.

"I'll get him a bicycle myself," Sara mumbled, holding back tears.

Mr. McNevin put his fatherly hand on her arm.

"That would never do, would it now?" he said.

And she nodded, realizing this was the hardest lesson the teacher would learn that year.

Suddenly Joey was running alongside the truck, his hand on the truck window frame on Sara's side. He hung on for a moment, and then let go. The truck passed through the gateway, turned onto the road leading to the railway station on the river flats. She looked back and imprinted on her mind forever was the image of that small boy standing in the middle of his lane waving at her, the Gatineau Hills as his backdrop.

Try-out in Toronto

Into Decker's class, interrupting a discussion of the sucking mouth parts of the sea lamprey, came word that Gus was to report to the principal's office for a long-distance call. Decker nodded permission. Gus bounced from the room and took the two flights of stairs down three at a time, knowing that they wouldn't call unless he had been tagged for try-outs.

It was Finney Mulligan, the Leafs scout.

"You're on, kid," he said. "Be at the station tonight to catch the seven o'clock to Toronto. Try-outs tomorrow at the Gardens."

"I'll be there," promised Gus. "But what about dough? You know."

"I'll have the tickets and all expenses are paid. See you at seven sharp."

As Gus hung up he realized his hands were sweating. He looked at the school clock. It said 3:45. Should he go home or back to the sea lamprey? His news would be more welcome in class. He took the stairs back up to class, three at a time.

In class he couldn't contain himself. As soon as Decker turned his back Gus leaned over to Joey and whispered, "That was Finney alright. I'm to try out tomorrow."

"Jes us!" said Joey, making his mouth O and crossing his eyes. "And Jesus again!" because everyone knew that trying out for St. Mike's was as good—almost—as signing a contract with the Maple Leafs.

The class became whispers and glances as word went round but Gus played it nonchalant, pretending he was carefully listening to the

Decker description of the death of a Lake Ontario trout by parasite. But he was really roller-coasting inside.

At the gong there was a stampede as everyone crowded around Gus, the guys slapping him on the back, calling out "Good going, Gus," and "Give it to them, Gus," the girls making little gurgly noises of admiration—even Andrea Crerar, the well-stacked "class" who hadn't given him so much as a look all year.

Decker broke through the crowd and said, "I take it they've asked you, Gus?"

"Yes, sir," said Gus, and would have said more but just then the more boisterous of the crew hoisted him on their shoulders and started him down the stairs to the strains of "He's a jolly good fellow," and he only caught the echo of Mr. Decker's "Good luck!" as he became part of the mob's momentum.

Outside, the crew deposited him on the back ledge of Duke Brazalone's Purple People-eater, an old Packard convertible, customized and traffic-stopping with a re-paint job. As many as possibly could scrambled over the doors, over the ledge, into the seats, girls and fellows three tiers deep, piled on top of one another, limbs sticking out in different directions. Some scrambled for the fenders, others clung to the bumpers and the Duke gave them a roaring, screaming, singing, muffler-roaring ride right up to Gus's front door, a thing the mighty Duke had never condescended to do before.

In his dash through the apartment halls Gus for once was oblivious of the smell of turnips which perpetually seemed to pervade, or the odour of the Newfie fish which the people in the basement had sent to them every week from home. Today the little, overcrowded, untidy sitting room didn't stir him to resentment against an absent father. In the kitchen he wasn't bothered as usual by the fact that his worn and troubled mother was using a Wednesday afternoon off from Reitman's to do a whole week's washing and baking.

He picked up a biscuit still warm from the oven, threw a leg over a chair with great bravado and said,

"Hi, Mum, I'm trying out for St. Mike's tomorrow."

He braced himself for the harangue which usually followed any mention of a hockey career. But there was none. Instead of chewing the rag about her "working her fingers to the bone so he could go to school," instead of harping on the mistakes his father had made that she "didn't want her son to make," instead of a big lecture on the merits of education in relation to "supporting of a family," instead of pleading, begging, nagging, his mother just said "Hmph" and trimmed the edge of the pie with furious movements.

It made Gus uneasy that she didn't lash out, hoping as she always did to whip the inevitable by sheer force of words. He watched her quick fingers fit the top crust, crimp the edges, prick the crust with a fork. Suddenly he realized that her hands were performing the task automatically, that the rest of her was shaking with sobs and that she was crying into the pie.

"Oh, God!" he thought. "Why does she have to make it so hard?"

Stricken with remorse, he jumped up, went over and put an arm around her.

"Mom, take it easy. This is our chance to get out of this, get some of the things you need, fix it so the other boys can go to school, so Babs can have—"

"None of us need those things so badly that you have to ruin your whole life as your father did before you."

"Can't I profit from my old man's mistakes? Can't I ride the gravy boat and get off before it grounds?"

"You're too young. You don't know what it's really like. You'll get caught in it, swept up and sucked down into the gutter just like your father."

"Isn't that just it! Don't I just remember what happened to my father, to all of us? Don't I just have to make up for that? Don't I just have to prove—"

Gus was yelling now and his mother was white-faced, holding on to the cupboard edge with her floured hands. She turned on him and yelled back,

"You don't have to prove anything here except that you can finish high school—"

Gus wanted to call her a stupid old bitch. Instead he wheeled into the bedroom, slammed the door and began frantically rummaging in the closet for his father's old duffle bag, one of the few useful mementos of his father's career with the Toronto Maple Leafs. He was throwing socks and underwear into it, sick with an unmanageable rage, when the door opened and Babs hurtled herself at him yelling, "Oh, gee, I heard, Gus, I heard" and then tight in his arms, saying, "Oh, please, make it, Gus, please, please make it."

And he squeezed her wriggling nine-year-old self and swore he would make it for more reasons than his little sister ever guessed. He might get his mother out from behind the lingerie counter at Reitman's, maybe buy a little house where his kid brothers, Dave and

Bill, could have some breathing space, a backyard, a place to bring their young teenage cronies home to. And Babs wouldn't continue to rip apart all their hearts crying for things she couldn't have now and would cry for more and more because she was reaching the stage when the things she couldn't have might set her apart from all her trendy peers.

He loved the brat so much. And he didn't know why except that maybe it was because she was born at a time when his father and mother seemed to have nothing much left together but rows and he, even at eleven, had been old enough to sense it in a dreadfully hollow-hearted sort of way and to realize that Babs, born later into the marriage, was to be virtually fatherless. At that tenderly naive and idealistic age he had honestly believed from the things that his father DID—like disappearing for days, weeks, even months on end—and the things his mother SAID in retaliation, that they only hated each other. Of course, he was older and wiser now and had some inkling of their teeter-totter love-hate relationship. But still somehow he was cast in a role where he was always trying to make up for things missing in his family. Like space to grow, and more money, and a father to lean on, to go to in time of trouble, to ask for advice and help.

After supper Dave and Bill, noisy, jubilant and excited, tried to help him by insisting upon piling his gear at the door. Babs helped too, and together the three of them managed to lose one of his skate guards. There was a great scrambling and searching, under chairs, beneath cushions, in the bedrooms. It was finally discovered in the kitchen where his mother, aloof from the furore, was putting dishes in the sink.

By then it was time to dash. He tried to collect his bags but Babs grabbed him by the leg, Davie climbed onto the arm of a chair and arm-locked him around the neck while Billy swung on his arm. Their farewell frenzy reminded him of the times his father had dashed for the Chicago or Detroit or Montreal train; it was a bit different with him, though, because he had been a man who liked to make the train wait—which it did—the coach had spoken to his mother about this and the news had shaken down into the children's minds so that his father's departures, while they were big exciting moments, were also times of agitated anxiety. Would he make it or would he not? Someday he was going to miss his train. And what dreadful thing would happen then? He looked at his mother to see if he could read what she was thinking. But she averted her eyes and said, "Alright now, children. Gus has to go."

She turned her cheek for his kiss, a dual signal of resignation and disapproval, one which he so well remembered his father often savoured.

"Here's a little extra, son," she said and pressed a bill into his hand.

In the hall he looked back because he sensed something strange and stiff about her and he could not know that she was numb with vision of a pattern repeated.

That picture of her stuck in his mind. Later when he was safely on the train, her face came up on the poker cards and through the lovely haze of rye on the rocks poured down in the men's john out of the eye of Finney who was sent down by the Leafs as their nursemaid to see that they didn't break training rules. But after a while, Finney got suspicious and kept saying, "I smell alcohol." He felt their overcoat and jacket pockets, searched under the seats and they had to play a real canny game of hide-the-bottle. Bertie Higgins, a try-out from St. Pat's, finally convinced Finney that the smell was Handy Henderson's imported after-shave lotion.

Of course, Gus kept his drinking "strictly under control" but some of the guys got really bozzled, that is, really smelling of after-shave lotion. And the poker game started out very quietly, too. But it got out of hand when Des Marker ran out of money and threw his hockey gear into the kitty. Finney Mulligan leaned over, put his hand on Marker's shoulder and said, "Now lad, you don't want to do that." Marker was feeling his rye and was ugly-tempered anyhow. He looked at Finney and said, "No third-rate has-been had better try to tell *me* what to do."

Finney drew back as though he had been kicked in the balls. They finished the hand and Marker lost his gear. He stood up and said, "What the hell! I can always go to college," put on his Peck and Peck overcoat, and swung off the train into the night at Port Hope.

Something about his insolent unconcern made Gus see red. He turned to Higgins and said, "That bastard talks about going to college as though he were going out to buy shoe laces. I suppose that's easy to do when your old man buried all the hoi polloi in Ottawa. I think I'd listen to my old woman crying about education if it was that easy to get to university. Old Decker keeps telling me I can do it—if I could only be sure—but what the hell's the use of plugging through senior matric when after that I'd just drop off into limbo, get some stinking job in a store—like my mother—selling socks, or pushing cash out to somebody else in a bank, or lying to sell rotten houses."

"That's what I say," Higgins affirmed. "This is real. We make these try-outs and we're into the big time, big contracts, ten thousand a year, bonuses for goals, assists, play-off games, Stanley Cups—"

"Just think of it," said Gus leaning back in the seat and putting his arms behind his head. "Just think of it—Of course, I'm going to take care of my family first—I'm the man of the house now—but I think after that I'll buy a car and you know what? I'd like to take Mr. Decker for a hop—maybe a play-off game in Montreal—he takes a real keen interest in me—bit like a father—"

"By the say," said Finney from across the table, "Where *is* your father?"

"Well, that's a bit of an embarrassing question," said Gus. "I bet I'm the only guy here who doesn't know where his own father is. But I'll take a guess. The darling lion of the Twenties, roaring no more, may be lost in the jungles of the D.T.'s. Right?"

"Yah," said Finney, "that may be right."

"Or he may be waiting death in a ditch singing 'We are poor little lambs—'"

"Right," said Finney, "but you don't need to be a young punk about it. I remember your dad. He was one of the finest."

"Yah," said Gus, "I remember him too, slugging it out on the home front with my mother, losing this job and that job, drinking our house out from under us—"

"That may be true," said Finney, "but you don't know it all, kid, you just don't have a picture of it all. You go pretty high to fall that far. Your dad was great—he was beautiful—there was no one ever like him—even Connie Smythe said so—"

"Nuts," said Gus, "I'll be just as good and I won't leave my son with a dirty smell about my name, a dirty smell he'll have to live with and try to blow out."

"There hasn't been a hockey great yet that produced a son that could even touch him, let alone follow in his footsteps," Finney retorted.

"Well, I'll damn well be the first."

"There's always a first. Maybe it's you. But if you get into the big league you'll see just what a tough game it really is, what it does to a man. I don't mean the games themselves. They're pie. I mean the sudden high living. And the crazy headlines spinning in your head. And the power-laden sportswriters on your back. And the people looking for handouts. And the girls that line up outside the dressing room door. And the rich bastards that buy you drinks so you can amuse them. And the crowd in your blood. And the sudden way you go out, flat on your prat, jobless, no training—"

"Ah, I know all about that," said Gus. "It's different today. The kids don't make the same mistakes. They play it smart, invest their money, get into a business, have a pension fund—"

"It's a bit better that way. But when you've seen as many as I have you know that they're still divided into two groups, the savers and the spenders—"

"Well," said Gus viciously, "I'm of the first group. I have to take care of the family my father left."

"Take it easy. Don't go hot-headed on me, kid. I'm only giving you the benefit of some things I've picked up on my way around."

Gus drew in his horns. The rye and the rhythm of the express train was beginning to have an effect on the passengers. Some fell asleep but Gus was too stirred up for that. He thought about his big day tomorrow and how his father once might have sat on a train going to fortune and fate, young and flesh-proud and invincible as he. Gus wondered where he might be now, in what down-at-the-heels joint in Ottawa, or Montreal, or Toronto. It was funny to think of your father as a possible shadow moving down some unknown street. He thought how his father would be better off dead; he was no use to himself and a worry to the family. Dead, he would save them all the anxiety of never knowing when the phone might ring and a voice might tell them to come and get Old Gus, dead-drunk in some place he wasn't wanted, or dead in a place where it didn't matter. They never knew when the door might open and their father would return for a time of endless rows, sleepless nights and near violence. They never knew when a knock at the door might announce the law with some dreadful pronouncement; he'd killed a man in a brawl, or left some soul by the side of the road in a hit-and-run, or taken some family to doom in a drinking and driving tragedy.

These thoughts frightened Gus and he turned to remembrance of the glorious days when his mother and father kidded and goofed in the kitchen and fell asleep on Sunday afternoons on the chesterfield even though you'd never believe it would hold two. One of his fondest memories - funny how some silly little thing sticks in your mind - but one of his fondest memories was that of making the Christmas stuffing. His father and mother always made it together. They cut the onions, weeping tears into the frying pan, and broke up loaves of bread and put the grinder onto the kitchen chair seat and ground it all out together. It fell into the basin wafting its delicious sage and thyme seasonal odour throughout the house.

He remembered his father's returning from "away" games, his arms laden with great big American trucks and trains and boxes of dresses spilling perfumed tissue paper. He remembered Christmas presents from avid fans, and women calling the house asking for Gussie in sweet tones, and headlines with his father's name two inches high, and his father on the front of the rotogravure section, and people saying to him incredulously, "Why! You're Gus Brannigan's son! I can't believe it!"

The phrases of disbelief slipped into the rhythm of the train wheels. And Gus slept into Toronto.

They were quartered at the Royal York—nothing but the best—but it wasn't big enough for them. They spread themselves all over the lobby, the elevators, the halls, the dining rooms, kids from Brockville, Belleville, Elora, North Bay, even Cochrane, from all over the country, talking in over-loud voices hoping to be overheard, flicking their ashes on the floors, making excuses to call the bellhops, pretending phone calls, paging themselves on the intercom, reading aloud to one another press reports of the try-outs.

After they had eaten high-protein breakfasts under the watchful eye of Finney, he left them sprawled all over the tables like a bunch of monkeys gabbling about the times they licked the shit out of the Whitby Dunlops and the Belleville Macfarlands and the Duchies, and how many girls they would lay when the try-outs were over, and where, and how often. And Gus walked over to the Gardens alone, although he knew it would be more "big-time" to pack into a cab with the rest of the boys.

But he had knots in his guts and he knew from experience that a walk and a whiff of air, even if it was the contaminated variety of downtown Toronto, would help to "can" his case of nerves. He couldn't afford shakes. This was his big chance. AND HE WOULD DO IT.

It wasn't far to the Gardens. Already a small crowd had gathered to watch the young gladiators go in. When they saw his gear the crowd made a path for him. He went through and entered the windy, empty corridors of an arena without the seething turmoil of the game crowds.

After the Ottawa Senators had folded financially and his father had gone to Toronto Maple Leafs, they used to come here every winter and take an apartment in North Toronto. They took turns, he and his brothers—for Babs wasn't born then—coming to the Gardens and sitting with their mother in the section reserved for players' wives, watching their father play and listening to 15,000 people rise and yell for him. That had all finished eight years ago, yet the smell of liniment and sweat and skate leather rose up around him and roused the same old excitement in the very pit of him.

He was standing in a dream looking at pictures of his father on the Gardens' wall—All Stars '31, All Stars '33, Stanley Cup '27, '29, '36—when the doors opened to a crowd of young players who had come in cabs. They swept over him and moved him along like a log caught in a current. The force of that propulsion reminded him vividly of a terrifying time when he had been a child here at a Stanley Cup final, a game that was won by his father's goal. After it was over and the crowd had littered the ice with symbols of their spectator jubilance, he and his mother had waited for his father at the dressing room door. But they barely had time to greet him before the wild crowd caught him up, pawed him, clawed him, slapped him, mauled him and, finally, lifted him up and bore him away out of sight. Gus and his mother had been almost stampeded into the ground although the policemen tried to pit their weight against the onslaught. He had been terrified. Being so small and feeling the pressure of the mob he had been certain they would kill his father. He had called out after his father and started to cry and one of the big burly policemen, sensing his terror and fear, had picked him up in his arms and carried him so that he was the same height as the disappearing figure of his father far up ahead in the arms of the mob.

In the Gardens dressing room they piled onto the benches. Finney came in and told them to climb into their gear and then to file out onto the ringside seats.

"The line-ups will be announced there," he said. "And keep your noses clean," he warned. "Smythe would as soon lop you off the list for fighting as he would for skating on your ass."

Gus found his pal Starkey and they laced together, silent with the tension of the moment and the psyching up of their inner resources. But there were the loud mouths too, in the crowd, guys who verbalized their anxiety. Gus vaguely heard two of them on the benches over behind them.

"Probably got here on pull," one voice said.

"Yah, his old man may be a drunk but he can still probably talk to the right people."

"Why worry about him though. He'll just be another one of the 'Sons of the Great' to fall flat on his ass—"

Gus felt himself redden. Were they talking about him? He was afraid to look. He stole a glance at Starkey. He either didn't hear or was pretending not to hear.

The other voice went on, "I hear his old man lost everything, even the house they—"

Gus stopped lacing, started to straighten up and turn around. But Starkey put a quick restraining hand on his arm.

"Easy, boy," he said. "They're trying to bait you. Knock you out of competition."

Gus bent his scarlet face over his skates again. It wasn't the first time that he had overheard his family's dirty laundry hung out to air. Once in a restaurant he had listened to total strangers at a nearby table discuss how much his father had lost in stocks, how much he drank, and how many cars he'd smashed up. Then, as now, he had had the same insane desire to smash in the faces of the gossipers. He was glad Starkey was there to hold him down. He stole a glance in the direction of the speakers and was instantly halted and held in the smirking belligerent stare of a red-faced bruiser with blond curls. Gus marked him well; it was a face and build easily remembered in any situation.

Finney came in and said, "Okay, guys. Let's go! Ten minutes free skating. Loosen up, now!"

Close to a hundred young hopefuls, praying to be noticed, streamed onto the new-laid ice like horses out of the starting gate, racing and stopping, backwards and forwards, heads high, skates flashing, whirling and turning, loosening up the superlative young limbs that might carry some of them this day into the soaring temples of their dreams. When the whistle blew, like cattle beneath the prod, they piled into the ringside players' benches intent upon Finney who was calling out the names for the first try-outs. They had been divided into Red Teams and Blue Teams. That's pure identification with Toronto Maple Leafs and Les Canadiens, Gus thought to himself. He hadn't been called for either on the first run but he watched Starkey go out into the arena to be tried.

Gus looked around the Gardens, mostly empty and echoing the days of his father's glory as one of the best right-wingers in the history of the game. God! Could he ever describe the pride with which he had watched his old man shoot and score, shoot and score. "He shoots! He scores!" rang around him.

Here and there scattered like huddled birds throughout the empty seats the odd lonely man watched the proceedings intently as though his life depended on the outcome of these try-outs.

"Probably Poison Parents from all over the Goddam country," Gus thought to himself.

"Well, I sure don't need to worry about that one!" Gus observed silently. "There's sure as hell nobody pushing me onwards and upwards! Except myself."

Directly across from where Gus sat on the bench was a small group of personnel including bigwigs whom he recognized easily—Selke, Irvin, even Smythe—all huddled together over clipboards, scribbling notes, muttering amongst themselves, watching the play, scribbling some more, arguing. "The Waterloo Gang" someone had dubbed them. Right on, too, Gus thought. Sitting in his agony of waiting, his adrenalin running down, Gus remembered one of his mother's many many favourite, pithy and sometimes wise sayings, "Oh, just wait. He'll meet his Waterloo."

At the next whistle Finney called out, "Brannigan for Blake. Get in there, Gus."

Finney gave him a supportive pat as he shot over the boards onto the ice.

As Gus took up his position at right wing he realized he was face-to-face with the big loudmouth blond guy who had gassed off in the dressing room.

"Hi, Curly," Gus muttered under his breath. "Got lead in your feet today?"

The whistle blew at face-off. Gus's centre was lousy but the guy on the left wing had some go in his legs and they shoved in two goals together, Gus taking one, and one assist. He was skating like a fool and his stick-handling was dead on. He carefully stayed out of a tangle with Curly. He didn't want to have to pull any rough stuff with him; he just wanted to use him as incentive to skate circles around. He remembered his father often saying, "Don't let them get your goat; just skate circles around them. Make them look like assholes."

He was called off after five minutes and found himself looking past the Waterloo Gang into a little crowd of fedora-hatted spectators. Suddenly he was struck by a shock of recognition. Down from the Smythe crowd and right against the boards was a face that looked like his father's. It was hard to tell from the bench. He leaned over the boards to get another angle. As he did so, the figure on the boards put a bottle to his lips and took a quick nip. Something about the movement was so familiar that Gus's heart almost went into spasm. It couldn't be—

"Brannigan, get onto that right wing again," Finney's voice commanded. He sprang to the ice. Curly was gone and so was the left wing he had run so well with last time. He missed two passes and a sure-fire shot on goal. He got off-side and then missed another pass. It was damn hard to play teamwork with someone you'd never seen before. He was thinking excuses for himself when a voice from the sidelines called out,

"Put him back on the bench. Put him back, put him back. He's a disgrace to the name of Brannigan."

Gus recognized his father's voice, but he played on. He took the pass thinking at the same time, "Father, Father, what are you trying to do to me?" He skated down towards the goal with the puck. "Haven't you disgraced us, shamed us all enough?" He broke up a forward rush. "I hate your lousy stinking drunken guts for doing this to me in front of all these people!" He took a body check, went down, saw stars, got up, and was called off.

On the bench he leaned on his stick for support, looked straight ahead and tried to compose himself, pretending that he didn't even know. But his father's voice was rising now, growing more clamorous, the slurred s's becoming clearer. He was berating and praising in turn, the old pro at the sidelines letting the newcomers know that they didn't know anything.

"Take him off, take him off," Old Gus yelled, pointing out one young player. "He can't skate. Can't you guys see? He can't skate."

"He's got lead in his ass. Bench him, Connie. Bench him for gawd's sake."

And of another, "He's got it. Yesirree, that boy's got it. That's the way, son. That's the way!"

Old Gus had always had a kind gentle way of calling every young lad "son." When Gus was young he had been proud of it, the good way his father had with young boys trying to come up. But now, as the one betrayed, he felt only scorn for his father's indiscriminate use of the word. "Son, be damned," he thought. "No father would do this to a son."

Now Old Gus, his father, was banging the boards with the flat of his hand yelling,

"Bring on Brannigan! Let's shee Brannigan again."

Up to this point the fellows on the bench hadn't tied Gus in with the loudmouth old drunk. Some of them were too intent upon the game to even raise their eyes from the ice. But most of them were mildly amused. He heard them snort and chuckle and query one another about the identity of the solitary figure who made up the cheering section.

"Some old wino," he heard one remark to another.

"Some old shit-disturber has-been, I'd say," said another lad on the bench.

Someone sent Finney down to remonstrate with Old Gus. Gus watched Finney try to quiet down, even reason with his father. Gus watched his father put his arms around Finney, lean on him and talk into his ear. Gus could just imagine the promises his father was making to Finney, the old worn-outs like, "I'll never take another drink," "I'm through," "I swear, I'm through."

Then Gus remembered vividly, painfully, that all would be quiet for a few weeks on the home front. Very quiet because his mother had a tight-lipped unforgivingness, a cold hurt resignation which was applied without words. The children withdrew; they were uncertain of their father. Gus, although he couldn't put it into words, found his loving idolatry turning into pity. His father wore his hangdog begging look for a short time and then went on another bender, benders which came closer and closer together—until the separation. Gus had always kept to himself the dreadful secret that he was glad, glad when the old man finally fell off the wagon, glad as though the axe had finally fallen. Why would you be so glad when you knew your father was killing himself, destroying his marriage and the family? He was asking himself this question when the guy next to him poked him in the ribs.

"Hey! You're on, Brannigan. They're calling you for defence on the Red Team."

"Defence?" he thought. "Why defence? They must be taking a look at me from all angles." But he was rattled and he let a couple of the Blue Team through to score two goals. Then he tangled with an opposing player, just missed a penalty.

They were facing off after the second goal he let through. Suddenly there was a commotion from the sidelines and they all turned to watch his father scramble over the boards and start across the ice, a clownish, unsteadily-gaited bottle-swinging figure in an oversized overcoat—a handout no doubt—which flapped as he walked.

They were all mesmerized. The referee had the whistle at his mouth. But he didn't blow.

Old Gus walked right up to Young Gus until he was so close Young Gus could see the worn shirt collar and the spattered tie and the gash down his father's cheek.

"Here," Old Gus said, "Hold this and gimme that stick. I want to show you how to stick-handle."

Young Gus found himself standing on the ice holding his father's bottle while Old Gus slithered and slipped down the ice in a soft-shoe demonstration of stick-handling as done by one of the greatest the game had ever seen. He dodged and feinted, swung with his imaginary puck, hearing the echoing cheers of ghostly games, dodging the figures of old opponents, muttering away to himself.

Laughter went up from the benches and the players on the ice. Cries went up, "Give it to them, old-timer!" "You're great, Daddy."

The refs got a signal from the bench. They moved in on Old Gus. But he, degenerated as he was, was still too quick for them. He moved on down the ice, eluding them, stick-handling his imaginary puck.

"Come on now, fellows," he said, "I gotta show my kid how. I got a right here—"

He was like an eel and, when they finally did catch him, they were angry. They took him by the elbows as though he were a bag of rags and skated him off the rink, his feet helplessly kicking in the air. Young Gus skated over behind them, saw his father safely deposited behind the boards again.

"They'll have you tossed out, Brannigan, if you make any more fuss," the referee warned.

Gus stepped up to his father. "Please, Dad," he begged.

"Okay, okay, jush gimme back my bottle," his father slurred out.

Old Gus put his arms around Young Gus, "It's good to see you, son. It's good to shee you." He squeezed Gus's arm until it hurt. Gus saw that there were tears in his father's eyes. He tried to disentangle himself. The referee called out in an angry voice, "Get out of here, Brannigan. We've lost enough time with that old bum."

Gus moved into the line as though stung by a whip. The whistle drove the try-out teams into heroic action again. But his father's clamour from the sidelines grew louder. He hammered the boards with his bottle, yelled, sang and roared like a lion. He baited the players, tagged them with obscenities. Finally, Finney went over and said something to him again, trying once more to save the situation.

"Fuck Smythe!" Old Gus yelled. "Fuck the Toronto Maple Leafs! Fuck 'em all!"

They took Gus off again. The rest of the bench-warmers moved over to let him in. No one said a word. It wasn't funny anymore. They all wanted to get on with the try-outs. When his father went over the boards again, there was an angry grumbling. The referee blew the whistle hard and long. They all moved in on Old Gus.

Old Gus fought back. He swung punches, harmless drunken ones. But the refs couldn't really get a hold on him, and some of the players, fed up with the interruptions, moved in, too. Old Gus slipped, went down on the ice and the crowd of skaters closed in on him.

Smythe called out, "Get him off!"

Gus heard his father's voice but he couldn't see what they were doing to him. Then the crowd opened up a little and he realized that they were prodding him with their sticks and trying to pull him across the ice by his feet.

Gus saw it all then, all of it. He jumped the boards, pushed through the crowd and said, "All right, you bastards, take your paws off my old man."

They saw the look in his eyes and they moved back. Gus leaned down and said, "Okay, Dad, let's go. Let's get out of here, quick."

He helped his father to his feet, put his arm around him. Even as they moved together across the ice, even before they got to the gate, the whistle had gone for the next face-off.

The Damn Best Builder from Kanata to Carlsbad Springs

Because of its remoteness and inaccessibility in the early days, the Ottawa Valley established from the very beginning of its history a cavalier attitude towards the law of the land, and a clear tendency for taking the law into its own hands. It required 20 years of long hard struggle in Renfrew County before the due process of the law overthrew the feudal system of the last Laird MacNab. For many years (and who knows, maybe even to this day!) fugitives from justice, outlaws and rogues hid themselves out at Rogues' Harbour on the Madawaska River above Calabogie; if necessary they were outfitted there for a flight to the United States. On numerous occasions the nineteenth century timber trade in the valley has been called "the crookedest business in the world." Certainly cheating, trespassing, illegal cutting was rife and, if the government, and later even the "robber" timber barons themselves, tried to make laws and regulations for the trade, how could laws and regulations be enforced in a vast timbered wilderness? From all the stories I have gathered it would appear that, on one level, the Ottawa Valley was one vast network of illegal stills and outlets. And I have been told stories of revenge castrations, rival clan huntings and killings, unsolved murders that I dare not think about, alone repeat

Although in a diluted form, this tradition of outlawry is maintained into more modern times in the Valley. It is still told that, during the First and Second World Wars, particularly on the Quebec side of the Valley, whole communities of draft-dodgers were hidden out in the bush. Poaching, hunting and fishing out of season has never ceased as a Valley tradition and is continually played, even today, as a game by "the boys" who will not be men.

Cheating on the government, on insurance claims, unemployment insurance, welfare are everyday occurrences regarded as old stale jokes. I know of people who have never filed an income tax form in their whole lives; others who have run illegal stills for a lifetime. On the roads in the redneck back country I have met characters straight out of the film "Deliverance." "Fight-night" still exists in the Upper Valley; men are still dreadfully hurt and maimed.

Into this part of the darker scene in the Valley, the image of the sociopathic builder, renovator, developer fits without any real problem. Indeed, just as the image of the hockey hero succeeds from the lumbering hero so the image of the crooked developer may emerge from the earlier "robber" timber baron.

The kernel of the idea for the development of the character of Charlie "Chain-Saw" Channigan was given to me in an interview with some young people in the Valley several years ago. I wore my oral historian-folklorist hat to that interview. But when I got the tape home and listened to it I realized that I had already written about a man just like Channigan. And so I put on my short-story-writer hat, built further the character of Channigan, and added considerable "creative biography" to the original handful of stories. I could not and did not resist the opportunity, in this particular case, to become the story-teller.

Channigan, the amoral builder, may have sprung from the Valley. But his stereotype is international. Readers may well laugh over some of the Channigan stories but also, at one time or another in their lives having been victimized by a man like Channigan, they may contemplate weeping.

Charlie Channigan is now in Fort St. John doing his con jobs. Peter's wife saw him there a year ago. He only stays about five years in one place and then he has to move on. They run him out of town. He was around Carleton Place until about ten years ago. We all worked for him at one time or another when we were in our teens trying to make an extra buck to spend on beer and girls—in that order. I still have nightmares about my part in his con jobs. And I sometimes wonder about the poor people he victimized—yes, sometimes even wonder if they have survived his perfidies!

Charlie was a little guy who always smoked a "cigah"—an expensive "cigah." And he lisped. Lithped. Otherwise Charlie was not at all what you'd expect a businessman to look like. Or even a con man. He was a slob. He bought his clothes at Second Time Around and the Salvation Army. He sucked on his expensive "cigahs" all day long and looked as though he had only half a brain up there. But, all the time, he was taking it in, taking it in. He missed nothing.

I'll tell you right off that Charlie Channigan's gig was that he would buy cheap old houses and do ONLY cosmetic jobs on them before he put them back on the market for sale. And he really did—the rumour is absolutely correct—have T-shirts made for all us lads who worked for him, off and on. On the front of the T-shirts it said "Charlie's Chainsaw Gang" over a drawing of a great big chainsaw.

Charlie was always running ahead of the building inspector. It was like a game of "Cops and Robbers" to watch. Charlie always had five or six houses going at once, being cosmetically transformed, perhaps one or two in town, three or four scattered throughout the surrounding countryside, towards Almonte or maybe even Pakenham using any cheap labour he could scratch from the area. He had to be on so many sites at once, it made it very difficult for a building inspector to catch up with him. He was as elusive as a loup-garou or a will-o'-the-wisp. When a building inspector would finally catch up with him Charlie would say, "Excuse me, a moment, I have to go to the bathroom to have a leak." And he would disappear for another three weeks.

Now one of the owners of a major industry in Carleton Place had a really beautiful house, architecturally designed, overlooking the whole countryside in the Almonte Highlands. Charlie bought a strip of land right across from him (can you imagine any council letting that happen? unless they were bribed, had their palms greased?) and proceeded to put up these cheap pre-fab jerry-built houses. Before they were even halfway finished, Charlie put them up for sale in the hands of one of the real estate companies in town. That always used to get to me, too, that the most reputable real estate companies would deal with him.

Anyway, one day one of the real estate men in the company went to Charlie and said to him, "Look, Charlie, this woman is really in a bad way. She had to get out of her house and she has nowhere to go now. She is really going to buy and she wants it by next Saturday."

"No pwoblem. No pwoblem," said Charlie, flicking his "cigah."

"I said she wants it," the real estate man repeated, "but it has to be all finished and landscaped by next Saturday."

"No pwoblem. No pwoblem," said Charlie, flicking his "cigah."

Of course, the whole site was mayhem even as he said this. They were only beginning the finishing carpentry and it was spring and all the lots were a muddy mess with scattered pieces of lumber, cement bags, garbage, strewn around.

But on Saturday the real estate man showed up with his client. Everything was beautiful. New sod. A little rock garden in the corner of the lot with a white birch gracefully draped in it. Blue spruce, pine, shrubs around the foundation.

The woman bought immediately for the asking price. But you know what happened in about three weeks, of course. Everything except the sod turned brown and withered down. Charlie Chain-saw Channigan had simply sent his lads out into the bush, had them cut down some small trees and bushes, haul them back to the house, dig holes for them, and stick the trunks in the holes.

Another time I worked for him, he bought an ancient shack of a house in Middleville. There had been an old wood furnace in the basement and the chimney hole—a very large one—came up through the kitchen. Charlie put the kitchen stove in front of the hole and covered it with linoleum. No subflooring, no two-by-fours, no nothing down under it to cover the hole.

"Well, nobody's going to walk behind there anyway," Charlie said to one of his workers who questioned the procedure and who later confessed to me, "My God! I often have visions at night of someone going through that hole with one leg!"

As I said before, Charlie was always two or three steps ahead of the building inspectors. They played games and he almost always won. He would *never* get a building permit. But, he would take—on each site he was working on—a piece of paper, stick it on a piece of cardboard, tear the centre out and leave the four corners hanging, cover it with the usual plastic, and hang it on the wall of the building he was working on. When the building inspector would come and ask for his permit, Charlie would point to his handiwork on the wall.

"Oh, yeth," he'd say, "I had one. You can thee what's left of it there on the wall—these damn local kids, you know—vandals, pure vandals."

One time I was working for Charlie on this house he'd bought in Carp. It was the old jail and it had the big thick walls and the bars on the windows and everything, and he was fixing the place up, making it into a house. At the same time he had also bought Scissons Hardware—it had gone out of business there—and he had bought everything. You couldn't believe the stuff there! Been there for a hundred years or more. Charlie gave him $500 and Scissons said, "Take everything." You wouldn't believe the stuff! There was a couple of Rubbermaid display cases, jars and jars of old nails and screws, parts of old machinery. But Charlie thought he would find a use for all of it—someday. So he brought it all over and dumped it in the yard of the house we were making out of the jail. There was also a zillion board feet of old lumber with nails sticking up out of it. When the building inspector told him to get the nails out of it Charlie would always say, "Oh, yeth, yeth, I'll have to hire some local kids to pull those nails out." But he never did.

Charlie was always being hassled by the building inspectors. It was an "in" joke with all of us who ever worked for him. Whenever and wherever we'd meet—on the street, in a bar, at a house—we'd always yell out, "Here comes the building inspector!" and then we'd all run off in different directions, as we had learned to do when working for Charlie.

But finally one day this young building inspector caught up with Charlie in Carp at our building site where we were making the house out of the old jail. Charlie happened to be there, by mistake.

"Let me see your building permit," the young building inspector said to Charlie.

Charlie pointed to the torn and bedraggled piece of paper on the wall, the centre ripped out and just the corners hanging there under the plastic.

"I had one," he said, "but these damn local kids, you know-"

The building inspector looked out into the yard full of debris and this old lumber with the nails all sticking up out of it. So he invited Charlie to walk out in the yard with him.

"All that lumber has nails sticking up through it," he said to Charlie. "You know that is against the regulations."

"No pwoblem. No pwoblem," Charlie is saying to the young building inspector. "We always keep kids away from the yard."

And Charlie, as he is walking and talking fast to the building inspector, he steps on a piece of old lumber and the nail goes right up through his foot. And he's trying to shake the nail out of his foot without the building inspector seeing it. And we're all stopped work and standing watching this. And Charlie's really in pain. You can see it on his face. But he's trying not to show it.

"No pwoblem. No pwoblem," Charlie keeps saying over and over again, shaking his foot with the nail sticking into it and the piece of lumber attached to him, and trying to hide the pain.

And the young building inspector continues his inspection, never stops walking and keeps pretending he doesn't see a thing.

Another one of Charlie's renovation secrets was wallpaper. If a wall was defective in any way, he would just say to his men, "Wallpaper. Just wallpaper the whole thing over."

He was always making deals that were just short of very crooked. That's how he got his houses. I heard about one time he made five thousand dollars without crossing the room. That was one night at the Newborne in Arnprior. Charlie used to sit in a corner and smoke his "cigahs." And he'd be talking there. And he'd know all the "fahmers." And this one night he bought this farmer's place at eight o'clock in the evening. They had worked at it, and drank at it all day long, and at eight o'clock the farmer signed his place over to Charlie. For about $12,000. The guy left pissed. But Charlie had the deed. By the time the farmer left, Charlie crossed the room and sold it to another "fahmer" he knew for $17,000, a "fahmer" he knew beforehand really badly wanted the property. Charlie knew it and he wheeled and dealed all day and made himself a neat $5,000.

Charlie owned and still owns a lot of property around Manotick. Don't think he didn't have any money, lots of it. He was making a thousand here and two thousand there all the time.

One time he bought this huge big lakefront and landlocked a local lawyer who owned property on the same lake. Charlie knew this, of course. And he waited. When the lawyer came to him complaining about the situation, Charlie just said (the way he always said) with a shrug of his shoulders, "Well, it's for sale."

So the big small-town lawyer had to buy the whole huge lakefront property from Charlie who, naturally enough, charged him enough to make it worth his while, being as he had the guy over a barrel and knew he would pay almost anything. Charlie charged the lawyer so much money on the deal that the lawyer had to divide the piece up and develop it in order to survive financially.

Nobody knows, as I said before, where Charlie comes from or where he is going. But everybody is curious, mighty curious. One day when we were working on a shack at Ompah I asked him, "Charlie, where do you come from?"

"I grew up up North," he said.

"Come on, Charlie," I said, "that's a big place."

"Well, yeth it was," he agreed. And that's all he would say about it.

"What's Channigan?" I asked him, not giving up so easily.

"Irish-Chinese," he replied. "Way back in the Ping Dynasty, B.C. The Chinese invaded Ireland. A very ancient family we are."

People always wonder how Charlie gets away with his scams. But, to my knowledge, back in those days in the boondocks, he was never sued for all his deceits and deals during the time I knew him in Carleton Place and environs. But, oh my God, he should have been!

Like the time this elderly gentleman, a retired farmer, was going to buy one of Charlie's "castles."

"Does it have running water?" he asked Charlie. This was pretty important to the old man. He was coming in off the farm and, after using the pump and the backhouse for 50 years, he wanted all the luxuries.

"Running water? Sure thing," said Charlie.

Of course, the old house didn't have any more running water in it than the farmer's old house back on the homestead. But right away, Charlie got two 50-gallon drums, put them in the attic, filled them with water, attached a hose down through the wall into the kitchen taps. So, when the elderly farmer retiring to town came to see the house and tried the taps there was indeed, "running water."

One thing as I have mentioned, always puzzled me. Charlie Chain-saw Channigan got away with a lot of his scams because he was associated with reputable mortgage and real estate men in Carleton Place. So, some people trusted him because of his association with the reputable. And I guess even the most reputable real estate companies in town dealt with him because they knew they would make money. He turned over houses as fast as pancakes on Shrove Tuesday. And that was enough. And Angus MacDonald was backing him with good mortgages. Charlie would buy a place for $2,000, mortgage it for $6,000, use $2,000 of the $6,000 to fix it up—cosmetically, of course—put $2,000 in his pocket, sell it to somebody for $1,000 down, ask $1,000 down in cash payment, and they take over the existing mortgage. He walks away with $3,000 cash. And he wasn't the only one who functioned that way in the Ottawa Valley building business.

He always had a dozen scams going at once, making one or two thousand here and there. I worked on two or three places for him in one week, one near Clayton, one in Lanark, one in Scotch Corners.

Shortly before he left Carleton Place, one of the real estate men in town said to him, "Charlie you'd get $1,500 more, maybe $2,000 more for that lot on Easy Street if it were treed."

"No pwoblem. No pwoblem," said Charlie. And sent some of us chain-saw boys out to the bush to cut some trees and "transplant" them to the lot on Easy Street.

When Chain-saw Channigan left Carleton Place in the middle of the night, nobody knew where he had gone. A lot of people knew they had been left with substandard housing, bills they couldn't collect and a number of impossible second mortgages. The boys who worked for him—well, we had our T-shirts.

We thought we had heard the last of Chain-saw Channigan in Carleton Place and we settled down to a quiet uneventful life again. We heard he had moved to Moosonee to work amongst the Indians there; someone else said they had seen him in North Battleford, putting up substandard shacks for an oil company; he had been sighted in Newfoundland. But all the rumours, as it turned out, were false. Charlie had done his apprenticeship in the boondocks and he had decided he was ready for the big-time in the capital city of Canada. Either he was ready for it, or it was ready for him. Looking back, I've never been sure which it was.

Anyway, one night I got this phone call from Charlie in Ottawa. He was into a big housing development there and he wanted me to come and be his "kitchen cupboard man."

"The rest of the house can be klutz," he said, "but it's the kitchen that wins the little woman. In these days of militant women's lib, the men are scared to death to say 'no'. They're scared shitless, to put it plainly," Charlie said. "You're a good kitchen cupboard man," he went on. "I want you to come. I'll pay you well." He offered me double what I was making.

I listened. Because things were really getting tough in Carleton Place. Half the town was on welfare or pogey. In the meantime, I had married, had a couple of kids.

"But Charlie," I said, "what about the building inspectors in Ottawa? I heard they're really tough."

"No pwoblem. No pwoblem," Charlie said. "I've learned what ones can be bought and what ones can't. You have to get a building inspector who is older, corrupted and whose palm twitches. I've got one."

So I went down to Ottawa to see Charlie. He had done the impossible. In the fashionable west end he had bought the tail ends of some of those older lots that were real long, put them all together and created a new cul-de-sac circle, which he called Greenwoods. There wasn't a tree in sight, but I already knew his skill at landscaping.

Yes, by buying up the butt ends of long lots on the periphery of his intended circle, he had invented a new street, had the "minimum requirement" of footage to present the city with a subdivision plan. He had even been lucky enough to have some of his new lots on the north side abut onto the Ottawa Parkway and overlook the Ottawa River. He had promised to build there only "quality expensive housing" and the city council, dreaming of high taxes on very small pieces of land—indeed, of high where no taxes before had even existed—gave immediate approval to the plan, zoned it A-1 single-family, had the city engineers juggle up plans for a totally inadequate road area.

"What did you have to promise in return?" I asked Charlie.

"I promised them I'd put up a street lamp," he said.

Charlie had also learned a few other lessons, particularly in the advertising field. He had himself billed as "The Best Damn Builder from Kanata to Carlsbad Springs" and he was running ads on both radio and television. He had hired the advertising company that does a famous fast-food-chain ad and convinces the whole world that a mix of sawdust and bad meat makes the greatest hamburger in history. In no time at all, it seemed Charlie Chain-saw Channigan was recognized as The Best Builder from Kanata to Carlsbad Springs. By buyers, by other developers, even by architects. It was something like *The Emperor's New Clothes*.

I commuted for a few months and went to work for Charlie on Greenwoods. Oh God, those houses looked good on the outside! But those of us who worked for him looked down at the ground and around and about or disappeared into the park on the west side when the buyers and the real estate men came by. We knew all about the timber so green that it was moulding and the cinder blocks below regulations, and no insulation, and the garage doors and the landscaping.

I was working on the kitchen cupboards in one of the unfinished houses on the cul-de-sac Channigan made for himself out of nothing when the first house buyer came home with a new car. He got into the garage but, once in there, he found the walls so close he couldn't open the doors of his new machine to get out of it. He could get his Gran Torino in but, when he got it in, he couldn't get out.

He backed it out of the garage and yelled for his wife like a bull moose in rutting season. His wife, who was always on the phone, was on the phone and did not immediately hear his cries of rage and frustration. He headed towards us and we quietly laid down our tools and disappeared into the park. Needless to say, the second thing which the Gran Torino owner did was phone Charlie, the Best Builder between Kanata and Carlsbad Springs. Naturally, Charlie was out of town. The case dragged through the courts for months and finally the *Monopoly News* stopped covering the proceedings. The strange thing about the whole case was that Charlie continued to be acknowledged as the Best Builder from Kanata to Carlsbad Springs. Not only did people continue to say it, but his ads on radio and television continued to say it as well.

Even I got sucked in eventually. It was wintertime and the houses were going slowly—only three had been sold to date—and Charlie needed the cash for another scam he was involved in in Brockville. So he offered me one of his houses at almost cost price. I knew all about the insulation, the green lumber, the below-standard construction. But I knew I could correct most of it. And at that price! I was tired of commuting and my wife was hankering for a fancy-looking house on a cul-de-sac with a low number on it—like 17 Greenwoods. Say, you can think you've moved into society with a number like that one! My reasoning was that I would humour the little woman, for a while at least. And since Charlie had established a reputation as the Best Builder from Kanata to Carlsbad Springs, I was pretty sure I could sell the house at a good profit, if we had to.

So we moved in. Right off, the Gran Torino guy refused to speak to me. And he and his wife never speak to my wife. But the other houses were selling and we had a variety of neighbours.

I'm no great hand at what makes people tick. All that psychology stuff. But there was something working in Charlie that made him a two-storey man. He wouldn't allow anything except a two-storey to be built on his cul-de-sac. But since the cul-de-sac was so small—some houses on the circle had frontages on their pie-shaped lots amounting to 12 feet—you got the effect of too-high houses perched on little rises of landfill, leaning over into the tiny circle below. On windy days in the winter, my wife said, you got the effect of toppling. After she said this to me I thought about it a lot and I decided that on very windy days you got the feeling that, only owing to the genius of Charlie Chain-saw Channigan, did your great hulking two-storey house stay hooked into its window wells. Our next-door neighbour, Ferris Fotheringham from the Philosophy Department at Carleton University, dubbed the circle "the amphitheatre." My wife and I didn't make the Roman-Greco connection, as he called it, so he showed us pictures in books on Greece. And then we could see what he meant all right.

I remember the first time Ferris Fotheringham's en suite bathroom off the master bedroom froze solid in that first winter. He knew I had the biggest plunger on the street and he came rushing over to me. "Please come and bring your plunger," he begged. "Our upstairs bathroom is plugged solid."

I got my plunger out of the basement and went over. It was a terrible spot for me to be in. I looked into his toilet. It was as I already suspected.

"Professor," I said, "I hate to tell you this, but your toilet isn't plugged. It's frozen."

"But," he cried out, "this can't be! This is a Channigan House. This is a Centennial House! This house was built by the Best Builder from Kanata to Carlsbad Springs!"

It was six months before Professor Fotheringham got Charlie on the phone—by mistake. And the court case dragged on for months.

Charlie's little cul-de-sac was so well situated in Ottawa and his houses looked so good on the outside—he was a master of cosmetics by now—that his houses were bought by very choosy buyers—by small businessmen, professionals, university people. Babe and I, out of the boondocks in Carleton Place, were very definitely the outsiders or low-lifers. Professor Fotheringham next door described Greenwoods as a "very conservative establishment upper-middle class type of street or community."

Well, it may have been all of that, Babe and I weren't sure. And didn't really care.

But we definitely learned there wasn't very much difference

between what went on with those folks and the folks back home in Carleton Place. There was a *ménage à trois* in Number 9 Greenwoods. Mrs. Weatherall's redheaded toddler was probably best explained by the redheaded man who came every Wednesday afternoon in a white convertible. Arnie Askwith, the computer man, really did break his leg throwing his Weight-Watcher wife over their patio railing after a New Year's Eve party on the circle.

It is also quite quite true that Dodie Denton, the dentist's wife, one Hallowe'en got all masqueraded up in a black coat and face mask with nothing, absolutely nothing, on underneath, and came to his door as a caller. When Denton answered the door, she threw open her black coat and said, "Trick or treat!" Doc Denton laughed so hard he fell off the porch, landed on a concrete planter and broke three ribs. When the ambulance came to take him away he was still laughing so hard that Dodie had a hard time keeping the attendants from certifying him on the spot.

And it is also quite true that Chris Cane, the one-cent candy man from 11 Greenwoods goes to Florida every year on the money he made on the stock market. He got a hot tip from a candy-bar salesman that Neilsons were going to put nuts in Sweet Marie. He bought the stock and it went straight up.

We stayed on Greenwoods. Charlie was developing in Smith's Falls and he wanted me to be his kitchen cupboard man there—for the same reasons—and Babe and the kids had got attached to Greenwoods, so I commuted again. For five years or so everybody stayed—all the original buyers in their houses keeping their secrets, the Gran Torino man with the two-by-four garage, Professor Fotheringham with his upstairs en suite toilet that froze every time the east wind blew in the wintertime. Those we all knew about. But when Harvie Garvie, the government man, was moved to the UIC offices in Sudbury he sold to Peter Pontillo, the Portuguese decorator. What was going on in all those cosmetic houses on Greenwoods that Charlie had built finally leaked out. No pun intended.

None of us will ever forget the shock of that night when Pontillo, shortly after he had moved in, blind drunk and looking very much like a Christian who had been thrown to the lions, ran around the "amphitheatre" yelling up at all the darkened windows, "You bastards! You knew it leaked!"

Truth to tell, Harvie Garvie had kept the secret well—who wants everybody to know they have been taken? For six years, as it turned out, the Garvies had run around the family room when it rained and put pails under the leaks to catch the Channigan run-off. When we learned about all this, we finally understood why it had been that sometimes Garvie was seen crawling alone along the eaves at night with a flashlight. Why they had ripped off their brand-new roof, torn apart their upstairs dormer windows. They had never found the source of the leak and they managed—after greasing the palm of their real estate agent—to sell the house on a sunny day to Pontillo the decorator. He put it back on the market in December in advance of the spring rains.

The house was next bought by Dan Daily, a draftsman for a drainpipe manufacturer. That April everyone on the Greenwoods circle discovered that the house leaked in more places than one. One rainy night when I was watching our basement fill up with water and was running around by flashlight in the dark trying to put things up on boxes and blocks and wondering if the furnace would be drowned in the night, Dan Daily came to my door. He was dripping rain.

"My God!" he said. "Is your basement flooding?"

"Heavens, no," I replied, "dry as a bone."

He turned and fled, yelling backwards as he ran.

"I have to keep bailing her out!"

Randy Robertson, the Fire Chief, was the next purchaser and he, in time, solved the leak problem. He heard from an ancient clairvoyant the house was actually built on limestone caves through which ran an underground river. He tore up the entire back garden to get at it, and then, when the underground river couldn't be found, he put a sump pump in the basement. Rain still leaked into pails in the family room on bad days, so Robertson devised a cosmetically disguised run-off pipe—it was an exact replica of the fireman's pole in the firehall—which ran through the outer wall and into the swimming pool which he had had built in the backyard to catch the overflow from the house.

Well, the job we were working on in Smith's Falls was coming to an end, and me and the boys were getting a little worried about what next. Was Charlie moving on? Would we all be out of work? We heard he had gone to Florida for a vacation to look over the deluxe condominium situation there. Then somebody said no, he was going into Quebec where there were very lax building and zoning bylaws and building inspectors were as rare there as an honest politician. Pierre Picard, a guy I worked with who came from Quebec said to me, "Shit, yes, Quebec! That's where you can still build a cottage on a lakefront with the backhouse on the beach and the water supply to the family sink running through it."

But then one day all our worries were over. There was a big

announcement in the paper that Belleville was to have the largest covered mall in North America built at its north end, right on 401, and that the OMB, after sixty-three hearings at an estimated cost of $33,674,123.29 to the taxpayer, had chosen the plan submitted by none other than Charlie Channigan, the Best Damn Builder from Kanata to Carlsbad Springs.

Charlie turned up on the Smith's Falls site one day when we were just putting in the finishing touches on some of the landscaping. I was getting scared about my mortgage payments and their relationship to my not having a job any longer. So I said to Charlie, "Well Charlie I hear the big news about the mall in Belleville. Good going. Good going."

"Yeth," Charlie mused, flicking his "cigah." "Good news travels fast these days."

"I don't suppose you'll be needing me on that site," I said.

"Why not? Why not?" Charlie asked.

"Seems to me that you won't be needing a kitchen cupboard man on that job."

"No, that's true, that's true," Charlie mused, "But stick with me anyhow. I want you to do the plumbing."

The Journey from Feakle to Dublin

I wish to tell you all, my good companions of the road in Ireland, of the adventures I encountered after I stood on the hill at Feakle in front of Smith's Hotel and waved you all good-bye—with real regrets. I went back in to Mrs. Smith's tales of the Tax Man who came down on her fold and demanded last year ten thousand pounds more, and of her hiring of that young man named Sean as General Manager and Accountant to swing her "out of the red"—which he did—and of their ongoing visitations to the bank to borrow huge sums of money to build an addition onto the hotel. Once more, as she had done on my previous visit, she mourned her dear, dead husband—"I took to the house for nine months after his death, you know"—and assured me that Myself and Mine would always be "well looked after" should Myself and Mine come again to lovely Feakle in County Clare.

"The train leaves Limerick at one o'clock," she warned me as I took off with my camera to walk the town and countryside. "We'll make sure you get there on time."

I asked her for directions to Biddy Early's little house. It had been buried in overgrowth when, three years before, I had walked to it with Betty White and Freddie Billingslea of Alaska.

We had poked all around the ruins of her house and its outbuildings.

For the second time as well Mrs. Smith sounded out a caution, conveyed her forebodings and superstitions to me. "Don't go in at all," she said. "Just say a prayer for her at the roadside."

I am somewhat at a loss as to why Mrs. Smith's fear, and general fear in the countryside, surrounds Biddy Early for, as Irish story-teller Eddie Lenihan says in his book *The Search for Biddy Early*, "she did good for all and sundry." He quotes an old man from near Kilishen, "T'was good things she done all the time. Sure, the Devil never cured anyone, only made them worse if he could. He has nothing to give you only what he has himself. That's his trade." Lenihan continues on to write that, in all his travels to collect stories related to Biddy, only one could be said to prove that she used her power irresponsibly and, even in that one case, there were mitigating circumstances.

Biddy was renowned for her consistent cures, predictions of unerring accuracy, and casting of spells. She also was renowned as a genius tutelae or guiding spirit. Lenihan says that throughout Ireland the best-known of the stories associated with Biddy casting spells is the one in which she stuck the priest and his horse to the road at Feakle for a whole day as punishment for "cursing her off o' the altar an' giving her a woeful hand, ordering the people not to be paying heed to her; that they shouldn't be listening to her at all."

An old woman in Ballylee remembered Biddy saying, "There's a cure for every known evil between the two millstones of Ballylee."

She accurately predicted that Clare wouldn't win an All-Ireland senior hurling title until the last member of a certain team had died.

The first time I went to Biddy Early's site I found it, but went without my camera. This second time I had my camera but could not find the exact site although I walked past where I thought it should have been several times. It may be that Biddy does not wish to have her spirit photographed—or her aura disturbed by outsiders.

Frustrated, I took the road back to Feakle town. At the top of the hill near the church, I met two people chatting—a tousled, ruddy-faced Irishman on the sidewalk and, on the road below him as though to emphasize her size, a teeny tiny woman who meant to grow into a fairy but was prevented because she "too often sat by the fire at night, a bad thing to do because you crowd out the old people on the other side, the people that's gone who like to come in around the fire after a certain hour, talking about old times, maybe seeing loved one's faces asleep." As I joined their duet I noticed the man was carrying a pail of fresh milk.

"You've just milked your cow," I said to him.

"Over in the field there," he said, laughing through his missing front teeth.

They posed for me at the door of the Feakle church hall, were keen for more blather from an obvious foreigner. But I was reluctant to hold him up, seeing that black moving specks were already appearing on the surface of his pure sweet-smelling milk. I ambled on down the road to the end of the village.

I looked at my watch. Twelve. I hurried back to Mrs. Smith's to gather my bags, check my peas in the pod and arrowroot biscuits for the journey to Dublin. I was delighted to see the new green van standing at the inn door and both Sean, the accountant who had saved the place from bankruptcy, and Mrs. Smith who had failed to understand the tax man's demands, both awaiting me at the reception desk. A full hour then, to get to Limerick for the train.

"If you could make me a quick sandwich, ham, chicken, whatever," I said to Mrs. Smith, "I'm ready to go."

"Oh," said Sean, "the train from Limerick doesn't leave until three."

"Oh," said Mrs. Smith, "I thought it always left at one."

Sean phoned and, sure enough, the train from Limerick to Dublin left at three.

I sat in the empty dining-room and ate my lonely sandwich where the night before we had all laughed together and Bev had done that memorable farewell eulogy which had left me speechless and quite unable to improvise. I got out my notebook and added some new material to my ongoing (15 years now) *Aphorisms and Absolutes.* "Every person seeks a love through which they can enter The Forever."

In Smith's dining-room, mulling over my journey and its infinite possibilities to go awry, I suddenly realized that my forthcoming check-in time at the Dublin Airport hotel was six o'clock and that they wouldn't keep my room past that time because it is so busy there in high season. So back to Sean to get him to phone the airport hotel and say I would be late. They'd keep it until seven, they said. I paid for the phone call and the sandwich, another five pounds sucked into the journey from Feakle to Dublin to catch a 10:10 plane homewards, and sat around.

I was grateful when Sean announced that he would leave at a quarter to two "In order to make sure," he said, "we get there on time." There really wasn't much doubt about that, though. It was a hair-raising lickety-split charge of the Young Man Feeling his Power as Manager and Saviour after seven years of training in hotel management, including apprenticeships in Switzerland and Spain.

But on the positive side he gave me insight into his generation in Ireland when he said he certainly considered himself one of the privileged of County Monahan where his parents ran a five-star inn and glad, indeed, he was that his education and background would make it possible for him to stay in his beloved Ireland and not have to flee to America and Mississauga as hundreds of his contemporaries have had to do in the twentieth-century immigration flood.

He went in with me at the train station to the ticket wicket. Another 25 pounds.

Mrs. Smith had assured me that the train went straight through from Limerick to Dublin.

"Does this train go straight through from Limerick to Dublin?" I asked the ticket-seller.

"You change at Limerick Junction," she snapped.

I groaned. More baggage hauling. If it was any distance at all I knew I could never make it alone with my big bag—the hard case—and my carry-on, grown so heavy with spoils.

Sean made arrangements with one of the uniformed employees buzzing about the combined bus-and-train depot to carry on my luggage at train time. So I sat and watched the motley Irish and the few tourists parade, women with babies in the grubby heat, life partners communicating in nods, snappy feminists carrying the chip on their shoulders in back-packs, hippies in heaven, cyclists wrapping up their bicycles for the baggage man, day shoppers opening and closing the rental lockers facing me, shoving in parcels, taking out parcels. The resident pigeons walked around and between peoples' feet, looking for food on a crumbless grey slate table. Lean pickings. I broke up an arrowroot and slid it surreptitiously through the slats of my seat.

I sat facing a neon-lit schedule of Departures and Arrivals, the platform numbers listed as well. While I waited there the light switched from Dublin Platform 3 to Dublin Platform 2 and then back again, several times. I was about to panic when a young slip of a thing, the uniformed employee, came out of a side door and up to me. "Can I help you with your bags?" she asked. "The train is boarding now for Dublin—on Platform 5!"

She hoisted my bags and got me onto the train to Dublin, brought them into a car, tried to shove the hard case in between two seats, but failed. Another pound. I got into two seats facing each other and put a bag on two of them, myself on the third, leaving only one seat free. A woman with her husband got on, took a look at my situation and snarled, "Look at that, will you? Taking up three seats herself." I thought she looked like the kind of a woman to make a troublesome scene about what might be construed as foreign greediness or ignorance. But her husband bunted her in the behind with his carry-on, and she passed me by.

I should mention here that not only did the train stop at Limerick Junction but several other unmentioned places before that, Illmore, Ballymore, Dunmore, and, I believe, More-and-More. Since I had been told by the ticket seller that the train only stopped at Limerick Junction before Dublin, the first time the train stopped I leaped up and yelled out, "Is this the stop for Limerick Junction?" The regulars looked at me as though I were loony and maintained a masterful silence. But one woman volunteered, "I'll tell you when we come to it, dearie."

A voice from the depths of new Irish technology finally did announce Limerick Junction and I arose to try to struggle my way out and across to a new train. Just as I pushed out of my seat, bent over with my burdens, a long arm reached out behind me and said, "Let me take that for you." And the big bag—the hard case—which I could barely lift, was hoisted as easily as if it contained feathers instead of the spoils of Ireland, sweaters, jackets, fairies, leprechauns—for my grandchildren—and books.

Another train was waiting across the platform.

"Is this the train to Dublin?" I asked, full of apprehension. What if it were the train to Belfast? Or even Donegal?

"God! I hope so!" said the tall tweedy man who had become my porter voluntarily. We got ourselves into four more seats facing each other and sat down in the sweltering heat—no air-conditioning, again—although this train, too, was clean and fairly modern with non-functioning air-conditioning vents above us looking down like black teeth.

The tweedy man complained about the heat, took off his coat, loosened his tie and began his life story. Retired to his garden, he was or had been a radio and wireless operator from aboard ships all over the world, later London Airport and Dublin Airport. He began to tell me stories of his adventures on Greek ships, Italian ships, Spanish ships, but alas, I was dying of heat and thirst. Although the conductor would not and did not ever manage to sound out the upcoming stations, he managed, "Dining car with a bar, to the rear." I excused myself from the tweedyman's story of waking up on the wrong ship, and went back to the dining car for water. Cool clear water. (A rare request in Ireland).

Although there were two uniformed attendants at the bar, some terrible confusion seemed to be tearing them apart or putting them in immobilizing conflict so that the four people waiting in line were just waiting in line like patient cattle. I hung out with them for a while, gradually growing paler and more faint, until one young man turned to me and said, "Can I help you?"

"I just want a glass of water," I gasped to him.

"Give this lady a glass of water," he said authoritively to one of the attendants who appeared to be hiding behind a partition.

The glass of water was put in my hands and I started back to my seat. On the way I noticed that the tall, long-armed, tweedy good-looking man who had become my porter was seated in the dining-car eating what appeared to be fish and chips. A fine way to cool off, I thought, after all that complaining about the heat.

I was relieved he had left me although I knew I would need his services again. I was so anxious and apprehensive about getting to the hotel at the Dublin Airport before my deadline that I really could not concentrate on his stories. They were floating around me and about me like patches of clouds, half into consciousness, half out.

Back in my seat I closed my eyes and tried to imagine my leap from the train to a taxi to take me to the Dublin Airport. My big bag—the hard case—had little roller coaster feet on it and in my carry-on I had carefully tucked into one of the zipper compartments the snap-on pull-along which belonged to it. But I knew that my big bag—the hard case—was so lop-sided now with the spoils of Ireland that it would only go a few inches before it flopped over and lay on its side like a winged partridge. I would have to inch my way down the aisle, out the door, across the station, to the taxi stand, unless—

At that very moment my Irish porter returned to the seat across from me, wound up his long legs, and began again. After a number of trips to the Old Sod and countless encounters with monologists I have evolved the theory that the Irish of the south, so long impoverished, discovered that the only gifts they had to give to the world were the gifts of language, story, poetry. Hence the ability for the uneducated to talk exquisitely, for the remarkable facility with story, for the language verging on poetry, for the simplest of folk to tell you the folklore and history, for regaling by the roadside. As some races think aggressively (the Germans) or monetarily (the Swiss) or ruthlessly (the Spanish) the Irish think only in story. Everyone. Without exception.

"I'm going to Dublin for my sister's wake," he announced. "She died of cancer of the lung. So young. My youngest sibling."

Being Canadian I had nothing to say to such a revelation of personal loss and tragedy.

Being Irish he continued.

"My brother died of cancer of the lung."

(Appropriate Canadian restraint).

"My other brother died of cancer of the lung."

(More of the same).

"I quit smoking years ago when I was a radio operator for an Irish line out of Shannon."

He had long slender fingers and I thought of them tapping out SOS's, storm positions, maybe even wartime messages. How old was he? Timeless as Ireland. I looked at him more closely. He had a fine labile face and, as only some of the Irish can do, mixed elegance with a kind of intangible seediness, as though the poverty of centuries cannot be varnished over in a lifetime on Grafton Street.

I did reason, however, that he was a seasoned traveller for his carry-on was so collapsed that he could only have thrown into it clean underwear and a razor, maybe a clean shirt, although it had to be a thin one judging by the space taken up.

He changed tack, began to talk about his garden, never mentioning "we!" Irish tomatoes don't ripen until fall. He had just discovered zuccini. He could grow red basil. His name is Johnny Kielly. I come to immediately, out of the strangling heat and my clogging anxiety.

"The Ottawa Valley was largely settled by the Irish," I offered, "and one of the people I taped on the Opeongo Line was a lively old man, a widower, living alone, named of all things—can you believe it!—Johnny Kielly! You are Johnny Kielly the Second."

"Probably related," he said. And I had to concur. Both were the same long lithe streaks, full of surprising strength, only truly handsome when they smiled. The Kielly genetic pool had crossed the ocean on some famine ship and cloned itself on the Opeongo Line, I thought to myself.

I was secretly freaked by entanglement in this circle of intercontinental Kiellys. Some years before I had taped the life story of Johnny Kielly the First on the Opeongo Line—it was the most poetic tape I ever collected—and afterwards he had pulled out his mouth organ and played while I danced on his sparkling linoleum floor. Maybe I was destined to dance with another Johnny Kielly? Some supernatural power of Biddy Early of Feakle foretelling my future even although I did not actually find the ruins of her hidden house?

But why was he heading for the airport outside Dublin when his sister is dead inside Dublin? He complained more about the heat, lack of air-conditioning on the train, described Ireland as "A Third World Country."

"Let us share the taxi fare from the station to the airport," he suggested.

"Fine by me," I replied. I have already figured out that this trip from Biddy Early's Feakle to Dublin Airport hotel would cost me in the neighbourhood of two hundred pounds by the time I stayed over in the hotel, paid for dinner and breakfast.

The train began to slow but again there was no announcement. You are simply expected to know that this is the Dublin stop, centre of the universe, the way the woman driver when hit from behind turning into her driveway yelled at the other driver, "What's wrong with you? Don't you know I always turn in here?" They do not expect tourists to take the trains. They rent cars. Or take planes. But trains! Well!

"Is this then Dublin?" I asked him.

"Well, I guess so!"

Johnny Kielly unwound from the seat, stood above me, put on his tweed jacket—countryman's jacket I had decided—picked up my big bag—the hard case—and his little collapsed nylon carry-on. I followed behind him with my overladen carry-on which got heavier and heavier as we travelled across the cavernous jammed station towards a taxi. At the curb one taxi was already filled and the other was taking off.

"Only two cabs?" I muttered. "Can't be."

"Is there a taxi stand?" I asked the taxi driver of the already filled cab.

"Yes," he said, pointing. "Over there across the station."

Johnny Kielly turned and I followed him back across the jammed vaulted station. He kept casting his eyes back to see if I was still with him.

"I'm following you," I kept assuring him. His height and broad shoulders broke trail for me.

At the taxi stand there were numerous taxis waiting empty.

"How much to the Dublin Airport?" Kielly asked the driver who came up to us.

"Oh, ten, twelve pounds," the driver said, laughingly, shrugging.

"Better be ten," Kielly warned him.

But I didn't care. It was six-thirty and my deadline was seven.

We were off to the airport.

"Why are you going to the airport when your sister is dead in Dublin?" I asked.

"I'll catch a cup of coffee at the airport and then head for where she lived," he replied smartly. "It's six of one and half a dozen of the other."

Since my geography of the Dublin area is very vague, I accepted his reasoning. But faintly far-off—

Side by side in the back seat of the taxi we flew towards the Dublin Airport, the cabbie driving so aggressively most other drivers on the busy rush-hour lanes made way for us. I recognized the early part of the route from previous runs to Dublin Airport. But then strangeness sets in. Is he taking a longer route recognizing me as an ignoramus who won't know the difference? But Johnny Kielly is obviously Irish, has a Clare accent, and knows his way around. No. But it was all strange without landmarks, terribly New World, white concrete rising. My God! Maybe there's more than one hotel now!

Johnny Kielly shocked me back into the present.

"Do you always travel alone?" he asked me.

"No." I rapped out. "Never. I had to leave for Dublin a day ahead of my group. Travel agent error." The bells far off were ringing.

The taxi started going up ramps and round and round in circles. This was not the Dublin Airport of three summers ago! What had happened? Nobody had told me about the Americanization of the Dublin Airport!

The last time I was here I stayed in THE Airport Hotel, a simple two-storey prosaic building directly across from the entrance to Dublin's little friendly airport. One where you could yell across a welcome to incomers, a farewell to outgoers. I remembered trundling my hard case on its little wheels across the street from the hotel entrance to the airport entrance, a hen's pace it was, and a simple chore.

Panic struck again. Back at Smith's Hotel in Feakle, Sean, the young manager, when he verified my reservations, had not given me the name of the hotel. I simply had assumed there was still only one. What if there were now two in this insidious Americanization of Ireland and I was at the wrong one? I shuddered at the thought of further expensive taxi travel around and around the one-way circles.

I had assumed that Johnny Kielly would go on to his sister's wake-house with the same driver after I got out of the taxi. But wrong again.

"Please stop at the airport entrance," he said to the driver.

Around a few more circles and we were at the airport entrance. Johnny Kielly got out on his side, leaned in the taxi, put six pounds in my hand and said, "I'll go in and have a cup of coffee here at the airport."

Well, maybe he wants to go and visit his old pals in the radar tower, I thought to myself.

"Good-bye, Johnny Kielly," I blurted out, "and good luck to you."

The driver pulled out before I had even thought of alone conveyed out loud all my thanks for his help on the road.

The taxi then made three or four more circles through the new concrete maze and pulled up to the front of a grand new totally unrecognizable hotel called Forte Crest.

"Is there only one hotel here?" I demanded of the taxi driver.

"There it is," he rapped out, turning around and looking at me.

"That's twelve pounds."

I got out, put fourteen pounds, six of Kielly's, six of mine and a two pound tip in his hand, asked for a receipt and stood in front of the hotel steps, a full flight up. Tipped or not, the taxi driver dumped my bags at the foot of the stairs up, and blew off quickly. I was in the process of figuring out how to haul them up. Should I trust one at the bottom, and only take up one at a time? Or should I try to do both at once.

"Here. Let me help you," said another big Irishman, and whisked my bags up to the reception desk. I thanked God that when the British impressed the giant Irishmen for the lumbering trade in the Ottawa Valley, they hadn't captured all of them.

The receptionist on the desk, after taking my Mastercard imprint, gave me the key to my room, directions to it, and said "The bellboy will be up shortly with your bags."

The ninety pounds worth of bed and bath was almost as welcome as if it had been home, but there was no soap and no wash cloth in the room. I crept back downstairs, told the receptionist and asked for my bags, please. I was sweaty, hot, tired and irritable, four hours from Feakle and a new maze of circles from the airport, all one-way.

I stood around until the bellhop came trundling my bags along and I started off with him to Room 381. Turned out that the hotel, so new it still smelled new, had no elevators but only lifts for the luggage. I left him loading at the lift and headed for my room again. Some time and two pounds later I had all my luggage in hand once more, and fell into the bath. A chamber maid arrived at my door and 50p later I had soap and a wash cloth. Plus a huge bath towel which I viewed as a good omen for the rest of the journey.

At eight o'clock when I went into the dining-room for dinner I asked the receptionist to give me a wake-up call at 7:30. "My plane leaves at 10:10 a.m." I reminded her. But I know how many things can go wrong yet in this scenario, line-ups for Value Added Tax, lineups for boarding passes, lineups for bathrooms, lineups for taxis, lineups for bellboys to haul baggage, lineups to pay my bill.

I was already up the next morning when, true to her promise, the receptionist gave me my wake-up call at 7:30. Another good sign on this journey. By now I was on a roll, had a quick breakfast, went back to my room and packed, throwing out everything disposable, called for a bellhop to take my bags down. Once more they disappeared into the luggage lift and turned up at the desk just as I was telling the desk clerk that I would leave them there and go early to the VAT office in the airport to avoid line-ups and get my sixty pounds back to pay in Irish money on my hotel bill.

"I want to get rid of my Irish money," I explained to her.

"Our man will run you over in the van," she said.

The van pulled immediately up to the hotel door and, along with another early bird, I jumped in. We went round and round the one-way circles again and finally arrived at the airport, only a few feet away as the crow flies but 3.5 km away as the concentric circles run, designed no doubt by a road engineer entirely on the side of underdogs like taxi drivers.

"There is a white phone right inside the door," said the van driver. "Pick it up and you'll get the hotel. Tell me when you are ready to return."

If my tweedy friend from Limerick considered Ireland a Third World Country, Dublin Airport, now, is no Third World Airport. It has escalators, restaurants, cubby-hole offices, a mile of Aer Lingus counters and gorgeous Irish girls making older women remember what they once were (and didn't know it then). However, you can only catch a glimpse of Irish beauty as Canadians cannot any longer fly Aer Lingus unless out of Boston or some other God-forsaken American mega airport.

To get my VAT money, I was sent off to find the Customs office and, after fifteen minutes of labyrinthian running came to a door marked "Customs." Inside it said, "Ring Bell for Service." I did, and after an Irish while, a uniformed woman, soured on something or other in life, came to a little window. I shoved my VAT slips in at her.

"This is Customs," she snapped as only people with false teeth can do. "VAT is upstairs and to the right."

I sprang to the up escalator and ran right, looking at my watch and figuring how many minutes left to countdown.

There was a line-up at VAT. I assessed the shortest one. When I got to the wicket and pushed in my VAT slips, the VAT lady kindly retaliated by shoving out at me a two-foot-long questionnaire with carbon paper inserted between two of the sheets. Americanization of VAT.

I took one look at it and threw it back at her.

She shrugged.

"You can mail it to us," she said.

I ran downstairs to the white phone and phoned the hotel to tell the van driver I was ready. Indeed, I was more than ready.

"He'll be along in a few minutes," she sallied off to me. "Wait outside the front door."

I went outside and waited. I waited and waited. I paced and I paced. I looked at my watch and counted the minutes to countdown. I phoned the hotel again.

"I have a plane to catch, " I yelled at the cheery voice on the other end.

"He'll be along in a few minutes," she said, unperturbed. She probably has taken that seven-year course in hotel management, I thought to myself, and learned how to lie to the tourists.

I waited for half an hour and then ran up to the taxi stand and said, "Take me to THE Hotel." By now I knew there was only one.

With one accord all the taxi drivers hesitated.

Finally one brave lad stepped forward and said in a sighing, sacrificial way, "Oh, all right. I'll do it."

We wound round and round the one-way circles again, gradually as the circles narrowed, closing in on our quarry, the hotel Forte Crest.

"How much?" I asked, now shaking with anxiety.

"Three pounds five," he replied without so much as a wince.

Now staggering, I ran up the steps towards the receptionist.

"Now what," I said to her. "I'm here and presumably my bags are with the van driver arriving at the airport. But I couldn't wait any longer for him—and I had to take a cab—and pay my bill here—" I am now blithering.

"Oh," she said, looking at me pityingly, "The van driver is here—with your bags."

"But you said—oh, never mind."

Her smile, I can see, is not removable.

"Give me my bill."

She put it in front of me. It said something like one hundred and twenty-two pounds. I paid by Mastercard. Eyes glazed over by now. You're supposed to line up an hour before boarding — I'm a greenhorn. Now panicking.

The van driver went around and around the circles again. Oh Christ! The Americanization of Ireland! The frenzy of Free Trade Ireland! The end of Third World Ireland! Don't these dolts realize that I and thousands like me come to Ireland, cherish Ireland, long for Ireland because we need to get away from the Americanization of our Canada!

The van driver took my hard case and we started running around the airport looking for Royal Airlines Sunquest charter to Toronto. We found it with line-ups the length of soccer fields in front of it. I gave him five pounds. He looked unhappy. I didn't care. I was beyond consistency or calculation.

I think to myself, I must be living right, or be doubly blessed to have arrived here at this spot on the planet in time to catch my plane to go home.

All the way across the ocean I am haunted by the pros and cons of Johnny Kielly the Second from Limerick. Who was he really? And what were his motives?

I recuperated from jet-lag in the garden, rose-scented, tree-cooled, of Gail and Chalmers in North Toronto. We ate there and drank there and talked there and I told them all about my incredible story-telling tour through Ireland and of my encounter with Johnny Kielly the Second. I recuperated for a day and a half in that cloistered garden amongst those dear friends. The second morning, when we were having breakfast in the garden before Gail drove me from Toronto to my home near Kingston just so she could have a swim in my lake, Chalmers said, "All day yesterday at work I was haunted by Johnny Kielly the Second."

Back at home near Kingston I regaled and entertained friends and relatives with re-tellings of my journey from Feakle to Dublin. Johnny Kielly the Second became a man to haunt everyone who heard the stories. Without exception every North American listener in speculating about his motives gave out the opinion that his intentions were dubious, to say the least.

When I wrote down the story of the journey from Feakle to Dublin without exception every North American reader was of the opinion that Johnny Kielly the Second was "on the make," "looking for a one-night stand in the Forte Crest Hotel."

But when my Irish friends heard or read the story, the perspective was quite different.

"He was sent as your guardian angel for that journey."

"You travelled under the benign influence of Biddy Early."

Although I am North American and at first sided with the cynical North American attitude towards Kielly, the more I puzzled over the details and nuances, the conversation, impressions and events of that journey the more I sided with the spiritualism of my Irish friends.

The more I began to side with my Irish friends in their assessment of Johnny Kielly the Second, the more I regretted that I had not in the least degree thanked him enough for his help on that Limerick-to-Dublin leg of my journey from Feakle. I decided to write to Eddie Lenihan, one of the Irish story-tellers on Ray McGrath's Heritage Ramble and the author of the book on Biddy Early from whom I had received a copy. He lived, I knew, in Limerick. I sent Lenihan the story and asked if he would Xerox out of the Limerick phone book the page including the name of Johnny Kielly, explaining to him how sorely I needed to thank Kielly.

Lenihan was prompt. He sent back a Xeroxed page from the Limerick phone book.

On that page were the names, addresses, phone numbers of twenty-four Johnny Kiellys!

"From where I stand," Lenihan wrote to me, "I think you should be thanking Biddy Early for sending Johnny Kielly to you as a guardian angel."

The Dead-End Road

Marina was at a publisher's party in Ottawa when it came to her like all life-changing messages—surreptitiously and as a tiny voice at first bleating far-off but rising to a blare—that she should abandon all hope of finding a mating man her age and equal in High Tech City. Or, as her Toronto friends disparagingly dubbed it—Deadsville.

She had purposely gone late to the Hexagon party to facilitate her unobtrusive absorption into the scene, but almost instantly realized her mistake. The champagne had been flowing for over an hour and her obvious sobriety put her out of context. She spoke briefly to a couple of people she knew including Philip Brackenworth (by then eschewing his consonants), hosting without his wealthy wife who was rumoured to keep him afloat in the crucifying business of publishing in a country unfortunately next door to the United States of America. Only the masochists are left, she observed running mentally down the list of recent bankruptcies, mergers and takeovers as Canadian publishers fought to survive.

Marina returned the curt nod of Dexter MacIvor, an aesthete who ran the only remaining "quality" press in Canada and who hated women—although he didn't know it. "Dexter probably goes home at night," she said to herself, "and says to himself, 'What did I do to her to make her react like that?'" Philip Brackenworth came back and introduced her to Cavendish McCullough, the Rabelaisian who ran the wine column in the Ottawa *Evening Star*, the only daily left in the capital city of Canada. Since the *Ottawa Advocate* had fallen victim last year to the accelerating movement to monoliths in the Western World, the *Star*, always second-rate, had plunged to new depths of mindless mediocrity. In desperation people in Ottawa were now buying the Montreal *Gazette*, the Kingston *Whig-Standard*, the Eganville *Leader* and the *Gatineau News*. After any death, Marina had thought to herself, the members of the tribe run around frantically trying to reassemble the pieces and fill in the gap. But this death would make history for it sounded the death of the newspaper in Canada.

She had dressed carefully for the occasion. A widow, aged 50, she was aware of approving glances. Well, maybe two approving male glances, she smiled to herself. The ratio of men to women in the cocktail party crowd was the usual in Ottawa—ten to one. And half of those are gay, she calculated with a sinking feeling in her gut.

She remembered that, at that point, she had thought about exiting but was cornered by Danielle Dagg, one of the young divorceés who worked in the office of *Hexagon* magazine. Whoops! Trapped! she thought and reached out for more champagne. Danielle had three daughters she was trying to raise alone on sporadic alimony and the salary she got from Hexagon. Recently she had been harried also by housing problems and had had to find a new place for herself and her brood at a reasonable rent—something which was becoming increasingly difficult to do in Ottawa as real estate prices climbed at a dizzying pace reminiscent of Toronto a few years previously.

Having raised three of her own alone for the past score of years, Marina was very sympathetic to Danielle's problems. But, God forgive me, she thought to herself, I am sick to death of women, women everywhere. I want to talk to a nice male man—even if it is only for a few hours. At this juncture they had been joined by Sondra McMartin, a freelance writer and leader of the Women's Movement in the capital. Marina was tempted to sing out "If you could read my mind," but had resisted. Sondra launched immediately and forthrightly into the recent scandal which had rocked the capital and the country and led to some sensational resignations—that of Chairit Mavis Sanderson, head of the Advisory Council on the Status of Women, and Floyd Flaxworthy, Minister of Employment and Immigration. Marina was certain that she and Danielle would have been bludgeoned with a vitriolic description of the methods by which Flaxworthy should be hung and quartered if it had not happened that Sondra sighted Mavis Sanderson in the next room surrounded by a group of followers and admirers.

With Sondra gone Danielle said, "Well, what do you think?"

"Of the party?"

"No, no, of the ratio." Danielle laughed. "I saw you taking stock there when you first came in."

"Pretty hopeless."

"What's Hopeless? Reagan and his War Hawk Haig or inflation in Canada with Trusty Trudeau at the helm?" Karen Carruthers, another freelancer chimed in as she joined them. Karen had set a record in publishing circles by living with the same man for 15 years; she was often heard to boast that they even went on holidays together.

"No," said Danielle. "It's the male-female ratio that's hopeless."

"I agree totally," Karen said. "Traditionally Ottawa as a civil service town has always been a woman fortress. But in recent years the situation has deteriorated due to the fact that, in our society, we are killing off more and more of our men earlier and earlier. Worse still, even the two eligible men in this room won't make an ultimate commitment. It's unfashionable now to make a total commitment—"

"That's right," Danielle cried out with a passion which Marina knew arose from a recent painful break-up and separation. "And that's why I'm teaching my daughters to get all the education they can get and learn to be self-sufficient and independent because some day they'll be left—"

Marina found the talk of these younger people, the despair of this "Transition Generation" more depressing than anything Reagan was doing or Trudeau wasn't. They were talking about the inalienable right to mate as passé, as a lost cause.

"And if it is hopeless for them what does that make it for me?" she had asked herself. And went home.

Back at the apartment—nobody had asked her to join them for dinner and she couldn't afford to take herself—hoping for some positive word from some source, she went to the mailroom with her chain of keys and got out her mail. As her protest against monoliths she left her telephone bill in the box—it could rot there for a while—and took out two personal letters. One was from Kate and Bertie Belanger, her tenants at the lake house north of Kingston. They were splitting—what else was new?—and could she please let them out of their mutual verbal agreement? They would like to leave by the end of May.

It had been both bad news and good news. Modest as it was, she really needed the rent money. But the thought of the lake house suddenly freed for herself for the whole golden summer was dazzling and unsettling. She had resigned herself to another summer in the highrise, plugged in to the air conditioner.

The second letter contained word from the apartment manager. Her condominium had been bought (it was a MURB) by an investor who insisted on her signing a lease. Would she please come to the rental office and do that immediately?

She had sat down on her bed and fired her shoes at the concrete walls.

"No! I won't sign a Goddamn lease. I hate this place!" she cried aloud. "What ever made me think I could live in a Goddamn highrise apartment?"

She surprised herself by picking up two books at her bedside and firing them at the walls as well. A year and a half of pushed down feelings were suddenly released in an overwhelming flood. She had taken the apartment hoping to meet some male singles. But in all those months the only friend she had made was Grace MacMillan, an older woman on the penthouse floor who ran a florist business downtown. And even she Marina had met in her shop before she ever moved into Park Place. No. Not even the view of the Parkway and the Ottawa River at Deschênes Rapids compensated for the concrete coldness, uniform sameness, chilling impersonality of the twenty-eight floor highrise.

The two concurrent events put Marina in immediate conflict and that night she lay in bed tossing and turning, juggling the pros and cons. Maybe she should stay in Ottawa where, over a period of three years, she had established herself both socially and professionally? But, ah, the lake house north of Kingston was paradise in summer. True, an isolated paradise and isolation was something she had to guard against. But the developer she had sold to had now sold almost all his lots and people from as far away as Toronto and Montreal, as well as from Kingston, had had him put up custom-built and, in some cases, exceptionally attractive houses: there were now neighbours on the land. Besides, it would give her a chance to sort out her papers, to get another batch ready for Queen's University archives, to rid herself of some more material things in keeping with her ongoing thrust to simplify life and eliminate "the garbage," to regroup for her next plateau of life. She had been increasingly aware deep down inside herself for perhaps the last six months that she was preparing for this.

In her tossings and turnings and weighings of pros and cons, she had had to consider the dangers in returning to Kingston, the dangers of resuming out of unmet needs old and dead-end relationships, the dangers of slipping into the partying, hard-drinking, well-heeled crowd she had moved with in her years in Kingston. How rich even she had been in those pre-inflation gravy days!

In 1981 she found it hard to believe that in the fat Sixties and early Seventies she had been able to hire a waiter, bring in the hard liquor and have a party for a hundred people. Or take a day off from her work, cook and bake all day, have ready at seven a five-course dinner for eight complete with aperitifs, dinner wines and liquors. Now, if she could manage a simple dinner for four she was lucky. And hers wasn't the only income level hit by the whole economic mess. Her old friends the MacIntoshes, both doctors who moved in the medical clique, had recently commented to her that the first thing to go in their belt-tightening programme had been entertaining. BYO parties had become fashionable.

She smiled to herself in the dark as she remembered Jim MacIntosh saying. "And now it's not just Bring Your Own liquor but it's bring your own everything—including your own plate and knife and fork!"

Back in the late Sixties and through the Seventies almost everyone in her Kingston circle had been in their promiscuous forties. Not only had the social world been characterized by feasts of food and orgies of liquor but it had also been rife with extra-marital affairs. Dan and Gwen Donaldson were former Kingston friends who had moved to Ottawa some years prior to her own move there and with whom she had evolved a real friendship. She recalled that just a few weeks ago at their house in Sandy Hill they had been quietly reminiscing about times past in the very "small town" of Kingston, a reminiscing instigated, no doubt, by the death there of an old friend, quickly taken out by cirrhosis of the liver.

"You know," Dan had mused, "in those days in Kingston in our forties there was a lot of excess sexual energy at the parties."

He had made his statement with such a clinical examining-room manner that Marina had hardly been able to keep a straight face. "To look at them now," she had thought to herself at the time, "who would ever believe that they had been involved in an endless and competitive succession of affairs!" Now it was "home to roost" and "share the spoils!"

She suspected that, in terms of her maturation, going back to Kingston was a form of regression or marking time—yes, that was better—but she felt she was strong enough now to resist the temptations. And how delicious was the mere contemplation of three or four months without paying rent, getting her feet back on the earth, falling into the lake a dozen times a day, putting in a garden, having a few old friends in to dinner on her own chairs, with her own dishes.

And then, deeper into the night, had come creeping across her consciousness another good reason for returning to the lake for the summertime. Yes, maybe it was time now for her to accept the fact that she would never find, at her time of life, a man of her own to love and cherish, to share with and grow with. Other people seemed to be able to accept such realities. Some of her single women friends even confessed to her betimes that they loved living alone. This always chilled her to the bone; she was unable to accept it as a healthy way of life.

On the other hand, why couldn't she be content with an affair? An ongoing weekend romance such as Bettina Compton had? For the past twelve years Bettina had been flipping from Toronto to Montreal every weekend to see her George, a married man with five children. Or how about the way Diana Doolittle did it? Every spring Diana decided to fall in love and every autumn she ended the affair and went back to work. Yes, indeed, wasn't half a loaf better than none? Wasn't it a bit late for her to stick to an all-or-nothing principle? Wasn't that hopelessly old-fashioned? Why couldn't she just have a big summer fling with Simon? He was waiting there for her; in a way, had always been waiting there for her. For the past ten years since they first had their close encounter. Away back then when she had finally demanded space for the relationship to grow beyond the confines of an illicit affair, Simon had said he couldn't leave "until the children were grown up." And she had broken it off because she wanted and still felt it possible for her to have a second chance at a real mating.

"When my three girls are gone, then I will leave her," Simon had said, his jaw set to emphasize his resolution. For some insane reason at the time she had suddenly thought of another lawyer in town who, when his son was 14, had said to his wife, "On the day Joey turns twenty-one, I will leave you." And on Joey's twenty-first birthday, in keeping with the incisiveness of the legal mind, he had the moving van brought up to the door of his house. But even back then she had known that Simon was not made like that. Simon wanted to live his life without hurting anybody and so he would not live his life, but rather endure it, as all martyrs do. And would end up hurting himself most of all.

Still, all that did not mean now that they could not resume their old love affair, be close for the summertime at least, pick up where they had left off five years ago. After all, it had never been just a loose arrangement, a casual affair. They did, indeed, deeply care for one another and Simon had proved it a number of times by offering her money when she was out of funds, by taking care of her income tax returns, by giving the best of his business advice. Once he had even fought a case for her with the Income Tax Department when they decided to tax her as a developer because she had sold off three pieces of her farm at the lake.

"There now," he had said, holding her tightly against him, "You've just had $6,000 worth of my time. Don't say I don't care."

And once, a year or so before she sold her house in Kingston, with her children all gone off to university, they had indeed resumed their old love affair. One afternoon in September she had been standing by a parking meter downtown about to put a nickel in the slot when that familiar arm had gone around her and inserted the coin. And they had gone home together.

When she was leaving Kingston he had looked after all her financial dealings, selling the house, investing the money. At their farewell once again she had looked at him longingly, hopefully. And he had read it once more.

"I have to get the girls through university. Maybe after that."

She had smiled sadly, partly because she suspected that he was probably prisoned forever, partly because of his lost self and destroyed potential, partly because she knew that maybe that was what she wanted to hear. She really was deeply loathe to break up a marriage, no matter how bad it was. And perhaps she was subconsciously like her friend Marie who had come to her in a panic once and said, "My God, here I was having an affair with a married man, thought I was absolutely safe. And what does he do? He decided he wants to leave his wife and marry me! What ever shall I do now?"

For four more years after that second parting her search had continued. And still no one to love and cherish, to share with and grow with! She had thought of going north, or west, or to Europe where the ratio wasn't so sickeningly out of proportion. There—it was reputed—that the men weren't so threatened, that commitment was still fashionable. Really, her life was such a conflicting bind! It was probably self destructive, even masochistic, to continue living in a place where the probabilities were virtually nil; but on another level of her life her work was so immensely rewarding and the cumulative effects of her Ottawa-Valley-based writing were about to yield returns. Maybe, she said to herself, when I finish my next two books, already in the works, I will leave and go north or west or to another country. In the meantime, if there were no men in Ottawa there was certainly one at least in Kingston even if only part-time for the summer.

In the dark of her bedroom she winced a little when she thought of the parting to inevitably arrive at summer's end. Put to the test, she knew what he would say. "Well, I just have to get my other girls through university and then—" Or maybe he would say, "My wife is too old to leave now."

The previous summer, before she had rented the lake house for the first time to winter tenants, she had finished off an Ottawa Valley book in July and gone to the lake for the month of August to prepare for the newcomers by doing some therapeutic scraping, painting, refinishing. Somehow Simon had found out she was there, had phoned and invited himself out to the lake one sunny August afternoon. He had brought a bottle of wine and they had sat in their bathing suits and sipped it on the rocks in epiphanies of sun, hoping that time would find a stop. But when he reached out for her, she pulled away. "What's wrong?" he asked, putting his arms around her and trying to tilt up her face so that he could read what was in her eyes.

"It's so hard, it's just so hard," she rasped out against his shoulder.

"You mean it is so hard because I always have to go?" he asked, gently kissing the top of her head.

"Yes, yes," she sobbed out, surprised at her own vehemence. "The hurt is more than it's worth."

And it was true. During the tenure of their intermittent affair, he had always had to go, for a four o'clock appointment, for an eleven-thirty appointment, home for lunch, home for dinner, off to the dentist, off to pick up a daughter at school.

And he had let her go.

Over the last winter they had lunch a few times when she had to return to Kingston on business; and a couple of times, on her birthday and on Boxing Day, he had phoned "just to say hello." During the winter, as well, she had joined the indoor tennis club, taken skiing weekends she couldn't afford at Lac Ste. Marie, gone to lectures and parties she was too tired to go to—all in the hopes of meeting someone. And once again, she had met with total failure. Yes, indeed, time to compromise—

Marina phoned her tenants at the lake house. Kate had already left, gone west, and Bertie was there alone, sounding forlorn. She had a second of hesitation as she thought of the horrors of sorting, packing, moving. "I seem to have forgotten, too, how isolated that lake house is at night, that 20 feet from the door is wilderness." But her decision held. She told Bertie he was free to go. And the next morning gave her notice to the apartment manager.

When she returned to the house north of Kingston, it took her ten days or so to unpack, re-sort and rearrange, clean, air the rugs, bedding, winter clothes, get the lawn mower in for repairs, have the vegetable garden ploughed, ready her flower beds for seeding and planting. In ten days of pure physical labours she lost five pounds, felt her muscles tone, began to tan. The big city tension lines around her eyes and mouth faded out.

Finally one afternoon when she felt she was ready, she phoned Simon's office. The receptionist sounded mystified. "But Mr. Fairweather has taken an indefinite leave of absence," she said. Marina stifled a gasp. There was an awkward silence. "Is there something I can do for you?" the voice queried. "No, nothing," Marina stammered. "Nothing important. Just an out-of-town client calling." And she hung up.

She slumped back into the chair. What did it mean? He was ill? "Oh, no! Not that!" she thought, remembering that his father had died very young, and his elder brother the year she had left Kingston. No. He had just decided to take some time off. That was all. Still, she had never been aware that he could afford that kind of sabbatical.

The Donaldsons with two of their "late" teenagers came from Ottawa for a long weekend and it was the middle of the following week before she got around to phoning Simon at home. She had never done it before even when the relationship was at its most intense. She felt it should be very straightforward and couldn't quite explain her hesitation. She would just simply ask some kind of legal advice and then casually give him her new phone number at the end of the conversation. But when she did finally dial his home number, there was no answer.

She tried intermittently over the next two weeks but there was never an answer. She decided that they must have gone west to visit their married daughter in Calgary. Imagine that! An extended trip together! Maybe the marriage had arrived, as marriages often do when the partners are in their fifties, at a new stage involving some coming to terms with the deficiencies, some revitalizing of the strengths, some hope of grandchildren as a binding influence. She thought of one of her married friends who for years had proclaimed that he was always "on the make" because his wife never went to bed with him and who had recently (and joyfully) announced that she was suddenly (and inexplicably) interested in sex. Maybe Simon and his wife were on a second honeymoon!

Summer and the social life around her absorbed her for the next few weeks. Amongst the new neighbours on the developer's land, she found a kindred spirit, a widow who did public relations for the Kingston Psychiatric Hospital. When she had left the Kingston area to go to Ottawa, the nucleus of an artistic community had begun to develop around the lake. In the interim, as inflation drove more and more creative people into the boondocks for cheaper living, the area north of Kingston had grown into an identifiable community expanding in texture and numbers to include writers, poets, painters, photographers, even a starving architect who refused to be government or university kept and who was trying to make a living doing restorations in Kingston and area. There, suffering from a lack of stimulation and intellectual challenge provided by the big centres, the creative ones drew together in a small (and dangerously incestuous) clique to feed and encourage each other.

These gatherings—unlike those extravaganzas of her forties in Kingston—were spontaneous, casual, cerebral and always BYO. She was happy to resume a warm friendship—in the true sense of the word—with an English professor whose wife had recently left him to further her career and she actually found some good tennis partners including a famous Canadian novelist who, not too many years previously, had been Ontario Singles Champion.

There were two weddings out of town, one of them up the Valley, a country wedding which continued on for three days of visiting, dancing, drinking, story-telling—a circle of blood relations' warmth which she found difficult to leave. The second much more sophisticated affair took place on a yacht which sailed out from Toronto Harbour, the wedding ceremony and reception afterwards all taking place on board ship.

Each time she arrived back at her lake place she tried Simon's number again. But still no answer of any kind.

She had a week of intensive close work for a murderous deadline on her second book, researching, documenting and writing the captions for over a hundred archival photographs. And summer was deep in daisies before she got to Simon. A voice she judged to be young answered the phone and said, "Just a minute." She heard the speaker yell out, "Dad, it's for you," and realized it must be one of his daughters. After a considerable time he came.

"Mr. Fairweather, this is Marina Caldwell speaking."

He was definitely thrown, said nothing. She filled in his blank.

"I'm thinking of selling my lake place," she hurried on, "and I wonder if you could recommend a good real estate man—somebody who is trustworthy and tuned in to rural properties."

"Why, yes," he said (she could tell he was upset but she didn't quite know whether it was fear in his voice or surprise), "Yes, yes, I just happen to have (she could hear him breathing hard)—I just happen to have the name and number of a very reliable man here—" his voice faded off and she could hear him rustling through some papers. Then, coming up closer again, he said, "Yes, his name is Elliot Goodfellow and he had just gone into business on his own and his company name is (He WAS breathing hard. What was he so afraid of?)—Frontenac Real Estate—he's the best rural man around here." Pause. Breathing.

He read her off the phone number. She thanked him. There was another awkward pause.

"You wouldn't recognize the lake place now, you know. The hydro is in and there is even a telephone—listed under Harrowsmith—"

Silence. Breathing.

Was someone listening in on an extension? Was that what was terrifying him? Making his voice tremble like that?

"Well, I just thought I'd let you know—" she said. She found herself inexplicably laughing. And hung up.

From Kingston, Toronto, Ottawa, up the Valley, the visitors streamed in. The zenith was actually reached when one group left at 7:30 p.m. and the next group came in off the road at 11:00 p.m.

She had to go to Toronto to meet with a publisher concerning a proposed new book and then to Ottawa to go over the final paste-up of the one due out in October. And the days went by.

"Why is he wasting our precious time?" she asked herself at first. "He must have tried me repeatedly when I was out, out in the garden, out swimming, gone to town, gone visiting. Everyone I know complains that they can never reach me, that I should have an answering service. Besides, he would have to make excuses to get to a pay phone—the way he used to do when we were having our first big close encounter. He always used to phone from the Le Roi Motel and we'd make a date and he'd come at two and leave before four, always lying beside me, holding me, wide-eyed, keeping himself awake, afraid to do what was natural—fall asleep. I used to wonder even then what he was so afraid of. Did he really tell me once that his wife would commit suicide if he left her? Or did I just imagine that?"

She was invited away for several weekends, to a friend's cottage on Lake Wah-Wash-Kesh and to a relative's farm up in the Nickabeau. In actual fact she hated to leave her own lake place but a few days as somebody's guest gave her time to rest up for the next round of visitors—her son and his girl friend from Toronto, her daughter from Ottawa, some sixty-year-old newlywed friends from Edmonton on their way to the east coast, a niece and nephew from Renfrew. When her Ottawa friends, the Donaldsons, phoned and asked her if she would come to a weekend party at their Muskoka place on August 22nd she hesitated. "That's maybe too far off for me to say," she fumbled.

"It's next weekend," Gwen snapped. "Better phone me back soon." And she hung up.

Marina was shocked. Where had the summer gone? Where did it always go? Every summer like a high-speed train. It was the beginning of July and then, when you turned around, it was the middle of August and the bluejays, full of anxiety, were protesting the first tinge of red on the maples. And still Simon had not got in touch with her! What could it mean?

She pushed down some of the ugly possibilities and went off to her tennis game. When she arrived home old friends from Waterloo were at her doorstep. By the time they left—and the weather was so perfect they stayed a couple of extra days—she had to work frantically eight hours a day to finish a sample chapter of a book for a publisher in Toronto. That finished she went off to the Donaldson's for their weekend party. On her return home, she looked at the calendar. The twenty-sixth of August!

Simon was not going to get in touch with her. They were not going to have a summer-long entanglement, a part-time relationship. It really had been fear she had heard in his voice on the telephone. The reason he stayed in that arm's-length marriage was that deep deep down, because of that dreadful unnurtured childhood of his, he did not want and could not cope with a close relationship.

And it suddenly struck her that, even in his relationship with her, things went lovingly well when all that was involved was a blissful few hours. But faced with a summer of entwinement, with time undetermined to spend and no limits on the encounter, he had simply faded away to a frightened voice on the telephone. She remembered how she had laughed on the phone and knew that, even back then, she had felt the intimations.

Beloved Simon whose image she had carried within her the past years. Beloved Simon whose caring had sometimes vicariously nurtured her through hard times. Beloved Simon was a coward!

She was sad. Then she began to feel angry. For it came to her that her secret and innermost torch-carrying for this man had probably put up shields, barriers, invisible walls around her, preventing anyone else from getting through to her. Since the time of her first love at 16, she had been a one-man woman. Most men, even the provers and libertines, sensed that total commitment in a woman, almost smelled it.

She had been all too willing to project all the blame for her primeval loneliness on the ten-to-one woman-to-man ratio in Ottawa.

"I've never ended it!" she cried out loud. "I have to end it—pull out the fish hook!"

Marina jumped to the phone intending to tell Simon exactly what he was no matter who was at home with him, no matter who was listening on the extension. In order to free herself from him now and go forward, she had to speak her piece. The phone was ringing its first ring when she put the receiver down. What was the point of hurting all those people? Maybe his wife loved him. He was the one who couldn't love, no, not even his daughters whom he probably used as wife-surrogates the way all people do who live in fruitless limbo marriages, gratifying their unmet needs through the innocent ones.

So this was really why she had come back to the lake place! To see the truth of it, to discover this ugly immature part of herself, to come to grips with this childishly romantic illusion nurtured for so long as a substitute for the exciting reality of risking again. This, then, was why she had kept one foot in Kingston, fragmenting herself, preventing herself from cleanly entering a new community, from moving totally onto the new plateau of her life. Why, part of her psyche was still living with ghosts! And she had expected to integrate and become whole dragging a weight like that!

She had pretended to herself that she was keeping the lake place because she needed a "home base," was keeping it for her children and the unborn grandchildren, was keeping it because she couldn't emotionally part with it, was keeping it because the market wasn't right—Kingston was so depressed.

Nonsense. All nonsense. The thing was dead. Time to re-assemble the pieces and fill in the gap.

She opened the phone book looking for the number of a rural real estate man she knew and trusted.

The Opening of the Hunting Season in South Porcupine

Billy Buckmeyer lay looking at the peeling ceiling while the heavy rains on the roof destroyed his chances of becoming the Great Canadian Film Director. The budget of $200,000 would only allow for three weeks of shooting. It couldn't rain.

Already Ergo Vashinsky was on his back screaming into the phone from Toronto for rushes and yelling about the alimony he had to pay to his four living wives and what he would do to one Billy Buckmeyer if this fucking film didn't make its deadlines.

"Shit on it from a high level," Billy had yelled back. "We're freezing and starving to death up here in the Far North and you're sitting on your fat ass in TO complaining. Porcupine quills up your rear from South Porcupine!" And he had hung up.

Billy went to the window and removed the stick that was holding the old frame up. It was getting cold. He looked at the sky and the rain. The sky was lightening up a bit as though somewhere it was beginning to clear. He prayed devoutly to the Methodist gods of his deceased parents. As he went shivering back to crawl into Sally's warmth again, he heard the pitter-patter of furtive footsteps in the hall.

"Who the hell is crawling in with whom?" he wondered to himself as he lay in the dark.

He knew that Joey Jackson, the token American in the cast and the lead supporting actor, was into Rena the cook when he couldn't make Melanie Moorehouse, the leading lady, and he suspected that Pierre Longtemps, the sound man, was into Catherine Keenleyside, the writer of the screenplay, a prissy dame who had her tail all set for Mr. Perfect. Billy cursed Catherine Keenleyside as largely responsible for the fact, in Billy's books, that this motley crew and cast were trapped in the

Canadian wilds for three weeks and were being stabled—stabled was a good word for it—long past the end of any reasonable "season" in a mining magnate's old rambling summer place, run now as a tourist inn by Paddy and Fiona O'Flaherty, a matched pair of Irish crooks.

Of course, it was becoming apparent to everyone by now that he had cast Sally not because she was a second Shirley MacLaine but because she appeared to have possibilities as a first-rate lay and, indeed, his casting perspicacity had been dead on. He was also increasingly aware that some of the film crew were wearing down the halls at night en route to the beds of a couple of the young girls with minor parts—like that Theresa.

Billy was fantasizing about big-titted Theresa when suddenly there was a terrible crash downstairs. It sounded as though something had gone through the floor. My God, Billy thought, in this place something COULD have gone through the floor, like one floor could have gone through to the next floor. He jumped into his shorts and ran down the hall through the main wing and came to the top of the curving staircase. There at the foot of the stairs, dripping November rains by the gallon, was Joey Jackson with four of the crew members. They were carefully moving an old player-piano into the living-room.

"We got it! We got it!" Joey yelled when he saw Billy standing there in his shorts.

"Jesus Christ! Where did you get it?"

"From a farmhouse down the way."

"Do you know you can be jailed for that? Do you know that in this kind of country everyone knows every move everyone else makes, day or night?"

"I'm taking it home."

"If you get charged with this I won't bail you out. I'll fire you. I'll get another actor—"

"You can't afford it. You can't afford to reshoot anything. Look at it! Isn't it beautiful!"

Joey sat down and began to play. The piano emitted a twenties version of:

"When it's springtime in the Mountains,
I'll be coming back to you,
Little sweetheart of the mountains,
With your bonnie eyes of blue."

Mrs. O'Flaherty appeared in Paddy-green chenille.

"Take that thing out of the living-room of my inn," she yelled.

"But my dear Mrs. O'Flaherty," Joey began, "it's just for a couple of weeks."

"Take that thing out of the living-room of my inn!" Mrs. O'Flaherty screamed.

Paddy O'Flaherty appeared in duplicate Paddy-green chenille. He tried to soothe her. Mrs. O'Flaherty continued to scream.

"Take that out of my inn or I will have Paddy throw you all out."

Paddy took his Bushmills out of the pocket of his Paddy-green chenille robe and put it to her with soothing words.

"There now, Fiona, my love," he said, "we don't have to go that far."

Joey looked to Billy.

"It's all right," Billy said in a low voice. "You know, you son-of-a-bitch, that it is an idle threat, but get the Goddamn thing out of here so she will quit screaming!"

"Where will I put it?"

"In the barn."

"But it will get cold and damp in the barn," Joey protested.

Mrs. O'Flaherty continued screaming. The whole cast and crew were lined on the stairwell.

"Don't argue. We're cold and damp here," Billy yelled. "Why can't your fucking player-piano be cold and damp there?"

The four crew men and Joey heaved the player-piano up and began to move it out the door. This movement precipitated the instrument into beginning to play again.

"Once again I'll say I love you
While the birds sing all the day—"

"Oh, for Christ's sake!" Billy yelled and kicked it. It shut off like a stove with a loose connection.

Billy turned to the cast and the crew.

"It's all right now," Billy said. "Everyone go back to bed and try to get some sleep. We start shooting at eight-thirty sharp."

"Not in the fucking rain we don't," said Harry Hogarth, the lead actor. "I'll speak to ACTRA."

"Fuck ACTRA," Billy said. "With an over-size dildo."

They all trailed off to bed and Billy got in beside Sally and put his arm around her. It was politely removed. He lay on his back then trying not to think of the Great Canadian Film he was making and on which his reputation would be made or broken. The phone at his bedside rang. He looked at his watch. Two-thirty. It was either the police or Vashinsky. He lifted the receiver off very quietly. Vashinsky was hysterically swearing in Rumanian.

"I know you are there, you bastard. You call yourself a film-maker. You couldn't make a starving whore. Do you know—" his voice rose in octaves, "do you know that there are twenty feet of film in these rushes with Catherine Keenleyside—the *writer* of the screenplay I might remind you—casually floating through the scene with her head showing but no body? WE CAN'T AFFORD TO WASTE TWENTY FEET OF FILM. I REPEAT, WE CAN'T AFFORD TO WASTE TWENTY FEET OF FILM. ESPECIALLY NOT ON THE WRITER OF THE SCREENPLAY!"

Billy sighed.

"Catherine was out walking in the woods and her head came up above the little hillock behind which we were shooting a scene with Harry and Melanie and I hoped you would realize the humour of the thing."

"Verne!" Vashinsky screamed. "What the hell was wrong with Verne that he didn't realize a disembodied head was moving through the scene before he had wasted TWENTY feet of film?"

"I asked you before," Billy said, "to recall her. We don't need her here."

"Dave says she is to stay and learn from all you so-called film-makers. He says she is a great talent as a screenplay writer but she needs to learn the mechanics—"

"The only thing she is learning here is the sound of a sound man screwing—"

Vashinsky actually laughed.

"Very funny. Do they have a morality squad in South Porcupine?"

"They're all here—enjoying themselves with the film crew. Turns out they're gay to a man."

Billy hung up.

The phone rang again.

"This love scene between Melanie and Harry," Vashinsky said very quietly, "before he leaves to go and fight the War of 1812—it's Godawful. Melanie looks as though she has the hiccoughs."

"She has," Billy replied.

"It's ridiculous."

"I thought it gave it a nice sense of realism."

"How the hell do you make love with the hiccoughs? It's impossible."

"It's entirely possible. You just do less kissing, that's all."

There was a long silence on the other end. Billy waited it out.

"Those were very nice rushes," Vashinsky said. "Remember you only have a week left."

Click.

Billy wondered if he would feel any better and if he would be able to sleep if he screwed Sally. He ran his hand down her hip. Sally pushed him away.

"I'm fed up with Position Five," she mumbled.

At 7:30, Les Beauchamp, the manager, faithfully went down the halls of the old summer mansion, knocking on all the doors and rousing cast and crew by reciting his favourite poem, Rudyard Kipling's "If." After a while Les came back, knocked on Billy's door and then came in. Sally made a grumble of protest from the bed.

Billy said, "It's all right. I've asked her to marry me."

"Your mistake. You always do." Les snapped. "Melanie says she can't get up. She has her period."

Billy rose stark naked from his bed, half an erection on, and tore down the hall, rushed Melanie's door, pulled down her covers and yelled, "Up, up, Lady Guinevere! Sir Galahad is here at last and he will rouse you with this famous jousting tool!"

It didn't work. Melanie lay inert, hung-over, pale, sickly.

"Get up, Miss Moorehead," Billy said. "This is your director speaking."

Absolutely no stir.

"Don't give me that crap about having your period. You haven't had a period in ten years."

Melanie made an attempt to throw the alarm clock at him but couldn't lift it. Billy left.

"She's up," he said to himself. "Now to keep her sober."

He met Les in the hall.

"See that she doesn't have a bottle in her room," he said.

He dressed quickly reminding himself half-aloud that a coach must have the plays figured out ahead of the players, way way ahead. He raced downstairs. In various stages of agony and disgruntlement most of the rest of the crew and cast were already in the dining-room coping with O'Flaherty's coffee substitute.

Billy went out into the kitchen, the only warm room in the house, and confronted Mrs. O'Flaherty as he had planned the night before.

"My dear Mrs. O'Flaherty, my people can't exist on pork and beans and fried potatoes. They are not Canadian lumbermen; they are Canadian actors. But even at that they work very, very hard—"

Mrs. O'Flaherty put on her morally superior nose.

"At night," she sniffed.

"Please, Mrs. O'Flaherty. The army won't run on an empty stomach."

"We do our best. We have kept the inn open only for you. We are losing money every day, I tell you."

Billy turned to look for Rena, the cook. She was in the kitchen annex, her head in the freezer. Billy, looking over her shoulder and pinching her bottom at the same time, spied stacks of frozen sirloin.

"Ah, Rena, my lovely," he said. "Those are for tonight. Those are for tonight for your good friend Joey himself. You have to feed the beast."

Rena smiled blissfully.

"I mean it, Rena," Billy insisted. "We're starving. What have you got to lose?"

Rena shrugged.

"Nothing," she said. "If they fired me, they couldn't get anyone else."

Billy left triumphantly. For a moment, it looked like a good day. Then Catherine Keenleyside came at him just as he was pouring himself a cup of coffee.

"Billy, I want to talk to you," she said with her hands on her hips. "You are definitely making Sally too big in this film. She is meant to be a secondary character. Melanie is the lead, remember? No more monkeying around with my play, Mister."

Billy didn't have time to defend himself by attacking. Suddenly Mimi Hogarth, the wife of the leading man, Harry Hogarth, came running downstairs with her teeth out crying, "Rameses is missing! Rameses is missing!" Harry was following.

"Yes, yes," he verified breathlessly. "We have looked everywhere. Help!"

Rameses was one of the trio of toy poodles afflicting the making of the Great Canadian Film. Harry never put a foot on a set without Mimi and Mimi never put a foot anywhere without her three "itchums kitchums" toy poodles. Rameses was the male of the trio, a randy little bastard who even tried to screw the cat.

"Don't panic," Billy said. "He probably had a night out on the town."

"No, no," Harry said. "We have searched everywhere. He must be outside."

It being obvious that there would be no shooting until Rameses was found, some of the crew and cast went outside, to all outward appearances to aid in the search, but all secretly hoping that the creepy Goddam dog had been kidnapped or drowned.

Curious as well, Billy stepped out into bright sunshine and a blanket of snow on the ground.

"Holy Mother of God!" he cried. "Snow! Please God, we're trying to shoot early fall!" He got down on his knees and began to say Hail Marys.

"Get up, you craven infidel," Les said. "This kind of snow will melt in a few minutes of sunshine."

Across the lawns there was a cry of horror from Mimi. By the time Billy had crossed the area, Harry was covering her eyes with his hands. Rameses was floating in the garden pool, his little white ears stretched out of the water. "Itchums kitchums" was dead. Billy knew immediately that Rameses had been murdered.

"He must have chased the cat into the pool," Billy proffered, "and not been able to climb out afterwards."

"Mimi will have to leave. Mimi will have to go home, away from this dreadful place," said Mimi in the trance-like voice of shock.

"Yes," Harry quickly concurred, "you will have to go home. You cannot stay here any longer."

He looked at Billy with relief. He too, then, Billy thought, must hate or resent these monstrous child-substitutes. He motioned to Les.

"Make arrangements for Mimi to go home," he said.

"There's a plane coming in today to take Melanie back to Toronto to do that part in *Cat on a Hot Tin Roof*," Les replied.

"Good. Get Mimi on the return flight."

Things are definitely looking up, Billy thought to himself. Now if I just get rid of Catherine Keenleyside. He was savouring the possibility when Les again came through the crowd of people standing around the pool.

"Vashinsky is on the phone," he said.

"Tell him to go fuck his third wife," Billy said. "Let's go!"

As Les in his infinite wisdom had promised, the sunshine had melted the snow. There were still a few leaves chattering on the trees and Verne, the greatest living Canadian cinematographer, as Billy well knew from past experience could be relied upon to create the illusion of the replete foliage of September.

The cast performed beautifully. Nobody sabotaged. Melanie was sick in the bushes once or twice but never a word of complaint was heard. Nobody horsed around and clowned. Verne sailed up and down the railway-track dolly without a single hitch, smiling into his camera lens. Sally was a lovely bright spot on the day; she had arisen dewy from the crazy night. She was wearing a sweater and no bra; he decided on Position Eight for the night. A very difficult one but challenging. They were going to have steak for dinner. Things were almost too good—Then suddenly Billy realized it was Wednesday. Amateur Night at the Empire Hotel!

The whole cast and crew were addicted to Amateur Night at the Empire Hotel. The bar alone was enough to keep patrons addicted for years on end. Known as the longest bar in Ontario, it actually had "a mile-long-fish-tank" in which swam piranhas waiting to grow up. The seating area was almost a total black-out and the size of a hay-barn. On Wednesday nights all the locals sang country or blues, tap-danced, jigged, step-danced, threw their voices and fiddled. Between numbers everyone danced with everyone else and drank with everyone else and Joey Jackson was quoted as saying he had never had as much fun in his whole life in New York City and that he was going to stay forever.

"Yup, buy a little mine and stay forever," he would repeat ad infinitum after his first three double martinis.

Unfortunately, Billy had found Amateur Hour at the Empire Hotel to be his cruellest enemy, worst than Vashinsky as a stumbling-block on his rise to the top in the Canadian film world. The day after Amateur Night at the Empire Hotel, not only was everyone tired, cranky, aching, hung-over, but just last week a station-wagon loaded with equipment and four crew members had failed to make a ninety-degree turn on the road back to the inn and had gone into the river. According to Ontario Safety Rules for Car Immersions, all four crew members had waited quietly until the car sank to the bottom of the river, rolled down the windows and swam up to the surface, a distance, as it turned out, of two and a half feet. But the camera equipment had had to be sent back to Toronto for drying out and repairs and the station-wagon had no discernible brakes after the event. Hearing of all this, Vashinsky had threatened to give their licence plate numbers to the police in Timmins.

And that was not all. Pierre Longtemps, the French-Canadian sound man, a rare-spoken individual in the daytime, turned out to have an incredible repertoire of filthy jovial verse which, with his French-Canadian accent applied full force, he bellowed into the microphone on Amateur Night to the ecstatic delight of the crowds who laughed so hard they broke the laugh-metre, and he was given first prize by default. Pierre was to be brought back by popular demand but had to be permanently restrained from performing when Billy had a visit from a hostile delegation of mothers from the high school Parent-Teachers' Association whose underage kids had been at the Empire the night Pierre performed. There was to be a morals charge.

Remembering all this with pain and anguish, Billy decided to scotch all hopes of his cast and crew attending another Amateur Night at the Empire. Time was too precious now. There was less than a week's shooting left. They were behind schedule. The weather might not hold.

Suddenly Billy came to, realizing it had grown too dark to shoot anymore. Everyone was stamping feet and blowing on hands from the twilight cold.

"Okay for now," Billy said. "We'll break for dinner and then shoot the ball scene tonight with lights."

The groan was concerted.

Sally said, "Billy! You can't do that!"

"Goddamn it to hell, girl, I can," Billy said. "We have to catch up with schedule."

Pierre cleared his throat.

"How are you going to shoot that ball scene without Melanie?" he asked quietly.

Billy sat down on a log and put his head in his hands. Jesus Christ Almighty! Melanie had gone to Toronto to shoot *Cat on a Hot Tin Roof*!

The cast and crew slipped away. Harry Hogarth put his hand on his shoulder.

"Tough luck, old man, but you shouldn't try to kill ALL our fun."

Sally came up and sat down beside him and kissed his cheek.

"Would a little nookie help?" she asked half-teasingly.

"Would it!" he rasped and grabbed her. They rolled off the log and did it right there, never minding Position Eight; it was too damn damp and cold on the ground.

After that, the steak was fantastic. Billy had wine for just such an occasion squeezed out of the $200,000 budget. Afterwards everyone resumed civilities and roasted a little by the huge fireplace before they all got ready for Amateur Night. Billy didn't go. He had too much work to do. He and Vashinsky, when the place was quiet, usually spent three to four hours on the phone talking about the week's rushes. But he went to Les and warned him to keep the gang together and herd them all home safely. Les was already into the gin. Billy could tell by his sweet breath.

"Ominous," thought Billy. "Why have I been stuck with such a screwed-up mess of people? Ugh!"

In the peace of the place, Billy did some more work on script alteration, and then fell asleep with the re-write on his chest. He heard one of the crew wagons come back and then another some time later. He must have dozed again when he was awakened by Les shaking him.

"Billy, wake up."

"What's the matter?"

"Well, we've had a little trouble. Come on down to Joey's room."

Shaking, Billy got into some clothes.

They went to Joey's room. He was bleeding at the mouth and blackened on the left eye.

"I was fantastic," Joey said. "Never had so much fun in my life. I actually held my own with him, didn't I, Les, old boy?"

"Get some ice," Billy said. "As fast as you can. I'll get some cold water to him until you get back."

"Wait'll I tell them in old New York—I took on a Timmins miner—"

Joey was high but not drunk.

Les came back, running, with the ice.

"Never mind if he bleeds to death from the mouth," Billy said, "get that eye."

Les applied ice with vigour.

"I think some make-up will get us through. It's not as bad as I thought," Les mused, holding Joey under ice. "There's more though—Theresa has taken off with a construction worker she picked up last night at the Polish Hall—they're shacked up in his trailer out in Trailer Town."

"Oh, Lord," Billy moaned, "Thy servant is undone—she has a part in the scene tomorrow at the railway station—she's crucial tomorrow."

"I know," Les said.

"Keep trying to get her."

"But—" Les began.

"Keep trying to get her," Billy yelled. "No, I mean 'get her!'"

Billy slept fitfully that night and swore to himself by the gods of his deceased Methodist parents that, after this was over, he would get an honest job, something nine to five with union back-up, and a coffee break every ten minutes, and indexed pension, and paid holidays and medical-dental-psychiatric services, something like a postal worker's job, something with normal, non-depraved people.

Les came back at six o'clock in the morning, haggard and weak at the knees, saying that he had located the trailer in which Theresa was ensconced with her construction worker. Les had told her that Billy had said that she would be fired if she didn't return immediately but, Les reported, Theresa had only opened the window a little and laughed.

"Fired from a bit part when I have a big part here? Drop dead!" she had yelled at him.

Les said he had further pounded on the door and beseeched her but the construction worker had come to the door and told him to scram or he'd shove his balls right up into his eyeballs.

"Keep trying," Billy said.

"No dice," Les said. "The guy's the size could kill me."

Billy stood a moment thinking.

"Okay. Go into town. Get a girl off the street that looks like Theresa, is the same size as Theresa. Tell her she is going to be in the Great Canadian Film. Offer her—$25. We'll fake it—dress—make-up—we'll fake it."

"Now you're talking," Les said. "But one more thing. Who's going to the airport to pick up Melanie from Toronto?"

"Couldn't Jake do that?"

"Well, he's not accustomed to watching her for the booze."

"We'll have to chance it."

By ten o'clock Les was back with a flushed and breathless new Theresa, a dead ringer in size for Theresa. Size 38.

"We'll use a hat," Billy said, "and get Verne to shoot her only from the side the hat's pulled down on, and from the back."

"That should be easy," Les said.

"How's the American cow-puncher, Joey Jackson, and his black eye?" Billy asked.

"Well," Les said, "if you get Verne to shoot him from the left side *only* and pull his hat down over his eyes—it should be all right."

"Now, if we could just get Melanie here we might start the day's shooting." Billy said.

Even as he spoke the door to the inn opened and Melanie returned from Toronto, flat on her back, stiff as a board, carried by four crew members, clasping a bouquet of goldenrod to her breast and singing an aria from *La Traviata*.

Jake ran alongside the entourage wringing his hands and saying, "She got it from the pilot of the airplane. She told him she had an infected tooth and that the show must go on and he gave her a bottle of scotch—I have it here," he said.

He held it up. It was three-quarters empty.

Silence fell upon everyone assembled. Billy said nothing either. For a long time.

Finally he began quietly: "Melanie, do you think you can do the scene in the bush where you are leading the cow through enemy lines?"

Melanie sat bolt upright.

"An old pro like me! Of course I can!"

"Let's go then," Billy said.

It was one o'clock before they could push off to begin shooting. The camera crew threatened Billy with ACTRA because they hadn't had lunch but he put his head down and said, "Do you or do you not want a credit on your résumés for the Great Canadian Film?"

And they all put their heads down and went to it.

First take was the railway scene where Theresa's stand-in had to be tied to the railway tracks by a group of hostile Indians and then lie there while the train roared down at her. Theresa's stand-in was a little hard to convince at first but an offer of ten more dollars and her name on the credits softened her and they had a really good take there. Joey pulled down his military hat and Verne only shot him from the left side.

The next scene was a biggie, as Vashinsky always so crassly put it. It was to be set in the deep woods close to a large lake, a setting that could only be reached by a lumbering road rutted deep in mud from the November rains. Billy was proud of the way the crews put the sagging rented station-wagons over the route at a good 40-to-50-mile-an-hour clip, losing no time in their tight schedule. Melanie, fortified with a thermos of Mrs. O'Flaherty's coffee substitute re-heated, was full of her lines and ready to go. The brown cow was led forth from its trailer. Billy had three cameras on this one to give it the breadth and perspective it deserved. The scene count had been duly taken and Billy had given the signal for the cameras to start winding when all of a sudden throughout the woods surrounding them there was cacophony like a thousand guns going off and a thousand troops moving through the bush.

"My gawd!" Billy yelled. "What is it?"

"It's the opening of the hunting season!" Theresa's stand-in yelled. "They've mistaken the cow for a moose! Hit the dirt!"

But Billy was brilliant.

"No, No!" he shouted. "Keep the cameras rolling!"

Melanie led the cow on, speaking her lines louder than usual, oblivious of the rain of bullets about her head and shoulders. One of the cameras was taken out by a shot but Billy yelled, "Don't stop! Keep shooting! Cameras one and two keep shooting! It's great!"

Melanie fought her way to the lake, pulling a now somewhat recalcitrant cow by the halter. They both got slightly stuck in the mud at the lakeside and the rain of bullets continued from all directions. Pierre, the sound man, had been grazed through the right thumb but he calmly switched his equipment to the other hand. Melanie stopped and had a swig from a concealed bottle.

"Never mind," Billy screamed. "Keep rolling. We can cut it!"

Melanie continued on her designated route into Canadian history and finally doubled back and came out into an open space where Joey, riding up on his rented nag with his hat pulled well over his eye and the left side of his face turned to the camera, took her message and rode off to save the country called Canada. Melanie, the strain of her greatest theatrical moment now over, fell flat on her face in the cattails and Theresa's stand-in began to sob.

The rushes were flown to Toronto that night and the next morning an ecstatic Vashinsky was on the phone.

"The cow was great," he burbled. "The cow will win a film award, but I've never seen Melanie act so well—I think that will go down as her greatest scene. The railway scene was outstanding (who is that little thing with the big tits anyway?) and I think Joey should always wear his hat down like that—it not only gives him a mysterious look but it makes him look strong. The sound of the troops moving in the bush, why, that was a stroke of genius, sheer genius—gives real authenticity to the whole story. I think you have a winner. Of course, you've over-shot and you are over budget—but you have a winner."

In fact, it was a winner. The film won at Cannes, Rio de Janeiro and Capetown. It ran for months in Italy, New York, Russia and Roumania. Billy Buckmeyer became a famous film director and was invited to England, Los Angeles and New York to make films but, being a Canadian nationalist and a masochist, he chose to stay in Canada where he actually nearly starved to death. Vashinsky went on to Hollywood and made the Guinness Book of Records. Sally moved in with Pierre Longtemps, the sound man. She said she preferred men who were quiet in the daytime. Joey put a mattress on the top of his car, fastened his player-piano onto it and went joyously back to New York where he made a fortune in Wonderbra TV commercials. Theresa NEVER came out of the construction worker's trailer. When a reporter from the Sudbury *Sidewinder* finally tracked her down there, her description in detail of the differences between actors and construction workers as lovers was so graphic that the reporter couldn't file the story, but instead sold the idea to Baby Baby Blue Blue movies and made enough money out of it to move to San Miguel with two bisexual 16-year-olds from Quebec. Melanie married an insurance guy she met at Donwoods when she was in treatment; they set up AA in Timmins and eventually the whole county. It turned out that Pierre Longtemps, as Billy always had suspected, had actually been screwing the writer of the screenplay, Catherine Keenleyside, who got to like it so well that she quit writing screenplays, collected the royalties on her best-seller, *I'm Not Too Tired Tonight*, and went to live with a Maori chieftain in New Zealand. At last count they had had 16 children and Catherine was reported to have said,

"It beats writing screenplays for Canadian films, I can tell you."

There were only two residual rough spots from the whole affair and they were the two lawsuits which emerged from the shooting of the Great Canadian Film. Catherine Keenleyside sued Billy Buckmeyer for screwing around with her screenplay or, as she put it, making "unauthorized changes." Ace Rent-A-Car sued the film company for the destruction in three weeks of four brand new station-wagons.

Both cases are still before the courts.

About the Author

During her writing career, Joan Finnigan (MacKenzie) has published twenty-eight books, the majority Ottawa Valley inspired. Over that thirty-year period, she has done considerable work for CBC and the National Film Board; for her NFB screenplay, *The Best Damn Fiddler from Calabogie to Kaladar* she received an Etrog, now known as Genie. Recently, *The Watershed Collection* was shortlisted for the Pat Lowther Poetry Award and *Wintering Over* for the prestigious Trillium Award. Her fifth oral/social history of the Valley, *Tallying the Tales of the Old-Timers*, is planned for 1998. She also has ready a new poetry collection, *Second Wind; Second Sight*, is working on a third collection of short stories, a new children's book, *Nadja's Nut Museum*, and, as always, her long-projected book on the Opeongo Line, *Where We All Began*, to be a coffee-table treasure including many of her best photographs taken over the past twenty-five years. She has three married children, seven amazing grandchildren, and lives just north of Kingston, Ontario, on Hambly Lake.